C PLAN 29A   12/10/07.

ANGEL TOUCH

In late 1980s London – the era of Thatcherism and Loadsamoney – Fitzroy Maclean Angel tries to be in the right place at the right time. As he says, it's better to be lucky than good. When he comes to the aid of his neighbour, the sexy financial analyst Salome, he finds himself carrying out an undercover investigation into an insider trading scam amongst the coked-up whizzkids and mega-rich wheeler-dealers of the City – and things turn even nastier when a fatal car crash turns out to be anything but an accident...

ANGEL TOUCH

ANGEL TOUCH

by

Mike Ripley

Magna Large Print Books
Long Preston, North Yorkshire,
BD23 4ND, England.

British Library Cataloguing in Publication Data.

Ripley, Mike
    Angel touch.

    A catalogue record of this book is
    available from the British Library

    ISBN   978-0-7505-2761-3

First published in Great Britain 1989 by Collins

Copyright © 1989, 2006 Mike Ripley

Cover illustration © Telos Publishing Ltd.

The moral right of the author has been asserted

Published in Large Print 2007 by arrangement with
Telos Publishing Ltd.

Magna Large Print is an imprint of Library Magna Books Ltd.

Printed and bound in Great Britain by
T.J. (International) Ltd., Cornwall, PL28 8RW

O1 2924439

For Kate and Miranda; early fans

CHAPTER ONE

Salome was in a right two-and-eight when I took her birthday present up at sparrowfart; and what with everything else that happened later on, it was no wonder she threw a wobbler that evening.

I had her present already wrapped, and I'd just heard Frank pad downstairs and out for his early morning jog, so the coast was as clear as it ever would be. Not that I've anything against Frank, and he is fairly broad-minded (well, as much as, say, Attila the Hun), but the present was a bit special and quite likely to be misconstrued. Well, if it wasn't, I'd wasted 40 quid.

Frank and Salome had the dubious pleasure of living in the flat above mine. It was much the same as mine, except their compact midi system couldn't hold a candle to my ginormous Pioneer speakers (which can set heads banging in Tottenham on a clear day) and I don't have shares in Laura Ashley. But Frank and Salome wouldn't have to put up with me for much longer. Like the good BASUMs (Black Anglo-Saxon Upwardly Mobiles) they were, the Asmoyahs were on the move, having spent nearly a year converting a flat of their own in Limehouse. Goodbye rent book, hello mortgage relief.

So as this was likely to be Salome's last birthday in Stuart Street, I'd got her something special.

I'd always had a soft spot for Salome. Well, strictly speaking, it was a bit of a hard spot, but any serious attempt at Naughties was out of order because I quite liked her husband and anyway he was about ten percent bigger than me and two hundred percent fitter.

But I have my limits, and they were well strained that morning when she opened the door to my knock. So was the purple satin slip she was wearing. Strained, I mean.

'Angel! It's 6.30. What the hell are you doing up?'

I produced my trumpet from behind my back and did a double tempo version of 'Happy Birthday' accompanied by a basic soft-shoe shuffle. And that's not as easy as it sounds; it's a bit like trying to smile and whistle at the same time, like they used to tell Boy Scouts to do.

At least it made Salome smile, until she suddenly remembered the other residents and dragged me into the flat by the elbow.

'You crazy man, you'll wake everybody in the street!'

I kept playing, but pointed to the mute in the trumpet bell. 'You might wake Lisabeth,' she said seriously.

I stopped playing immediately.

A very wise man once said that you should try everything in life once, except incest and folk-dancing. I fully agree with that, but I would add waking Lisabeth, who lived in the flat below with her girlfriend Fenella. (I'd also add: country and western music, driving a Lada, piano lessons from Richard Clayderman, Pot Noodles and a whole bunch of other stuff.)

'Okay, killjoy. Happy birthday to you, Happy...' I sang quietly, then reached into my jacket to produce her present as suggestively as I could.

'What have you got in there?' Salome being coy was almost as cute as Salome being proud and imperious. Or Salome mixing concrete, come to that.

'Birthday girls have birthday presents, just as soon as I can whip it out.'

'I'll take the parcel instead,' she chirped, grabbing the package and wriggling by me into the living-room.

There was a birthday card propped up on her coffee table, which was of the sort that are designed to amputate shins. The card showed a gorilla beating its chest and bore the legend 'I'm Your King of Kongs.' I filed that away to use in evidence against Frank some day.

'My goodness ... it's...'

'Just what you've always wanted?' I offered.

'No, I can't say that. It's...'

'Something to put the magic back into a jaded sexual partnership?'

'No, it's just plain bloody rude! Anyway, who says I'm jaded?' Dangerous ground here, so watch yourself son. Don't let on that you'd noticed the absence of creaking bedsprings for the past four months. At one point in their marriage, you could set your watch by them, as long as you set your watch on Tuesdays and Fridays, that is.

'Just presuming, my dear. You busy busying in the City all day, Frank in training as a legal beagle – or should that be eagle? – and then both of you over in Limehouse every evening doing up the flat. All work, no play.'

'And this will help?'

'I guarantee it. Wear it at the office, especially when you have an important meeting and there are lots of old fogeys clocking you something rotten. They won't know what they're missing. Then, of course, you spring it on Frank one evening when the mood is right.'

'Don't be silly, it wouldn't fit him.' She slumped onto the sofa.

'Well, if you wanted a trial run, I'm usually free on Wednesdays.'

That day was Wednesday. I'm nothing if not subtle.

'Oh shit, it's Wednesday,' she said, throw-

ing back her head and almost all her won-
derfully-shiny hair.

'I can see you're totally underwhelmed by
my offer,' I said, pouting.

'It's not you, Angel darling.' She put out a
hand and patted my knee. It trembled. 'It's
just that I don't want to go to work today.'

'Well, of course not. It's your birthday. In
America, everybody has the day off. Some
American friends of mine have over two
hundred birthdays a year.'

I knew that would cheer her up, and like
most women she showed her amusement by
bursting into tears.

I said lots of 'There, theres,' and sat down
next to her, putting an arm around her and
cocking an ear just in case Frank returned
earlier than usual.

'C'mon, honey, tell Uncle Roy all about it,'
I said, much against my better judgement.
(Rule of Life No 52: when women decide to
tell you what's troubling them, if it's really
important they start with 'It's nothing...')

'It's nothing, really, I suppose,' she said.

Oh shit.

'It's just ... I've got bad vibes at work.' She
took a deep breath and shuddered. 'I'm
being blamed for information leaking out
from the firm, and the big chiefs are getting
paranoid.'

I felt my eyebrows rise. Salome was part of
a team of stockbroking analysts, the back-

13

ground boys and girls who keep industrialists well wined and dined whilst sticking to the Perrier themselves. Any titbit of information they pick up at a lunch table is recycled that afternoon in the form of a sector note telling punters what shares to buy, what to hold, what to flush down the pan. Salome's particular sector was the leisure business, holiday firms, travel agents and so on, but there are as many sectors as there are businesses with share listings: breweries and distilleries, cars, oil, banking, you name it.

If Salome was linked with information leaks, then it was serious. Just at the moment, insider trading carried a stigma in the City only marginally less repugnant than having your car clamped.

'Is it happening?' I asked carefully.

'Oh yes.' She sniffed loudly and stood up, looking for a box of tissues.

'Why does anyone suspect you?' My eyes followed her legs across the room.

'Somebody somewhere has acted on my last two circulars before they even got to our paying customers. Yesterday was the worst. I did a profits forecast on an airline and the shares were being bought within an hour of it leaving my typewriter. I'd had a tip I'm sure nobody else had got wind of. It helps being a woman in the City sometimes.'

'Now, that's a sexist remark, Salome, my dear.'

'No, it isn't,' she smiled.

'It would have been if I'd said it.'

'You could make a note to the milkman sexist.' Now there was female logic for you. 'I'd better get ready, I suppose. Got to face them.'

I stood up and put my arms round her from behind, keeping an eye on the door in the reflection from the screen of her TV.

'Come on, my dear, slip into your pin-stripes and have at them with your umbrella. They've got to be nice to you on your birth-day.'

'Yeah, well, I don't intend to do any work today, so they can't blame me if anything else goes wrong.'

'I've been saying that for years, but they still do. You've nothing really to worry about, have you?'

She half turned to me.

'Yes, I have to worry about it, Angel, but no, I haven't done anything wrong, if that's what you're asking.'

I shrugged, but kept holding her. She kissed me lightly on the cheek.

'I've got to put my face on. I'll be okay, don't worry. Thanks for the concern ... and the present.'

'Why don't you wear it today, eh? Cheer us all up.'

'No, I'm not in the mood. Not today. But I will one day. I've seen pictures of them

15

before, but I never knew they made them in suede.'

'I have contacts, you know,' I said smugly. 'I think you'll find it fits, but if you want to make sure...'

'Out.' She pointed to the door. 'I'll see you tonight.'

'Sure thing.'

'The boys are lined up?'

'Oh yeah, but it'll cost you in beer.'

I had arranged a small band to play at her birthday party after work. As it was Salome and most of the lads knew her through me, they were doing it for beer only, but I don't think Salome had any conception of what that meant in volume terms.

'So we'll see you about 6.00? Frank's coming on later.'

'Good. I'll get the first dance, then.'

'You can't dance and play... Oh yes, I've just seen you, haven't I?'

I smiled my best pearly smile.

'Oh get out, I'll be late.' She reached for a scatter cushion to throw at me. It was a little tradition we had.

'Okay, I'm gone.' I held my hands up and backed to the door.

She put down the cushion and picked up a hairbrush. She had long, lovely black hair, the sort that makes you think you could become a hair fetishist.

'But thanks for getting up so early for my

birthday,' she said.

'What? Oh, no. I was just getting in.'

She reached for the cushion.

I put the flat key in the lock with some trepidation, as I didn't want to wake the Werewolf. He was never at his best in the mornings. He was never at his best during daylight, come to think of it.

I needn't have worried; Springsteen had woken him up and he was glued to breakfast TV and half-way down a bottle of Guinness.

I suppose I'd better explain about Werewolf before you get any funny ideas. I've known him since we were students together, but if I'm lucky I see him maybe every three years. If I'm not lucky, it's more often. He appears, stays for a few days, then goes, leaving only a hangover to remember him by. He eats my food and sleeps on my floor, but he always brings his own booze – 'gargle' as he calls it – and a present. So far, I was down two Chinese take-aways and some kebabs from the local Stavros. My presents had included an ounce of first grade Moroccan black and an old lemonade bottle full of poteen, real vintage hooch at least a week old.

Werewolf was Irish, but his mother, he said, had been French. He could certainly speak French and Irish fluently, and swear competently in about six other languages.

With that natural skill and a first in philosophy, he was destined for great things, so he became a roadie – and a good one he was too, starting with bands like Weather Report, then Joan Armatrading around Europe and then the big one (for him), the U2 concert in Dublin.

'This is a feckin queer country, Angel,' he said between sips of Guinness. 'Mrs T'atcher gets elected for a third term and yet the LP charts are full of Housemartins, Communards and all the other pinkos with their samey sounds and their haircuts. Their bluddy haircuts.'

'Good morning, Werewolf. Good morning, Springsteen.'

I stepped over his sleeping-bag, which was anchored at the feet end by Springsteen at full stretch. As an obedient, loyal and loving pet, Springsteen of course hadn't opened an eye at my entrance. As a guard-cat, he was on borrowed time.

Werewolf must have had a proper name somewhere along the line. I mean, even the most doolally Irish priest would have insisted on something a little more in line with Catholic tradition for the christening. But I honestly couldn't bring it to mind these days.

He got his nickname because of his general appearance, the unkempt hair that looked like fine-mesh barbed-wire and the full, bushy beard that could double as a refuge for displaced badgers in a bad winter.

'That's a fine animal you've got there,' he said, prodding Springsteen with his foot through the sleeping-bag. Springsteen didn't wake up, he just flexed his front nearside claws, and Werewolf drew his foot back sharpish. 'Is there any chance of breakfast, then? I thought we was going to eat last night, but you did a runner after last orders.'

I took the mute out of my horn and balanced it upright on one of the stereo's speakers, then started to undress.

'I told you I had a date with Ruth,' I said, yawning.

'Oh, that night-nurse female I haven't met yet.' Too right, Werewolf.

'But I thought you said she was on duty?'

'She was; we had a Trivial Pursuit tournament in Casualty. Lasted five hours.' Well, we had interruptions. 'Anyway, get what you want, I'm hitting the sack. Don't forget we're playing tonight.'

'Sure thing.' He raised the Guinness bottle to me without taking his eyes off the television. I think he had the hots for the weather lady.

It seemed five minutes, but it was five hours, later when Werewolf shook me awake and put a mug of coffee down on the paperback edition of *The Third Policeman* he'd brought me from Dublin. The mug left a brown ring all over Flann O'Brien's picture.

He can be a real hooligan at times.

'C'mon, Angel, stir those stumps, you've got to run me down to Covent Garden.'

'I have?'

'Yus, you have. You said you knew where I could get an instrument for tonight.' He did a quick shimmy with his hips. 'It's party night!'

Oh God, I'd forgotten I'd not only invited Werewolf to Salome's birthday do but also asked him to play. He was just about the best banjoist I'd come across, I have to say it. But Salome's do was at least six hours away, and that was a long time to keep Werewolf sober.

'Yeah, right on. Let me grab a shower and a shave and I'm with you. I thought we'd pick up a frying-pan for you, then grab a bite to eat and maybe go over a few numbers with Dod over at his place.'

'Oh, don't fret yerself. I've never rehearsed in my life, and I'm too old to start now.'

As he turned to leave, I saw he was wearing his 'Adolf Hitler – European Tour 1938-45' T-shirt, the one that has the gigs listed down the back. You know: Austria, 1938; Czechoslovakia, 1938; Poland, 1939; and so on, ending in Berlin.

'We'll have to come back here to change,' I said to his retreating back, knowing that I was wasting my breath.

Going to Covent Garden with Werewolf was

tempting fate; I knew that. Let's face it, going anywhere with Werewolf was a bit like cooking chips in the dark.

But the Garden had so many potential hazards in its nifty golden rectangle that it was almost worth doubling the insurance premium.

First, there were the tourists Werewolf felt honour-bound to fleece any way he could. Not that I'm knocking that *per se*. I mean, I've survived more than one summer showing American tourists *(never* Japanese; they don't tip or buy you meals, they either give you a paper fan or just bow politely) around Cambridge colleges or Chester's archaeological remains without actually saying I was either a Fellow or an official guide. I can't be responsible if they jump to conclusions, can I? The only trouble was, Werewolf's approach was much less subtle. I have heard him approach tourist families and ask outright for their wallets – for safekeeping, of course, while he took them on a pub crawl of Dublin's down side. More's the point, they give them to him and never complain when they find out later that half their cash has been palmed. Well, I'm saying they don't complain; I don't know – I'm always miles away by then.

Oh yes, that's the other thing about Werewolf. If he wasn't so distinctive (i.e. if he actually didn't look like a werewolf) ... then he'd be the best con in the country. He's the only person who has ever made me seriously consider a body-belt for the rent money.

Then there were the women. A few models, a smattering of Sloanes (or should that be a stuttering of Sloanes?), a fair sprinkling of typists on their lunch-hours and the posh segment out shopping or having a nude swim and a massage in the Sanctuary. They were all targets for Werewolf, whose other T-shirt bears the legend: 'So Many Women, So Little Time.' (Although he bought it because he thought it was a Ramones LP. It probably will be.)

Most dangerous of all, though only by a short head, were the Garden's pubs and wine bars. These drew Werewolf like a moth to a hundred-watt bulb. Trouble was, Werewolf didn't go buzz-flutter-zubb and fall down.

'Will yer get a feckin' move on?' he yelled from the doorway. 'I'm starving.'

Oh dear.

Like the Eskimos have over 47 words for different kinds of snow (including 'yellow' for the sort you don't eat), the Irish must have a similar number for being thirsty.

I pulled on a sweatshirt and thought about a shave. Designer stubble was still in, but only just. Mine wasn't so much designed as crayoned on the back of an envelope. Still, it would do.

Pre-flight check: wallet, watch, packet of Sweet Afton (great Irish smokes but difficult to get in England), lighter, car keys, folded sunglasses, flies zipped. Ready to roll.

Hang on: watch. I'm a bit paranoid about my watches. No, that's not true. It's not paranoia; people really do stare at me if I'm not wearing one. I was quite proud of my new one (the old one was lost in, shall we just say suspicious circumstances), which I'd bought with some cash I'd come into. (No, don't ask.) Getting a Rolex would be like taking out adverts in the *Muggers' Gazette*, so I'd gone for a Tissot. Not the stone-faced with the red-and-yellow hands; no, too gross. I'd chosen the much more sensible Seastar, which would work underwater at depths long after I'd get the bends.

Needless to say, Werewolf had a Mickey Mouse watch that made an obscene gesture twice a day at five past 11.

'Are yer fit to be seen on the street, you old tart?' Werewolf yelled from the stairs.

'Okay. Let's be careful out there,' I shouted back.

Werewolf scampered down the stairs and out of the front door ahead of me. I winced, knowing what was coming.

As I came out of No 9, the mad Irishman was 20 yards down Stuart Street standing on the kerb looking everywhere but at me. He had his right arm raised and the index finger pointed.

'Taxi!'

All right, so I drive a taxi, and I get a lot of stick for it. Not that I'm a real musher, and I've certainly never done the Knowledge. It's just that where other people have 2.2 VW Golfs each or a clapped-out Cortina, and ill-mannered gits drive Escort XRis, because they can't afford BMWs, I have a de-licensed black London cab called Armstrong. So what's yours called?

But seriously, what else would you drive around London? What other vehicle doesn't get clamped, speeding tickets or hit by buses, and which other vehicle runs on diesel, can go twice round the clock and still run sweet as a nut, never has any trouble getting an MOT and can go down Oxford Street without getting pulled by the Bill? I'm surprised Ford are still solvent.

Werewolf, as you've probably guessed, likes riding in the back and shouting directions. He also waves to the pedestrians. I must have a word with him about that one day.

We made it down to the Garden with the minimum of fuss, all things considered, and I found a half-inch of parking space on Henrietta Street. I turned Armstrong around before parking him (Rule of Life No. 277: always park facing the way you're likely to make a quick exit), and turning through 180 degrees is another thing you can do in a cab in London without getting honked at.

'So where do we find this mate of yours?' asked Werewolf, his eyes following the buttocks of a young lady metronoming her way down the pavement.

'Given the time of day, the barometric pressure and this morning's horoscope for Aquarius, there's a fair chance he'll be in the Punch and Judy.'

'Would that be a public house by any chance?'

I could see Werewolf in the driving mirror. He still had his eyes on the pavement.

'There's some dispute about that in certain quarters, but roughly speaking, it is.'

'Then what are we doing here?'

We found Bunny in the downstairs bar of the Punch and Judy, and he and Werewolf got on like a house on fire.

Bunny is one of the few people I know good enough to play as a busker in Covent Garden and, more to the point, he's actually gone through the audition all the others impose. Anyone who doesn't go through the right channels soon finds accidents happening. You know the sort of thing: guitar strings suddenly catch fire, sax reeds get Dutch Elm disease, amplifiers turn out to be more use as microwaves, so forth, so fifth.

'So how much can you make here?' Werewolf asked him in between gulps of stout.

'Well, it's mostly tourists round here. A lot

25

of Dutch birds, the odd Yank, though they tend to go round in pairs, perhaps...'

'No, Bunny,' I said soothingly. 'How much? Not: who?'

'Oh.' All innocence. 'About a ton and a half on a good day. 'Course, that's if the bloody mime artists aren't around. They screw up the traffic flow something rotten.'

Bunny sipped orange juice, and I poured myself some alcohol-free lager. That was the second (and last) sensible move I made that day after brushing my teeth.

'And what about the police?' Werewolf pronounced it pol-lis.

'No problem,' said Bunny.

And he was probably right. Busking isn't actually an offence in British law, but obstruction is, and that's what they do you on. London Transport police, on the other hand, just move you on, though they're not so worried about the buskers as about the fly boys selling suitcases full of pirated cassette tapes. I tend to be more philosophical about them, as the tapes are so badly and loudly recorded that I reckon it's a plot to blow the eardrums of all the ginks on the tube wearing impersonal stereos. More power to their elbow, I say.

'So where do I get my instrument, then?' asked Werewolf, but not before he'd got another round in. He gave me a withering look as he handed over another non-alcoholic lager to me.

'Cricketer's lager,' he said scornfully.

'Eh?' said Bunny.

'Gives you the runs,' I explained.

'Oh. Five-string banjo, wasn't it?' Bunny the professional. If it didn't involve women, Bunny's sense of humour was strictly limited.

'That's the ticket. Got one?'

'No, I only deal in reeds and brass, but Tiger Tim will give you the loan of one for a tenner.'

'He sounds just my sort of man,' grinned Werewolf. I knew he was grinning; I could see his beard move.

Tiger Tim turned out to be a dwarf with three guitars and two banjos, all on stands, upright and forming the points of a pentacle on his pitch near the corner of the entrance to the old market. He wore his hair long over a faded denim jacket and kept it out of his eyes with a red bandana tied pirate-fashion. He had at least six pentacles on chains around his neck and two on an amulet on his left wrist. I'd lay odds that he hadn't been to a Round Tablers lunch for a while.

I let Bunny do the negotiating, but I found a tenner, which was only fair as I was bank-rolling the band for Salome's party.

There was a large lunch-time crowd drift-ing round the flea market and out of the shopping plaza and it was a bright, sunny afternoon. Werewolf couldn't resist it.

He tuned up Tiger Tim's banjo and produced an un-coloured bottle neck with the end ground down for safety, probably a souvenir of a Corona drinking session on his last California trip. He slipped the tube of glass over the middle finger of his left hand and tried a few chords before breaking in to the Boss's 'Spare Parts and Broken Hearts'.

Tiger Tim jammed along for a few seconds, then gave up. The crowd had never heard bottle-neck banjo before, and Werewolf was what they wanted to hear.

After half an hour, the regular buskers formed a committee and had a whipround. They elected a white-faced clown as their spokesman, which amused me because I thought he was going to do it in mime for a minute.

The clown sidled up to me in the crowd and hissed through the corner of his mouth. 'Get the mad Irish git aht of 'ere and there's a drink in it for yer.'

I felt my hand being tapped, and I looked down to see a couple of ten-pound notes tightly folded. I took them from the clown. Fancy, being run out of town by a Cockney Marcel Marceau impersonator!

I tipped Werewolf the nod and he finished with a flourish, packing up the banjo to the applause of the crowd (and cries of 'More' –

although some of the other buskers muttered 'Less'), who pitched another few quid into the banjo case.

When we were in Armstrong heading back to Hackney, Werewolf laughed.

'Nicely done, Angel me old mucker. I reckon we're a tenner apiece up on the day, even allowing for the rent of the instrument. We haven't pulled that one since ... when was it?'

'The Edinburgh Festival.' That time we got paid to leave by a consortium of fire-eaters, two street-theatre companies, a bagpiper (you ever heard a synthesised bagpipe?) and an accordionist. 'And you just couldn't resist showing off, could you? One of these days, they'll do you over rather than pay you off.'

Werewolf laughed again.

'I'm terrible aren't I? Some days–' he was being philosophical; I could tell, because he'd put his feet up on the glass partition behind my head –'I just shouldn't be let out of the house.'

CHAPTER TWO

Salome's birthday bash was held in a pub called the Pavilion End, because it had been done out like a cricket pavilion. Apart from the cricket bores from the City who haunt it during the summer, it's not a bad boozer. It's just behind St Paul's, on Watling Street, the old Roman road that connected the Kent coast with St Albans, though it beats me why anyone should want to go to St Albans.

There was a downstairs room for parties and where the pub occasionally had a jazz trio or quartet, but there was little space, so I'd limited our ensemble to five: me and my horn, Werewolf and Tiger Tim's banjo, a BBC producer called Martin who would take his trombone anywhere to get in a gig, and my regular co-conspirators Dod and Trippy. Dod is not only a passable drummer but he also has a van big enough to transport us all, and Trippy, when he's straight, is a passable pianist. (Actually, Trippy is a very good pianist, but only passably straight most of the time. He's not called Trippy because he falls over his bootlaces.)

Martin was there first, partly because he was keen – 'Jolly decent of you to let me jam with you'– and partly because the rest of us had arrived in Dod's van, which is never reliable at the best of times and certainly not in the City at rush hour.

I introduced Werewolf to Martin – he already knew Dod and Trippy – and we managed to set up Dod's drum kit and tune up before the pub started to fill. Well, I say tune up. Trippy opened the lid of the upright piano, estimated that there were at least 70 keys there and then headed for the bar. Werewolf took Tiger Tim's banjo out of its case, murmured, 'A man after me own thirst,' and followed him.

'It'll end in tears,' I said to Dod.

'Yer probably right,' he said. Then he tightened the last butterfly nut on his high hat and went to join them.

'Er ... can I get you a pint in?' Martin asked nervously.

'Might as well,' I said resignedly. 'Make it two.'

'Two? Each?'

'It gets very crowded in here.'

By the time Salome appeared, there were so many red-striped shirts so close together that I thought my vertical hold needed adjusting. The place had filled so much that the next champagne cork would probably constitute assault and battery.

You get the picture already. The *jeunesse-*

31

dorée-ever-so-slightly-blue (as Werewolf once described them) were there en masse. The young City slickers had taken off their double-breasted suit jackets and were flashing the shirts they'd bought at Next before it went downmarket, which they probably got their mums to wash. I wondered if it was true that they bought suits with an extra jacket so they could leave it over the backs of their chairs in front of their screens when they went to lunch. Not that many of them ever ate lunch. Just think, they might miss a couple of million between Mars bars.

We'd done a WC Handy selection, and I was quite pleased with my solo on 'Hesitation Blues', though I fluffed some of the fast high ones on 'Atlanta Blues' trying to do a Satchmo. Well, I get carried away. Then we'd done 'Tiger Rag', partly because Martin wanted to show off, and I've always thought it was a bone player's piece anyway, and then 'And the Angels Sing', which was a bit of a private joke between me and Werewolf involving distant memories of three Aer Lingus hostesses (and, yes, I know *all* the jokes) in the days way back when there was safe sex, or what we thought was.

Then I saw Salome's legs coming downstairs and we slid into 'Happy Birthday', which could be my theme tune I seem to play it so often.

Salome was wearing a blue jersey dress I

hadn't seen before, a red leather belt about a foot wide with a buckle no bigger than a portcullis, long red evening gloves up to the elbows and really dangerous red high heels. It was enough to impress an atheist.

There was a general increase in the hub-bub at her arrival. She seemed to be known by most of the crowd, and a fresh volley of champagne corks went off at the bar. I was beginning to know how Rommel felt at El Alamein.

It seemed a good time for the band to take five – which Werewolf deliberately mis-construed as meaning pints of stout – and mingle with the throng.

Salome was surrounded by people push-ing presents at her and saying 'Darling' or ''Ello, darlin',' depending on which side of the river they lived. I blew her a kiss when our eyes met, and she smiled back, but even at a distance, I could tell she was going through the motions rather than letting her hair down.

Werewolf and I made our way to the bar by different circular routes – an old U-boat tactic when hunting in packs. I kept an ear open and picked up the City chat.

'...saw it coming a mile off. Got out of dollars and into yen nearly a year ago...'

'...but it's basically bid-proof because of the two-tier voting structure...'

'...so I said orwite, son, you can 'ave what

I can get but there'll be a premium that'll make your nuts ache, and 'e said...'

'...and as I have never exactly wet myself over the trade figures, I don't see why my clients should...'

You know the sort of stuff; well, you would if you'd ever been in a bar within a mile of Bishopsgate after 5.00 pm, or after 4.00 since they changed the pub hours. There was one thing I caught, though, that made the hairs on the back of my neck stand up.

'...the spade bitch deserves the stick whether she's doing it or not.'

I turned as much as the crowd would allow, but it was impossible to tell where the voice had come from. It could have been any one of six pairs of large tortoiseshell glasses or about a dozen pale yellow ties. I'd remember it, though.

Werewolf had reached the bar about six feet away, and he sidled along until he was at my elbow, mouthing the words 'Pint o' stout,' and I realised I could lip-read Irish accents.

'So these are what yer call Yuppies, are they?' he asked between sips.

'Some are,' I said, after ordering a bottle of Pils.

We turned and rested our backs on the bar, like Alan Ladd used to do, except we weren't standing on boxes.

'Now he–' I pointed with my glass –

'probably is, because he's had time to go to his squash club or somewhere like Cannon's gym after work and break into just enough sweat to justify a shower and a change into his country casuals. His work suit's probably in the Porsche parked round in Finsbury Square.' The tall blond guy I meant was wearing enough designer labels to account for the GNP of, say, Andorra.

'But he, on the other hand–' I swung my Pils to the right – 'that's probably a Puppy.'

Werewolf squinted his eyes in curiosity, but I knew he wouldn't come out and ask.

'A Previously Upwardly-mobile etc,' I explained. 'Did very well out of the Big Bang but has found it very hard going a year on. Probably been demoted when his brokers got taken over by a bank or similar. You can tell, because he's still wearing Mr Harry suits even though they've been naff for – ooh – six months now.'

'I've heard of them, but I never thought I'd actually see one. It makes me feel like David-fucking-Attenborough.'

'And there–' I noticed my glass was nearly empty – 'is the future. The one drinking Coke from the bottle and trying to eat a pound of peanuts because he's heard protein is good for you. Looks like he hasn't taken O-Levels yet, and he probably hasn't, and now he won't 'cos he's earning too much.'

'As what?'

'They call them market-makers now. It used to be jobbers, you know, on the Stock Exchange floor. Before the Big Bang, the best he could have hoped for was a tick-tack man's assistant on a race course.'

Werewolf pushed his tongue into his right cheek until his beard bristled. It was his way of looking thoughtful.

'And the public school hangers-on?' he asked.

'Lombards.'

'Lots Of Money But Are Right Dick-heads?'

'Correct. Your round.'

Werewolf turned to the bar and noticed a couple of double-breasted suits using mobile phones. I could now sense the hairs on the back of his neck standing up.

'Watch this,' he whispered, and edged along the bar as if trying to get to the bar-man. As he moved, he sneaked up behind the two mobile users and gently nudged each one on the elbow.

I tried to assume my never-seen-him-before-in-my-life ('your Honour') expression as the two suits turned angrily on him, but Werewolf just smiled and said 'Sorry, sur' in his best bog Irish, and they let it go at that, moving away from the bar before trying to redial.

'They're very badly designed, those BT

mobiles, yer know. The "Off" button is so close to the ear-piece that it's ever so easy to cut yerself off, just putting them up close.'

'How do you know stuff like that, Were-wolf?'

'It's always happening with mine.' He handed me a pint.

'I never had you down as a slave to modern technology.'

'That's rich, coming from somebody who drives a black cab and smokes Gold Flake and probably still hasn't worked out how to open a Swiss army penknife.'

'And I refuse to own a Filofax, don't forget, on religious grounds.'

'What religious grounds?'

'For the love of God, I can't think what I'd put in one.'

He narrowed his eyes.

'Shall we resume and get the joint jumping?'

'They won't appreciate it,' I said.

'I know, but the sooner we do another set, the sooner we can get down to some serious drinking. This is supposed to be a party.'

There's no peace for the wicked.

I had to scout around for Trippy, and found him in the upstairs bar conversing with an Australian barman. Now there was a deal going down if ever I saw one.

Dod hadn't moved from behind his drum

kit – he trusted nobody – and Martin was where we'd left him, raring to go for the second set. We put together a fair enough selection, from 'Indiana' to 'St James's Infirmary' with 'Perdido' and 'Avalon' in there somewhere. Werewolf managed his Django impersonation of 'Moppin' the Bride' (a bebop version of the Wedding March), which actually drew a smattering of applause. Then Martin did a solo version of 'Do Nothing Till You Hear From Me', which was really very good, and we all clapped even if the revellers ignored it.

Not to be outdone, Trippy offered to fill in a few numbers, so we let him take over, although Martin looked a bit put out as he was on a roll and could have gone on all night. But he'll learn.

I looked around the party. It had thinned out some and the composition had changed. A few of the City slickers had slunk off either to their wives or to Cannon's health club or similar to work off the tonic water or Perrier they had been punishing their bodies with. The younger, brasher market-maker crowd were sitting tight and knocking back the lager like there was no tomorrow. For them, maybe there wasn't.

A posse of Salome's female friends had arrived to slightly redress the sex ratio but, like most things in the City, it was still weighted heavily towards the male. It was the sort of situation that makes me feel uncomfortable normally and one of the reasons I always avoid pubs that discriminate, however tactfully, against women. (Rule of Life No 13: as women form more than 50 percent of the population, they should be taken into account in all things. Don't be a General Custer – know when you're outnumbered.)

Trippy had started his potted history of jazz, a flexible medley that is really wicked when he remembers it all and could go on all night if you let him. He was somewhere between late cakewalk and early ragtime when I indicated to the rest of the band that we should pack up and, making the international tipping-wrist signal, head for the bar.

I waited for the crowd to rush us and demand an encore like they do in the Miller and Goodman biopics of the 50s, but nobody moved. To be fair, Salome did. She pushed her way through the crowd and put her hands above her head in the sort of clapping motion footballers make to the crowd at the end of a match. She mouthed 'Thank you' a couple of times before being dragged away by a new arrival, a stunning young black girl wearing a suede mini that Tina Turner would have turned down as too rude.

Werewolf made a low growling noise. He'd

seen her too.

'Down, boy,' I said in his ear. 'Let's get the instruments away first.'

'Aye, yer right,' he said, and packed up Tiger Tim's banjo, giving the case a double pat to show he'd approved.

As we were dismantling Dod's drum kit, and Trippy was up to Jelly Roll Morton, one of the suits came up to us. He had one hand in his pocket and one around a glass of champagne and was flashing his striped shirt and red tie at us.

'Jaysus, it's Robin Redbreast,' muttered Werewolf.

'Can I help you?' I asked as the nominal leader, though I've always wondered why it's usually the trumpet-player who gets lumbered with dealing with the hecklers and the request-demanders. I mean, the horn player is the one who can least afford a fat lip if they turn bolshy.

'I was wondering if your chum here on the banjo had ever worked with a band. He's rather good, I thought,' said the chinless wonder.

'U2, the Genesis Invisible Touch tour and George Michael's Faith gig,' said Werewolf without looking round.

'Oh,' said CW. 'So you're what they call a session musician.'

'No, I make the tea and drive the vans.'

'Ha-ha. Very good.' CW's laugh was like a

horse that had just misjudged the height of a fence, but he seemed happy enough and wandered off to tell his chums that he'd met a real live roadie.

Werewolf watched him push through the throng, and shook his head slowly.

'Where do they come from?' he wondered aloud.

'He probably made telephone numbers of money before you were on your second Weetabix this morning,' I said, handing Dod his bass pedal.

'Frightening, isn't it. They're all so bluddy alike. Just like country and western music, all style no substance.'

'That's very good, Werewolf. Where did you read it?'

Werewolf pursed his lips at me.

'Ooh, you bitch. You're so sharp, *you* can be in the shower scene.'

With not a little difficulty, we got the instruments out of the pub and round the corner into Dod's Transit van. I offered him a tenner for petrol, but he declined, saying it was for a friend and he'd catch me some-time for a drink. As he was in a good mood, I asked him to drop Martin off near the Central Line and to look after the instru-ments until I could collect them. He grunted a few times, which I took to be a Yes, Okay, Willdo. Dod doesn't waste words.

I wandered back into the pub. The plan

had been to keep things moving right along there until about 9.30, after which Salome would pass the word to a few select friends to reconvene back at our house in Stuart Street for a final fling. I hoped she'd warned the mysterious Mr Goodson, who lived in the ground-floor flat and was rarely seen after dark. She probably had; she's very sensible. Unfortunately.

As I made my way downstairs, I could hear that Trippy was up to Errol Garner, which was never popular unless he was playing to real jazz fans. With a lay audience like this one, he should have quit while he was ahead, say with Teddy Wilson, although he would probably get away with Dave Brubeck. I'm told there are still people alive who can remember when 'Take Five' was in the charts, though it's been used for so many TV signature tunes even some of these wunderkind would recognise it.

I ran into Salome at the bottom of the stairs. Literally.

'Oooh, sorry, Angel.'

'No problem. You've just made an old man very happy.'

She put her hand up and stroked my cheek.

'Oh, not that old,' she said coyly.

'Then you've just made a young man very randy. What time do we split?'

She looked at a gold watch so thin it could

have been a bracelet for rheumatism.

'We're okay here for another hour, so I'd like to thin this lot out.'

So would I, with a Bren gun, but I didn't say it.

She gave me a wide-eyed, up-from-under look. It never fails.

'I mean really thin this lot out, Angel. I don't want more than a handful back at the flat.'

'One handful coming up,' I quipped, doing a Groucho with my fingertips.

Salome narrowed her eyes. 'Don't ever say I don't feed you the good lines. I'm serious. I don't want you inviting all and sundry round to the flat; I couldn't face it.'

'Bad day at the office?'

'Uh-huh.'

'Fair enough, your wish is my command. Where's Frank, by the way?'

'He's chilling the wine and opening the peanuts back at the flat. This isn't his scene.'

'I never had him down as a caterer.'

'Lisabeth and Fenella are helping out.'

'My God, we'd better hurry.'

'I think he's safe enough,' she observed wryly. Then she looked over my shoulder at something. 'But you're not. Meet Beeby.'

I turned as slowly and coolly as I could manage, and I found myself virtually nose to nose with the stunner in the suede miniskirt.

'Sal says your name is Angel. Is it really?'

'If yours is Beeby, why not?'

'I'll tell you why I'm called Beeby if you tell me why you're called Angel.' She smiled, then sipped some wine.

'Seems reasonable. Shall we adjourn to the bar?'

'Sure.' Beeby smiled broadly. 'And don't worry, I really am a pushover.'

I smiled back.

'So am I.'

Beeby and I got on famously after she announced she'd got interested in the great lady blues singers after reading or hearing an interview with Sade in one of the music comics. That singled her out, as most of our audience that night were probably convinced that Whitney Houston invented jazz. I scored a few kudos points by saying I knew Sade (well, I'd stood next to her in a pub once), and offered to get her a refill.

The crush at the bar was still bad, but I clawed out a couple of inches with some nifty elbow work and waited to be noticed by a barman. (Rule of Life No 56: never shout at a barman unless you know him or her – in which case you shouldn't have to – just wave some money casually and look as if you couldn't care less when you got served.) I got served almost immediately, and while the barman was opening another bottle of wine, I scanned the heads and shoulders and spotted Werewolf at the other end of the pub. He was deep into serious chat with a tall blonde I hadn't even seen arrive. I somehow doubted he'd need the sleeping-bag that night.

Our drinks arrived, and as I waited more in hope than expectation for some change, I tuned in to some City chat. Actually, I wasn't really earwigging at all. It was just that I heard that voice again, the 'spade bitch' voice.

It wasn't saying that again, it was telling somebody called Nigel to 'keep it buttoned.'

I turned my head but, I still could not pin down the voice's owner. I did spot somebody, though, only a yard (and about six people) away. It was the Chinless Wonder who'd come up to the bandstand, and he was looking into the face of a clean cut, red-spectacled young man.

'Simon, all I told him was to get out of Capricorn Travel before the excrement hits the ventilator tomorrow. He's not a big holder, Si. It won't make waves. Dammit, Simon, I was at school with him.'

I didn't catch any more, as somcone who didn't work to Rule of Life No 56 yelled for a pint of lager right in my ear, presumably expecting the order to come out the other side of my head nearer the barman.

Somebody else surged in towards the bar,

causing a ripple of bodies, and to keep my drinks intact I had to step away. I took a long look at the one Chinless Wonder had called Simon, just to make sure I remembered the face. It's never a good thing to hate somebody on sight, but it does save time in the long run.

His eyes caught me clocking him, but he looked straight through me. I was pretty sure he wouldn't recognise me again unless I drew attention to myself, and I had no intention of starting a fight. (Rule of Life No 44: never start fights. Always aim to take out your opponent before he realises you've got it in for him.) Then again, I wasn't going to stand for any 'spade bitch' attitude near young Beeby. So I suggested we moved upstairs.

We actually managed to get a seat there, and I was able to get most of Beeby's life-story, particularly how she wanted to get into the music business. Why ask me? But I didn't say it.

Werewolf and the tall blonde emerged and left without a word or a nod in our direction. Ah well, he'd turn up somewhere, somehow.

Then the guy the Chinless Wonder called Simon emerged, buttoning up a camelhair coat. Sure enough, CW tagged along behind. He'd left his jacket somewhere, and I noticed, not that you could miss them, that

46

he was wearing red-striped braces to match the shirt, and the stripes all went in the same direction. How naff.

'Si...' said Chinless, offering a glass of champagne.

Simon turned on him and put his right forefinger up to CW's lips. Then he shook his head slowly, then he took his finger away, made an open palm with his hand and gently patted CW's cheek.

It was a curious little pantomime, which I thought I was the only witness to. As usual, I was wrong.

'What's so fascinating about the two irons?' asked Beeby, following my gaze.

'Oh, I don't think they're gay,' I said, thinking she meant 'iron hooves' as in rhyming slang.

'No, iron as in iron gates. The new Yuppies living in Docklands, where they have to chain up their windsurfers at night and they keep the real locals out with big iron gates. Those two look the sort. Cash registers for brains and no soul.'

'You could be right.' Such perception in one so young. 'But let's talk about you.'

And she did.

I have to admit that her attitude towards me cooled somewhat as she realised that I was far from the music-circle big shot she'd imagined. But then I told her about my friend Lloyd Allen and his recording empire (well, he manages bands and gets record sleeves designed) and she sat up and took notice. Basically, Beeby was mapping out a career as a pop star without the hassle of actually having to sing or play. She was quite open about it. She admitted she didn't have the boobs to be a page three girl or the class to be a model. Of course, she couldn't sing and she was pretty sure she was tone deaf too, but she genuinely felt she had something to offer pop culture. Her ambition was to be burnt out by the time she was 22.

Salome appeared in the nick of time, just as boredom was setting into my left buttock, with about a dozen revellers from downstairs. We followed her entourage out, and near St Paul's we managed to cram into three taxis. It was a novelty for me to travel in one in the back, and quite an experience to travel with Beeby on my knee. The musher driving complained all the way to Hackney that he shouldn't have more than four in the back, but for me the journey wasn't long enough.

Back at the house on Stuart Street, there were about a dozen people already boogying the night away in Frank's and Sal's flat. Well, to be honest, they were all sitting round sipping Australian Chardonnay and listening to Luther Vandross and trying to make it look like fun. I decided to liven things up by shouting 'Pump up the volume, Frank,' and slipped a Huey Lewis CD into his twee little Japanese midi system.

I claimed a bottle of wine and two glasses and looked around for Beeby, but she was busy checking out the guests for record producers. I doubted she'd find any, as most of Frank's friends were legal beagles or proto-fuzz. You know, magistrates' clerks and the like. So I checked in with Lisabeth and Fenella, who had ventured up from the flat below; a social outing for them of the same magnitude as, say, Scott's crack at the South Pole.

It was fairly obvious from the way she slumped in the corner of the sofa that Lisabeth was in a Huff, or at least a Mood if not a full scale Huff. I moved a *Next Directory* and sat down beside her.

'Did you know, Lisabeth old fruit, that the population of Hackney Borough is now greater than that of Iceland?'

She gave me a look that would have withered a clump of nettles at 50 feet.

'Are you drunk?' she hissed.

'Have I started juggling oranges?'

'No,' she said suspiciously.

'Then you're safe for now.' I poured a glass of wine for her. 'But it might be an idea to put the fruit bowl out of temptation's way. What's up? You look as if toothache might cheer you up.'

Lisabeth sighed deeply, and her bulk sent

a ripple effect along the sofa.

'It's Binky,' she said. It always was. 'She's a constant worry these days.' She screwed up her face. 'Ugh! What's this?'

'It's wine. Chardonnay, from Down Under. I think it's rather good,' I said honestly. 'I can't afford it.'

'Whatever happened to white wine that was sweet?' she puzzled.

'It was called Liebfraumilch, and only the lower classes drink it nowadays. So what's Binky done now?'

Fenella, apart from having the dubious honour of being Lisabeth's live-in lover, as the Trade Descriptions Act puts it these days, was cursed with the surname Binkworthy. Hence, Binky. (She also came from a posh family in Rye, wouldn't you know it, though I've never held that against her.)

Lisabeth fixed Binky with her best laserbeam stare. Fenella's a tall girl and was once probably very self-conscious about her height until flat shoes came back, and although I don't think I'm a foot fetishist, I reckon the Princess of Wales has got a lot to answer for on that score. She still had a pretty eccentric idea of casual clothes, though, and at the moment was wearing a light blue cotton dress and a darker blue blazer. It looked suspiciously like her old school uniform.

'It's not what she's done,' said Lisabeth

50

primly. 'It's her ... her attitude.'

She made it sound like a disease, and a contagious one.

'One of those *men* – that one–' she indicated a perfectly harmless-looking bloke in a snappy suit – 'asked her if she worked in some restaurant called School Dinners, and she giggled and has been talking to him ever since. Look out, they're coming over.'

'Don't worry,' I whispered, 'I'll get rid of him. Fenella love, where've you been hiding all my life?'

Fenella sat down on the sofa next to me, not Lisabeth, and smiled sweetly over the top of her glass.

'I wasn't born for most of it, Angel.'

'Very good, Fenella darling; you've been keeping up the postal course in witty put-downs, I see,'

'But Angel–' she blushed – 'you're always saying you taught me everything I know.'

'Well, not *everything*, Binky.' She went from red to scarlet. On my other side, Lisabeth snorted loudly. 'Anyway, who's your friend?'

The guy who had been chatting her up came over with a glass of wine for her.

'Angel, this is Alec Reynolds. He's in the City.'

I nodded to him and poured myself another glass. I realised I was well down the bottle and I still hadn't got to Beeby yet. I wondered if anybody fancied an exhibition of orange-juggling.

'Did I ever tell you my plan for making my fortune in the City?' I asked Fenella, ignoring Alec.

'Which one?'

'The Fish and Chips empire.' She frowned and Alec leaned forward, so I pressed on. 'It's easy, really. You just work on the basis that everybody in the City has more money than sense, novelty commands a premium price, and they all get hungry. So, what I plan to do is start up a fish and chip shop – or better still, a mobile one in a van – that serves cod and chips wrapped in the *Financial Times*. You could do a deal with the paper and get over-run copies cheap in the morning after the main deliveries have gone, and you could even specialise. Say, rock salmon comes in the commodities page, plaice is wrapped in the oil section.'

'You could do afternoon fry-ups in the *Racing Post*,' said Alec, catching on. 'And take-home suppers in the TV pages of the last edition of the *Standard*.'

'Exactly, and you could charge ten pounds a go in the City and get away with it. And you'd get tons of publicity, and within six months some restaurant or pub would offer to buy you out.'

'And would you sell?' asked Alec.

'Of course, just before the novelty wore off. Remember, there are 13 million mugs in London and they all need to come just the once to make my fortune.'

Alec laughed, and Fenella smiled uncertainly, not sure if I was serious. Lisabeth snorted again. Obviously Alec was getting too friendly.

'What would you do with your millions then, eh? I'm sure my firm could put together an attractive portfolio for you,' Alec offered.

I waved him away magnanimously and poured myself another drink. The bottle seemed empty.

'I have my own sources, old boy. I'd do some short term trading, keep my ear to the ground for good buys. Maybe I'll dabble in something like – ooh, say, Capricorn Travel. You know, buy when it's cheap and then...'

I had been showing off, and honestly didn't expect the reaction I got.

It wasn't so much that Alec's expression changed from amusement to one akin to chronic indigestion, or that his fingers whitened around his glass so that I felt sure he would snap it in half. What really threw me was Salome's scream.

She had been standing right behind me and obviously listening in.

'What did you say?' she'd yelled.

'Eh? What...?'

She'd almost given me a heart attack, but she was the one clutching her hands to her mouth.

'How did you know?' she shouted. 'How?'

Then she ran from the room into the kitchen, and the door slammed behind her. Frank charged after her, looking daggers at me as he passed.

'What have I said?' I asked nobody in particular, and nobody answered.

Me and my big mouth. I should have kept it well zippered.

It would have avoided a lot of aggro for Salome and Alec and several others, notably me.

It also meant I never got to find out why Beeby was called Beeby.

CHAPTER THREE

I surfaced next morning with a really Gothic hangover. All the classic symptoms were there: the overflowing ashtray mouth, the dreaded Whirling Pits where the sense of balance ought to be and the steam-hammer thumping behind the eyes as if somebody was pounding my head against the wall.

I opened an eye and saw that Lisabeth had me by the hair and was pounding my head against the wall.

'Oi! Florence Nightingale! Take it easy will you!'

'Wake up, Angel!'

'Leave it out. Just go easy on the violence, okay? Christ, I think you've loosened my brain.'

'So that's what was rattling. Now will you wake up?'

I opened one eye again. She was still there. If she'd handed me the Temperance Pledge I'd have signed it on the spot. Lisabeth could collect a lot of signatures this way.

'Orwight, orwight. I'm awake.'

'Both eyes, please.'

'Happy now?' She didn't look any better in stereo.

'Good. Now get out of that pit and come and talk to Salome.'

'Who? What? What for?'

'Get up.' Thump. 'And talk to Salome.' Thump. 'Before she goes to work.' Thump.

I caught her wrist with both hands. God, she was strong. It didn't even slow her down. Thump. God, I was weak.

'Okay, okay, I'm up.'

I flung back the duvet and swung my legs out of bed. Lisabeth saw I was naked and dropped me like a hot brick. She didn't actually scream but there was a definite sharp intake of breath.

'We'll be in the living-room until you're decent,' she said with as much dignity as she could muster while fixing her eyes on the ceiling.

'You could have a long wait,' I yelled after her.

I padded into the bathroom to soak my head under the bath taps, hitting myself this time, but by now I was probably punch drunk.

I brushed my teeth – carefully – and although they felt loose, they all seemed to be there.

I remembered that after Salome had thrown her wobbler at the party, I'd been taken out to sit on the stairs with Lisabeth acting as my minder. I must have slipped away from her at some point as I distinctly remember nipping downstairs to my flatlet to get the bottle of poteen Werewolf had brought me from Ireland. I even remember laughing about the label – a piece of lined paper stuck on with Sellotape on which was written 'Kerry Dew' in green crayon. They probably didn't allow sharp objects in the place it was made.

To be honest, that was about all I remembered. I just hoped I had managed to put down a couple of pints of water before I fell into my pit, to combat dehydration, otherwise I was going to feel terrible later on. (Getting drunk costs me a fortune in bottled mineral water ever since I found out that tap water in London has been recycled five times.)

I put a towel around my stomach – I don't

possess a dressing-gown – and jogged from the bathroom to the kitchenette. Two-and-a-half seconds. Good, my times were improving.

I found an unopened tetrapack of orange juice in the fridge, hiding behind a stick of celery. It took me a few more seconds to bite the corner off and drink. Aagh, lifesaver. The man who put OJ into those things deserves a medal, but if he hasn't got one, he's probably rich enough not to worry about it.

There was nothing else I could think of to delay me. Breakfast was out of the question in my state, not that I've ever been wild about celery. So I hitched my towel tighter and clutched my OJ like a gunslinger's .45 as I strode into the living-room.

'Hi there, Sal, my love, popped home for lunch?' I breezed in and parked myself on the sofa next to her.

I'd just assumed she was back from the office because she had her city slicker gear on: a suit jacket in grey and red squares so wide at the shoulder that Robert Mitchum could have acted in it; short, tight matching skirt; black stockings with red seams; and really high-heeled black shoes with a single silver star on the back of just the left one.

'I haven't gone to work yet, Angel. I was worried, and Lisabeth said you wouldn't mind a chat.'

I looked at my watch. Jesus Christ, but it wasn't even seven o'clock. Never mind, stay charming and make sure the towel doesn't slip.

'Anytime, Sal, as long as you let me say how smart you're looking, and I particularly like the really dangerous shoes.'

Salome tugged the hem of her skirt down a micron or two.

'Well ... thank you. But the shoes aren't dangerous.'

'You don't know what I'm thinking,' I leered.

'That's enough of that,' said Lisabeth. If I'd been wearing trousers she would probably have smacked the backs of my legs. 'Salome is worried.'

'Then tell all, Salome. You know what they say, A Trouble Shared ... is two people losing sleep.' I buried my face in the OJ carton.

Salome licked her lips and leaned forward. I wished she wouldn't do that when I was wearing only a towel.

'Do you remember what you said about Capricorn Travel last night, when you were talking to Alec?' Her eyes widened in hope. Lisabeth's widened out of sheer nosiness.

'To be honest, Sal darling, I can't remember last night, let alone Capricorn Travel or Alec. Alec who? Do I owe him money?'

'Angel!' snapped Lisabeth. 'Be serious.'

I shook my head to clear some of the

pebbles in there. They just moved position a bit.

'Okay, okay, it's all coming back to me now. Yes, there was this guy at the party ... no, earlier, at the pub. He had a particularly nasty turn of phrase that I didn't want ... Beeby. What happened to Beeby?'

'She left with one of Frank's friends,' said Salome, almost apologetically.

'A musician?' I must have sounded worried, because it startled her.

'No,' she said thoughtfully. 'Although Wallace has done some contract work for CBS and EMI. Why?'

'Oh, nothing. Skip it.' Wallace, eh? I wonder what his friends called him.

'Well, get on with it,' Lisabeth shouted angrily. She probably wasn't shouting, but it felt like it.

As quickly as I could, I told them about the Chinless Wonder and the guy he called Simon or Si and how I'd noticed him because of his mouthy attitude and devotion to the Eichmann school of racial harmony.

'I just remembered that stuff about Capricorn Travel. They talked about the shit hitting the fan today and tipping somebody off to pull out his stake. Later on, when we got back here, I was just being lippy and showing off. I don't know what it means, for Christ's sake. Is it serious? Don't tell me, it's serious, isn't it?'

Salome reached out and put a hand on mine. Lisabeth scowled.

'We could be talking unemployment, Angel. I work with Alec, and he knows you know something only I or he could have known.'

'But...'

'He's got to mention it today at the office and yours truly gets it in the neck. Then it's goodbye yellow brick road.'

'And goodbye new place in Limehouse?'

''Fraid so. We couldn't afford it just on Frank's salary. Yet.'

'Does he know?'

'He knows something's wrong, but not what exactly, and not how bad it is. You see, Capricorn Travel is one of mine. One of my companies. I'm the sector analyst and they're my particular tip – or they were – and our company are their brokers and...'

Her big eyes misted over and she swallowed hard to lock off the tears.

There was only one thing for it.

'Listen, love, is there anything I can do to help?'

As soon as I'd said it I wished I'd bitten my tongue.

'Well, actually, there could be.'

Bitten clean through.

So I had to go to lunch with Salome; what's so bad about that? Normally, of course, absolutely nothing. Normally an honour worth lying, cheating and maybe even wearing a tie for.

But this was lunch at the office. A working lunch, a real finger-tap table-top session. And I had a nasty feeling that I was being served up as dessert.

Come and have lunch in our Directors' Room, she'd said, with Alec and their section boss. Have a shave and put on a suit and find some black shoes, she'd thought.

Well, the suit was out for a start, as I don't possess one, or at least not at the moment. I'd had one once, but a lot of my possessions had formed a lengthy insurance claim after a previous residence of mine down in Southwark had sort of blown up one day. I'd learnt a lot from the experience: travel light and rent north of the river.

I settled for a dark blue blazer that I hadn't spilt much down, a baggy, grey-wool shirt with buttoned down collar and some black slacks that would have been pressed if I'd remembered to put them under the mattress.

That was going to have to do. I didn't really care what impression I made in the City; for Hackney I was sharp as a pistol.

I took a bus, not Armstrong, into the dirty old heart of the City. For a start, I was probably still over the limit from the pub and the party, and it would really peeve me to get breathalysed for a piss-up where I'd made a conscious decision not to drink and drive. You see, I can be socially responsible. And anyway, my hands were still shaking and I had trouble focusing – hence the dark glasses – and I couldn't remember where I'd left Armstrong's keys.

Salome's office wasn't actually in the Stock Exchange, but I didn't think it was my place to complain. It was round on Gresham Street on the third floor of a building occupied by, among others, a Japanese bank, a Malaysian bank and an Australian investment trust. I didn't have accounts with any of them, and I wondered if that meant I was deprived. Certainly, from the look he gave me, the doorman of the building thought I was.

I don't suppose they called him a doorman, mind you, even though he was wearing enough gold braid on the shoulders of his uniform to settle the balance of payments.

I told him I was there on business with a luncheon (note that: luncheon) appointment with Prior, Keen, Baldwin, and eventually he had to believe me.

In the lift, I allowed myself a significant thought. Why are there no 'ands' in the names of City firms? For example, Sal's firm: Prior, Keen, Baldwin, *not* 'and Baldwin.' Maybe Baldwin objected. He probably would if he knew the firm was referred to as Pretty Keen Bastards among the financial press, although knowing a fair cross-section of City half-life, Baldwin was probably secretly pleased.

If he'd done what most of the old brokers had done and sold out to the mega-nationals, he was probably in Switzerland teaching the gnomes to fish. In fact, Prior, Keen, Baldwin was almost certainly called something like Durban Kuwait Broken Hill Den Haag Prior Keen Baldwin Suisse nowadays. But as the switchboard operators could never get that out before the pips went, they stuck to their old name.

At the third floor, the lift doors opened on to a sort of lobby area with a big oaken desk and another uniformed ex-SAS man in residence. I trudged across a carpet that really exercised the ankles to get to him.

'Yes, sir? Can we help you, sir?'

There was nobody else around, so it must have been me he was growling at. He'd probably never seen anybody not in a suit before.

'I'm here for lunch with Ms Asmoyah and a Mr Reynolds. Which way's the canteen?'

'One moment, sir.'

He was impervious to my best charmer smile, but his eyes never left me as he picked up a phone and pressed a button or two. I couldn't understand it. There was nothing nickable around except his desk.

'There's a visitor for you, Mr Reynolds.' Then to me, with a smirk: 'Mr Angel, is it?'

'Yes,' I said seriously, 'of Fitzroy, Maclean,

Angel, Dealer and Bonk.'

'Mr Reynolds will be out directly, sir. Have a seat.'

I noticed one single, straight-backed chair near the lift doors, so I pulled it over to his desk, turned it round and straddled it, folding my arms on the back. I tried another smile on him and struck up a conversation.

'So what do you think of Arsenal's chances in the Cup, then?'

He turned red and made a strangled sobbing sound.

'No,' I agreed, 'I don't rate them this season either.'

Alec Reynolds appeared and rescued me before the porter could get to me across the desk.

He was wearing a double-breasted suit probably the equivalent in value to, say, the 19th Century cloth trade with India. His shoes had probably removed the crocodile menace from a grateful Third World country.

'Hello, there,' he said as we shook hands. 'Thanks for coming. It's Roy, isn't it?'

'Sure.' Among other things.

'I've already got quite a few punters interested in your fish and chips in newspapers ideas, you know. Hope you don't mind.'

I fumbled through the memory banks to remember what I'd told him the previous night.

'No, that's fine.' I smiled. Was he joking? 'I'll take ten percent.'

'Excellent.' He patted me on the shoulder. 'Come on through.'

He held open a pair of swing doors – the sort you get on kitchens in hotel restaurants, with round windows in them – and ushered me down a corridor. To one side, the offices had all been knocked into a single, open-plan unit with double banks of computer terminals and phones, including the sort of phone where you just touch a name on the video screen and it gets the number for you.

'This is our main dealing room,' Alec was saying. 'Though most of the real business is done before 9.00 am. That's the bread-and-butter stuff. The jam comes when the market opens.'

Only about half the swivel chairs in front of the consoles were occupied, and some of them only had jackets draped over them. No-one turned to look at us. Every five feet or so, there was a monitor tuned in to Extel or Ceefax or Topic, the Stock Exchange's private network, or a fax machine or a telex, and there was a teleprinter receiving Press Association copy.

Littered in between were sandwich wrappers, empty fruit juice cartons, glucose drink bottles and Mars bar papers, as well as a couple of hundred coffee cartons. A woman in an apron was working her way down the far side with a plastic dustbin liner collecting the junk. By the time she got to the end she could start again.

'The analysts and backroom boys – and girls–' Alec added as an afterthought – 'have a bit more privacy.'

He gestured to the left, where thin partitions had carved out about a dozen offices. Some of the doors were open to reveal a desk, two chairs and a hat-stand. With luck there might have been room for three people to stand in each. If they were good friends, that is, and it wasn't a hot day.

'And this is Salome's little empire,' said Alec, rapping a knuckle on the door frame.

The door wasn't shut, and I could see Sal coming round from behind her desk trying to slip her suit jacket on and speak into the phone at the same time. I thought for a minute she was doing a good juggling trick, then I realised the phone had one of those shoulder-rest attachments, which left her hands free. I made a note to ask her to get me one. That way, I could play cards and answer the phone at the same time. (Why else would I need one?)

'...Yes, of course. Naturally. Yes, certainly. I'll be back to Mr Stavoulos this afternoon. Yes, before three o'clock certainly. Thank you.'

She put down the receiver and allowed herself a brief smile.

'Hi.'

'Hi. So this is where it all happens, eh?'

'Too right. Let's go before the phone rings again.'

'Busy morning?' asked Alec.

'Somewhere between hectic and paranoid. Is the dining-room ready?'

'Yes, according to Mrs Pilgrim, but Terry will be a few minutes late joining us.'

I mouthed 'Who's Terry?' at Sal as Alec opened another door at the end of the corridor.

'Terry Patterson. He's our head of Security Systems,' Sal whispered.

'Your boss?'

'On this one, yeah.'

Alec led us into a dining-room complete with oak table, four place settings and a cruet that would have paid off my mortgage if I'd had one. At the far end was a bar.

'We've got everything except beer,' Alec said proudly, waving a glass in my direction.

'Tequila Sunrise, please.' I hate show-offs.

'Er ... sorry...' Alec looked in one of the cupboards. 'Except beer and tequila.'

'Just the orange juice then, please.'

'Coming up. Perricr, Salome?'

'Yes, please,' she said as if she knew she didn't have a choice.

We all three swirled ice cubes around for a minute, then Alec decided somebody had better speak.

'I don't think you told me what you *do*, Roy.'

'Oh good,' I quipped. 'I wasn't that drunk, then.'

'Now don't be hostile, Angel,' Salome mediated. 'Alec and I are in this together.'

I nodded sagely.

'So Terry's the one to watch, eh?'

Alec didn't say anything, but he looked at Salome as if to say, 'He's not daft, is he?'

'Don't worry, love,' I reassured her, 'I'll be on my best behaviour. By the way, it's the funny flat knife for fish, isn't it?'

She tried to smile, but it ended as a shrug of the shoulders. Behind me, the door handle clicked, and she jumped about an inch with nerves.

'Here we go,' I said under my breath. 'Lock and load.'

'Morning everyone, sorry to keep you waiting.'

Patterson breezed into the room. He was a big bloke and looked bigger, because his suit jacket had shoulder pads Joan Collins would have envied. His blond hair was cropped short at the back, but a long shock fell carefully over his right eye, and I just knew he would have to brush it aside every 90 seconds or so. He didn't look old enough to be a Prefect, let alone Salome's boss.

'Terry, let me introduce Roy Angel. Terry Patterson, Roy Angel,' said Alec.

'Good to meet you,' he boomed, crushing my hand. How did he know it was going to be good? 'Glad you could make it. Let's eat and talk.'

'Sure,' I said, being friendly. 'Time must be money to you guys.'

'Isn't it to everyone? There just aren't enough hours in a day.'

He took his place at the head of the table and pressed a bell-push attached to the table leg.

'I don't agree,' I said. 'My Rule of Life No 19 is that if a job can't be done between nine and five, you're either understaffed or totally inefficient.'

Patterson looked surprised. Not impressed, just surprised. I'd got that reaction before, and always from people with jobs. That's why I prefer to be my own boss.

The door opened behind me, and Patterson looked over my shoulder.

'Ah, here's Mrs Pilgrim. What's the recipe today?'

I bet myself he said it every day, and this was confirmed by the soft but distinct sound of Salome grinding her teeth and Alec looking straight down at his empty place setting.

'If it's Thursday, it's Chinese, Mr Patterson; you should know that by now.' Good for her, I thought. 'Crab and water chestnut soup, duck in hoisin sauce and then lychee sorbet.'

69

If I'd been expecting some ageing Lyons Corner House clippy waitress in black dress and white starched pinny, I couldn't have been more wrong.

'Mrs Pilgrim' turned out to be a tall, long-haired brunette wearing black leather trousers tucked into high-heeled boots and a long, white frilled shirt – a man's dress shirt – outside them. She had a waitress's notepad and pencil clipped to a studded leather belt, which held the shirt around her waist, and a bootlace tie added to the gunfighter image. I doubted if she got many complaints about the soup being cool. Instead of asking if someone was ready to order, she probably said: 'Feeling lucky, punk?'

'Is everybody happy with that?' was what she actually said. 'No vegans, gluten-free freaks or anti-salt campaigners?'

'We always eat our greens here, Mrs Pilgrim,' said Patterson with a sickly smile. 'Otherwise we don't get any pudding, do we?'

'Good. Then I'll serve.'

'Er ... one thing,' I said hesitantly.

'Yes?' asked Mrs Pilgrim sharpishly.

'Have you used fresh lime juice in the sorbet?':

'No.'

'Pity, it gives the lychees an extra tang.'

She smiled as if she'd just seen a child drop an ice-cream and turned away to open the door. She wheeled in a heated trolley and served out four bowls of soup, the bowls being fine china with lids on. I thought of my meagre kitchen back at Stuart Street, and I liked my grub, don't get me wrong. But this was how the other half lived without a doubt. Strike that; make it the other seven-eighths.

Mrs Pilgrim closed the door behind her, and Patterson dropped the small talk as subtly as if he'd banged for order with a gavel.

'I'm told you can help us with a slight problemette we have, Roylance. You don't mind if I call you that?'

Problemette? Roylance? Who wrote this guy's script?

'You're buying lunch, Tel, you can call me what you like.'

Patterson just stared at me, although I knew he was still alive, because I saw his jaw working a couple of times. To my right, Salome choked quietly on a water chestnut. To my left, Alec Reynolds started the deep breathing exercises his psychiatrist had taught him to help combat moments of stress.

'Er ... well ... good. Fine.' He spooned some soup to give himself time to think. He'd probably come across people like me before, but he'd never had to talk to them.

'I think, Terry, that we should tell Roy why

we wanted to talk to him,' said Salome, putting emphasis on 'Terry' and 'Roy' in the hope that we'd both notice. Well, I would if he would.

'Yes, Terry,' said Alec. 'We've got to put Roy into the matrix on Capricorn Travel.'

'You're right, Alec. Will you input or shall I?'

I finished my soup and leaned forward on my elbows just to prove I was an oik not to be trifled with.

'Listen. Before anybody plugs me into the mainframe, let me tell you what I know, and then you can tell me what the hell it's all about. Fair enough?'

Patterson and Alec looked at each other, their eye movements faster than Morse.

'Okay,' said Patterson slowly. 'You lead, but *pas devant les domestiques.*'

He pressed the bell for Mrs Pilgrim, and they small-talked among themselves while she cleared the table and served the next course – Chinese-style duck, served dry and fruity, with three-inch diameter pancakes, spring onions and shavings of cucumber accompanied by a small bowl of hoisin sauce. I gave her my best smile as she leaned over me, but I resisted the temptation to ask for chopsticks.

As she left, I asked Salome if she really was one of the firm's *domestiques*.

'No, she's the founder of Mrs Pilgrim's.'

I looked suitably blank and did a 'so?' shrug.

'Just about the most successful external catering company in the country,' she said in her don't-you-know-anything voice. 'It's a franchise deal supplying high quality function food to City firms. Cash for her, no overheads for us. It's a business she started with some girlfriends from university, apparently. There are four of them and they're all called Mrs Pilgrim when they're on duty. They're slick, reliable, and the food's good and...' She hesitated, hating to say it.

'If they all look like her – the men love it,' I finished for her.

'Got it in one,' she said.

Patterson coughed. I could take a hint.

'Very well, Roylance ... er ... Roy, if you'd like to kick off, Alec will fix us some more drinks.'

Alec did, but nothing more exciting than Perrier, although I didn't complain. The sniff of a pulled cork would probably have set me on a roll after the amount I'd drunk the previous night.

I skipped over most of the gruesome bits of the previous evening, concentrating on what I'd heard the Suits saying about Capricorn Travel. I also missed out the racist cracks I'd heard, so as not to embarrass Salome. This seemed a nice liberal firm, though. They didn't worry that Sal was black; they ignored her because she was a woman.

When I'd finished, Patterson asked one question: 'You are quite sure that this chappie you overheard said that the shit would hit the fan today?'

'Well, he actually said "tomorrow," but that was last night, so the answer is yes.'

Patterson hunched forward and said dramatically: 'Then we have a leak.'

'Don't shoot the messenger,' I said, and Salome smiled and patted my hand.

'To fill you in, Roy,' she said, watching Patterson all the time, 'I'd better tell you our interest.'

'I wish you would.'

'We've been suspecting a leak in the building for some time now. Sensitive information has been getting to the market before it should, and it's been information based on our research and analysis, quite definitely. In the past few weeks it's been mostly my area – the leisure industry.'

'Actually, Salome, it's been only your area,' said Patterson coldly. 'Yours and Alec's.'

'Yeah, well.' Salome shrugged. 'Anyway, yesterday I finished a pre-result forecast on Capricorn Travel. They report in about a week's time...'

'Ten days,' interrupted Alec.

'In ten days,' Salome continued.

'Report what?' I asked. They looked shocked.

'Their annual results,' snapped Patterson. 'Their profits.'

'Or lack of them, in this case.' Salome got back in her stride. 'We got to know – well, I found out – that they were riding for a fall. They'd overstretched themselves on discounting and special offers for package holidays in the early part of the season just after Christmas. There's been more cut-throat competition this year than ever before, and Capricorn just went over the top hoping to build up volume trade later on.'

'So they cut their own throats,' I said wisely.

'Yes, but they couldn't have foreseen how strong the pound has been, which made the US a far better holiday bet than some tacky hotel in Spain.'

'You don't have to race the Krauts for the sunbeds in Florida,' said Patterson, smiling. I think it was a joke.

'And apart from the usual problems of double booking and air traffic controllers on strike,' Salome continued, 'three of the eight hotels used by Capricorn are about to be closed down by the Spanish health authorities.'

'Things must be grim in that case,' I observed.

'Probably one dead dog too many in the swimming pool,' said Patterson – rather tastelessly, I thought.

'Consequently,' Salome soldiered on, 'my note – we call them notes – to our clients, who have a stake in Capricorn, was to sell in advance of ... of...'

'The excrement hitting the ventilator,' I said, and they all looked at me. 'Well, that's what the guy said last night.'

'But how did he know?' asked Alec quietly.

'Search me.'

'We do have a programme of body searches at random,' said Patterson. 'When people leave the building at odd times.'

'Oh, goody. I knew I should have worn my Strip Searches Can be Fun T-shirt.' I beamed at him, and he thought I was kidding, but I'd had one once, picked up for a couple of quid at a Notting Hill Carnival.

'No-one could possibly have seen my note last night,' Salome said angrily, but mostly she was angry with herself.

'Why not?' I tried to sound interested.

'The note would go to maybe a dozen people on our client list. The City investors, mostly the institutionals...'

I must have looked blank. She stopped her flow to explain.

'The big institutional investors – the insurance companies, the pension funds, the unions. Most of those are in the City, so their copies were not dispatched until this morning at eight-thirty. The private clients – individual shareholders, that is ... I put theirs into envelopes myself and stuck their address labels on myself and the stamps and posted them myself last night at Liverpool Street Station before I went to the pub.'

She obviously felt she had to explain. 'Liverpool Street because they do half-hourly collections in the early evening and it's the one place from which you can guarantee next day delivery.'

That at least was for sure. In West One district, for example, there were more troublemakers in the Post Office than there were in Dublin in 1916.

'I've been over all this with Salome,' said Alec, but he was talking at Patterson, not to me. 'And I saw her post the client list myself.'

'Well, somehow this friend of Roy's knew enough to be blabbing to all and sundry in the four-ale bar last night,' snapped Patterson again.

Where did he get his dialogue? What did he talk like before translation?

'No, that's not right,' I pointed out. 'The Chinless Wonder was explaining why he'd tipped somebody else off. He wasn't broadcasting the news, more like covering up a mistake. The guy he was blagging – he called him Si, I'm pretty sure – seemed to know already, but was just pissed off 'cos Chinless had grassed up some third party.'

Patterson stared at me. I don't think he followed. Maybe he didn't speak English at all; or at least not as a first language. Maybe he was Swedish. They speak English backwards; I'm convinced of it.

Alec pointed a finger at me in a thoughtful way. 'You are pretty sure about that?'

'Yeah. Definite.'

Well, almost. It was Thursday that day, wasn't it?

'It's Cawthorne,' said Alec. 'I'm sure of it, even if you're not.'

'You could be right,' said Patterson.

'Who's Cawthorne?' I asked, because I presumed I was supposed to.

'Simon Cawthorne,' answered Salome. 'He used to be something in the City before he retired. He was in the pub last night, but I didn't invite him.'

'Retired? The guy Chinless Wonder called Si was no more than 28.'

'That's him.'

'The point is,' Patterson interrupted, 'how did Cawthorne know?'

He held up a hand to cut off Salome's response.

'Coffee,' he said, and pressed his bell-push again.

'Mrs Pilgrim' appeared immediately, as if she'd been waiting outside the door, with another trolley. This one carried coffee-pots and cups and saucers. She began to collect up dirty plates.

'Great sorbet,' I said as she leant over me.

'But take my tip and use lime juice next time.'

'It's tattooed on my heart,' she said, through clenched teeth.

'Leave the coffee, Mrs P,' pronounced Patterson. 'We'll serve ourselves.'

She looked relieved and nodded to him, then left.

'Salome,' he said as the door closed, 'would you mind?'

'Yes, I bloody well would,' she muttered under her breath. 'Of course, Tel,' she said out loud. Then to me: 'Black?'

'Naturally.'

'So, we return to the question of how Cawthorne knew,' Patterson went on, unperturbed. 'He's not on our client list, and as far as I know, he doesn't work for any of our institutionals. You two–' he pointed to Alec then Sal – 'alibi each other, and we just have to assume that Cawthorne was at this party by chance.'

He left a lot hanging in the air, not the least the nasty implication behind 'alibi.'

'There was nothing particularly private about that party,' I offered in Salome's defence. 'I mean, it was in a pub and anybody could have been there. They even let me in.'

'Point taken, but question remains – how did he know?'

I didn't say anything, but I wasn't convinced by the coincidence theory. After all, this Cawthorne character had been muttering about 'the spade bitch' earlier. But I didn't say anything. Unfortunately.

'Come on, you two.' Patterson sat back in his chair and put on a ham American accent. 'If you ain't part of the solution, you're part of the problem.'

If he came out with stuff like that, I could understand why he didn't get Christmas cards.

Alec and Salome stayed silent. It was time for a diversionary attack.

'In my experience,' I said confidently, 'you'll have to look below stairs for your leak.'

'Your experience?' said Salome with an incredulity that hurt.

'Now listen, Sal baby, I may not be the high-flying executive type you're used to mixing with, but I've hung around more typing pools, loading bays, postrooms and company garages than you've had lukewarm entrees. If you want to know what a company's doing, ask a chauffeur.'

'He's got something there,' said Alec, making it sound a lit like a disease. 'You think that's where our problem lies?' Patterson looked keen. I should have been on my guard.

'I'm not saying it is, I'm just saying that's where I'd start to look if it was my problem. You take care of the directors' dining-room,

I'll hang around the staff canteen.' I shot a glance sideways at Salome. 'And question the catering staff.'

She smirked, but Patterson was dead serious. 'Would you do that for us? None of us could; well, not with any hope of results.'

'We could give him a cover story to explain his presence,' said Alec enthusiastically. 'And make it worth his while.'

'Naturally,' said Patterson. They were talking as if I wasn't there.

'We could go a K plus any out-of-pocket expenses.'

I began to feel claustrophobic and my stomach churned. Classic stress symptoms. It always happened when somebody suggested I get a job.

'Hold everything,' I said, holding up my hands to show I was serious. 'There are over two-and-a-half million people out there looking for work. I'm not.'

'It would be purely temporary,' Patterson enthused. 'And you'd do exactly what you want; just report to me every so often. I think we could go to K.2 and no questions.'

'No, I'm sorry.' Not even for K.2 – that's a grand, two hundred in the City. Even I knew that. 'I'm too young to start drawing a monthly pay packet.'

'If you have a tax problem or something, we could make it cash.'

'Brown envelope job, eh? You City boys

81

are too slick for me.'

Salome reached out and touched my hand. 'He means £1,200 a week, Roy,' she said, staring at me. 'Not a month.'

'When do I start?'

CHAPTER FOUR

Flushed with my newfound wealth, or at least the prospect of an expense account, I took a taxi – a real one – to Dod's place in Bethnal Green to collect my horn and Tiger Tim's banjo from the back of his van. He wasn't in, but his van was parked outside his block of council flats just asking to be nicked. I knew Dod had it well over-insured, but he might have given a thought to our gear. Some people have just no consideration for other people's property.

I helped myself to the instruments and deliberately left the back doors open slightly to encourage joyriders – I knew Dod would have wanted it that way – then hopped back in the black cab and asked for Stuart Street. The driver, a real diehard musher of the old (reform) school, didn't bat an eyelid at my apparent daylight robbery. Mind you, I got a reaction from him when we got to Hackney and I made him wait while I transferred the instruments to the back of Armstrong.

When he thought he'd been carrying a fellow musher, he didn't swear when I didn't tip him. For London cabbies, that's the next best thing to discount.

I got Armstrong wound up and headed for Covent Garden. I reckoned to catch Tiger Tim on his usual pitch, before the tourists and office workers moved out and he switched to his evening pitch outside one of the theatres.

Feeling lucky, I left Armstrong parked a few yards from Bow Street court and worked my way into the back of Covent Garden through the flea market. There were at least three different styles of music coming from the Plaza – unfortunately you don't get warnings of the white-faced-clown mime acts until you're almost on them.

One theme came across as worryingly familiar. If I hadn't known better, I would have sworn it was Werewolf doing his Eddie Cochran medley – a party trick of his that doesn't last long.

It *was* Werewolf playing Eddie Cochran, and hamming it up to the gallery something rotten. He was standing on Tiger Tim's pitch and had a fair to middling crowd around him. Across the Plaza, trying to compete, were a talented duo I'd seen on the comedy club circuit. They went under the name of Lord Snooty, or something pinched from an old comic strip, and one played soprano sax and the other sang and filled in with a miniature trumpet, Don Cherry style – except Cherry's good at it. I felt sorry for them. At the rate Werewolf was pinching their audience, if he got onto Chuck Berry then they might as well pack it in and move down onto the Northern Line.

I joined the crowd around Werewolf for what turned out to be his last number. He'd obviously just been minding the store while Tiger Tim went for a natural break. Tim's break had been as far as the Punch and Judy, and he'd reappeared with a pair of bottles of lager with the tops off. He handed one to Werewolf as he finished and unplugged Tim's guitar from the battery-run amplifier without even acknowledging the applause he was getting.

Tim raised his eyebrows at me and offered the other bottle. I shook my head.

'Better not, I'm driving,' I said.

'I shouldn't either,' said Tim, 'but I'm gonna.'

I knew what he meant. Since the pubs were allowed to stay open all day, the police had come down fairly heavy on drinking in the street. It was what politicians called a *quid pro quo* and what Tim and the other buskers called a fucking nuisance; but they had their pitches to think of.

'I loike this place, lads,' said Werewolf, in

between swigs of lager. 'I might take a sabbatical and work it for a year, or a summer anyway.'

'He's good enough,' Tiger Tim said to me. 'You could be too if you changed your style.'

I tried to look modest.

'I'm no good at the cocktail jazz that goes down these I days,' I said, trying to be self-effacing. 'My jazz is public bar, light-and-bitter, kick-the-chairs-against-the-wall stuff.'

'But you're playing to an ageing audience that by the nature of economic progress declines as affluence increases and other alternatives begin to show. Why do you do it?'

'Somebody has to,' I said, pretty sure that I followed him. 'And anyway, when did you get a degree in marketing?'

'Last year. I start my Master's in Business Administration at the LSE in September.' Tim wasn't flannelling.

'Just goes to show you can't trust anybody these days.'

I turned to Werewolf, pouting my lips.

'And you; you never came home last night.'

Werewolf pulled on a brown, soft-leather jacket I hadn't seen before. A price tag on a length of cotton hung from one sleeve.

'Ah well, something came up,' he said, grinning.

'I can believe that,' said Tiger Tim to himself as he examined the banjo I'd returned for scratches.

'I came round to collect my gear and invite you for a gargle but I was told you was out to lunch. I said you'd been out to lunch for the last ten years. Come and meet Sorrel; she's round the corner.'

Sorrel? Was this a person or some new street smarts Werewolf had added to his vocabulary?

'T'anks for the five-finger exercise.' Werewolf acknowledged Tiger Tim.

Tim looked down at the guitar case he used to collect his earnings. I guessed there were more pound coins in there now than when he sloped off to the pub.

'Anytime, big man,' he said. 'As long as you don't make a habit of it.'

'Oh, all my habits are vurry pleasant.' Werewolf smiled, then, for the benefit of the tourists, said loudly: 'C'mon, Angel, let's go.'

'Right behind you, darling,' I said, cringing; but with a name like mine, you get to cringe a lot.

'Nice jacket,' I said as we walked back towards the flea market.

Werewolf shot his cuffs and did a twirl.

'Yeah, I thought so. So I mentioned it and wallop – Sorrel bought it for me.'

'Did it cost over the ton?'

'And the rest, but Sorrel gets discount

from the other traders. There she is.'

A tall, statuesque blonde that I'd last seen on the other side of the pub the previous night was standing behind the end stall of one of the market rows. She was wearing the sister to Werewolf's jacket, but it looked better on her. I wondered how I'd missed her as I'd walked through.

'Hi, lovey,' she said as we got there. 'With you in a tick.'

She returned to the business in hand, which was wrapping an old brass miner's lamp in tissue paper for an elderly American couple. You could tell they were Americans – or maybe they were models for the Burberry collection – and they handed over a 50-pound note without a qualm. Sorrel didn't even attempt to make change.

After they'd moved off, she reached below her stall and produced the twin of the lamp she'd just sold. I knew a bloke in Kent who'd kept making them long after the pits closed, but I'd no idea they could fetch that sort of price. The real ones never had.

Werewolf slipped an arm around her waist. Not exactly lovingly, more like a wrestler would.

'This is my old mate I was telling you about.'

'Hi, Armstrong,' she said sweetly.

'Er ... that's not me.'

'That's his cab,' said Werewolf.

'Oh, sorry. Hemingway, isn't it?'

'No, dear. That's his sleeping-bag. This is Angel.'

'Oh yes, of course.' She smiled. 'The trumpet-player. That's right, isn't it? What do you call the trumpet?'

'Don't be silly,' I said, doing an 'aw shucks' routine. 'Trumpets don't have names.'

'You should call it Sultan,' said Werewolf seriously. 'As you're the last of the Sultans of Swing. Ever thought of yourself as a dying breed?'

'Thanks a bunch, that's really cheered me up, and just when I was going to tell you I'd got a job.'

'What? Oh Jeeesus!'

Werewolf did the full phoney swoon, the back of his right wrist up on the forehead, staggering backwards to clutch at the edge of Sorrel's stall and dislodging a collection of old blue glass bottles of the kind that some people find buried in their gardens and others pay good money for.

'Don't worry, it's only temporary and it's very well paid and I get an expense account.'

'Ah-ha!' Werewolf rolled his eyes. 'Exes – my favourite word in the English language.'

'Cut it out.' Sorrel cuffed him playfully about the head. 'You're making my junk stall look untidy. Help me pack up.'

Sorrel began to hand out boxes and give us instructions on which bits of bric-a-brac went where.

'So when do you clock on?' Werewolf asked, stacking a pile of old postcards as if he were shuffling a deck of cards.

'Tomorrow. I'm going to be something in the City,' I said smugly.

'Pretty Keen Bastards?' asked Sorrel without looking up.

Werewolf looked surprised.

'She's right,' I said, before he could butt in. 'Prior, Keen, Baldwin – it's Salome's firm. How did you guess?'

'Pretty bleedin' obvious,' she said, cool as anything. 'You were rubbing shoulders with most of their broking staff last night. I thought it was a firm's outing at first. Mind you, I didn't know they were recruiting from the orchestra pit. But it was either them or that bastard Cawthorne – or, of course, the pub could've needed a relief barman...'

She stopped and looked at me all innocent. I realised I'd dropped a couple of handfuls of silver-plated cutlery on to the floor.

'Cawthorne? You know a guy called Cawthorne?' I tried to sound casual while scrabbling around on one knee picking up spoons.

'I thought everybody who was anybody in the City knew Simon Cawthorne.'

'Be fair, love, Angel hasn't even clocked in yet,' said Werewolf, trying to balance about six boxes.

'It seems to be a small world,' I said as I straightened up. 'What is there to know about Cawthorne?'

'Oh, the usual City smut,' said Sorrel casually, busying herself with some ancient cosmetic jewellery. 'And then again, he runs his courses.'

I looked at Werewolf, but he just looked back at me and shook his head.

'Courses? Like accountancy, or French for beginners?'

'No. Courses as in assault courses.'

Naturally. Why hadn't I thought of that?

Salome was chopping okra for a gumbo when I got back to Stuart Street, though she scared the hell out of me by answering the door of her flat with a heavy Sabatier knife in a potentially eye-watering position.

'Come in, come in.' She waved the knife towards her kitchenette.

'Frank's working late but we're having a proper dinner tonight – to make up for last night's debacle.'

'Do I take it you didn't get to try on your birthday present?'

She raised one eyebrow at me and went back to dissecting an okra she had pinned to the marble chopping-board. I wondered why they called them ladies' fingers. I hadn't seen a woman with green slimy fingers since the last time I was down the King's Road on a

90

Saturday afternoon.

'Okay, well maybe tonight,' I said.

'I doubt it. He's playing squash until eight, and then he'll do his regulation 20 lengths of the pool and turn up here about nine well and truly cream-crackered.'

I leaned over her stewpot – regulation Habitat-issue as you might expect.

'Are you putting any sausage in that? It won't be a proper gumbo unless you do.'

She picked up a crab claw, and suddenly she looked more dangerous than when she'd had the knife.

'Quite a little chef, aren't we?' she said sarcastically. 'Sorbet lessons for Mrs P and now gumbo. Is there no end to your talents, Angel?'

I thought about this for a minute.

'Probably not,' I said finally.

Salome cracked some crab with a wooden mallet and dumped it in the pot, then wiped her hands on her apron.

'Okay, smartarse, down to bizz. Go through.'

She followed me into the living-room and we parked ourselves at either end of the sofa. She picked up a wad of folded papers from the coffee table and handed them to me.

'You'll need these,' she said.

I lifted a corner of the top one. It looked like an architect's plan with a map of the

Underground superimposed on it.

'What the...?'

'Wiring diagrams showing the telephone and computer link cables and the air-conditioning.'

'Silly question, I know, but why do I need these? I mean, it's not even as if I've finished my library book.'

'It's your cover,' she said impatiently. 'You're our new heating engineer. What's the matter?'

'Oh, nothing,' I sighed.

'You look peeved.'

'Well, I had a vague notion I could hang around as some smoothy stockbroking troubleshooter – and put the Armani suit on the expense account.'

'What do you know about stocks and shares?'

'Slightly less than what I know about air-conditioning.'

'Now don't sulk.' She patted my knee and I forgave her everything. 'I've seen you in your overalls, working on Armstrong. You look really professional.'

'Thanks a bunch. Is there a real heating engineer in the building?'

'Yes, but he covers the whole building. You just stick to the floor we occupy. Don't worry, we're always getting in plumbers and suchlike to do odd jobs. All you need to do is say you're checking out the conduit routes for additional cabling.'

'What does that mean?'

'I don't know, but nobody else will. Just unscrew a few panels and *look* as if you know what you're doing. If you don't interfere with the dealers or the market-makers, they won't even notice you're there. If anybody asks, say you reckon the job will take a week or so. Turn up sometime tomorrow morning – note: morning – and check in with Sergeant Purvis on reception.'

'Is that the guy who was on duty today?'

'Yeah. So?'

'So won't he think it weird that I turned up for lunch with the top brass one day and the next I'm back in the proletariat?'

'We've told him you are a computer buff with a new system and you always check out the installation personally.'

'Did he swallow that?'

To me he had looked like the sort of person you want to take on one side and say: what was it like in the Waffen SS?

'Yes, because Patterson told him it was "confidential."' She made quotation marks in the air with her fingers. 'And he loves secrets. In fact, he adores Patterson and refers to him as the Head of Security Confidential. Incidentally, we're all calling him Tel since your visit. He hates it.'

Well, that was all right then. As I always say (Rule of Life No 7): no day is wasted.

'Don't contact me or Alec, and we'll be polite but not friendly. If you spot anything or hear anything, find an internal phone and ring 2001. That's Patterson, and he'll arrange to meet you.'

'In a safe house in East Berlin?'

'Probably. He does go OTT on things like this. Oh – I almost forgot.'

She stood up and fetched her shoulder-bag from the table, delved into it and produced a wad of ten-pound notes.

'Expenses. Tel thought you could bribe the below-stairs staff, working on the premise that it's dead easy to bribe the upstairs mob.'

'Greed is all in the dirty old heart of the City,' I said gravely.

'That's very good.' Salome smiled. 'Where did you read it?'

'On the back of a sandwich-board man in Oxford Street. The other side said "Eat less Protein." How much is here?'

'Two loads.'

I was impressed. 'Load' was Thatcherite streetspeak for a hundred nowadays, with 'part load' being 50. Nothing lower merited a nickname.

'Do I need receipts?'

'No. If you did, then the heads of the various departments might. And there's this.'

She handed over an Amex card. It was valid for two years and had 'MR ROYLANCE

MACLEAN' printed on the bottom, along with 'PRIOR, KEEN, BALDWIN.'

Not bad. An Amex card within eight hours. With my credit rating, a personal one would have taken eight years.

'I like the name,' I said.

'I thought you might,' Sal said, smiling. 'It's not so much that we deliberately fudged your name, it was just that Tel-boy insisted you were called Roylance and...'

'And nobody had the nerve to tell him he was wrong,' I offered.

She patted my leg again.

'I never knew you had such a fine grasp of management psychology and office politics.'

'I may just be a humble heating engineer tomorrow, but by the end of next week I'll be the Lounge Lizard from Accounts.'

'You'll be wasting your energy, son. The City is a stainless steel machine for making money. Only politicians and civil servants go in for extra-curricular rumpy-pumpy. The City gets its rocks off reading the *Financial Times,* not Page 3.'

'Maybe I'll liven things up.'

'Keep your nose clean, Angel. And for God's sake don't fuse the electrics. If the screens go down for a minute, we lose telephone numbers in turnover and my quarterly bonus goes down the pan.'

'Along with the flat in Limehouse?' I probed.

'If I lose this job, yeah. But listen, you.' She inched closer. 'Frank knows nothing about this. Well, not the detail, anyway. So not a word. Okay? No point in two of us worrying.'

I looked at my watch. 8.30. I knew she'd want me out of there before Frank staggered home, so I had to make up my mind whether to get an early night with a good book or go down the pub and do some damage to my expenses. Ah, decisions, decisions.

'Don't worry, my dear, your guilty secret is safe with me.' Her face changed as quickly as a baby's goes from gurgle to sulk.

'I haven't got a guilty secret. I'm not guilty. Don't tell me…'

'No way, José. Not for a minute. I'm on your side.'

She calmed down a bit and took a couple of deep breaths.

'You think this guy Cawthorne is behind it?' I asked quietly.

She nodded.

'We're pretty sure he's the why. You only worry about the how. Okay?'

'But who is this guy? And who's Chinless Wonder?'

'They're not your problem. Just help us find out how he's getting the info if you can.'

'So you City types can keep the poo-poo undies out of the launderette, I suppose.'

'Something like that,' she said, shame-faced. 'Just go along with it, huh?'

And of course I did. What an airhead.

I left Salome to her gumbo partly to be out of the flat before Frank came back but also because I'd decided to go out on an errand. Business, of course, not pleasure. I was really taking this having a job lark seriously.

As it happened, I passed Frank on the stairs. He must have had a helluva workout, because he was taking them one at a time.

'Wotcha, Frank.'

I had an unlit Sweet Afton between my teeth. Frank looked at it with disdain.

'Still on the coffin nails, Angel?'

'First of the day, Frank, and still unlit.' Which was true. 'And you'll die before I do.' Which probably wasn't.

'Ha!' he yelled as I reached the bottom of the stairs. 'How do you make that out?'

I had my hand on the Yale catch of the front door and he was almost at the top of the stairs when I said:

'It's breathing, Frank. Think of the strain on your heart. Your chest going in and out all those times a day. It's bound to kill you after about 80 years. Have a nice night.'

I've always said it costs nothing to bring a little comfort into somebody's life. Duncan the Drunken believed that too, but then anything that cost nothing was tops in his book.

I knew he'd be in a pub in Leytonstone, because it was his darts night and he'd cobbled together a team of reluctant players from his Barking local to play 'away,' an excursion that involved about a hundred phone calls and the hire of a minibus to travel nearly three miles. I knew all this because Duncan had tried to recruit me into the team. I'd declined because I'd given up darts after a five-hour marathon at a university reunion, which had ended with me betting my double bed on a double eight and missing.

Duncan was an incorrigible optimist and a Yorkshire-man moved south to boot. Now, the two don't normally go together, but when they do, it's awesome. Duncan had appointed himself social secretary of his street, organising parties, outings for the kids, planning applications, petitions against planning applications and so on. He always said he didn't have the brains to go into politics. If he had brains, he'd be dangerous.

But he was a soft touch and an ace mechanic, so it was best to keep in with him if you wanted anything, and I usually did.

He was propping up the public bar with a pint of bitter in one fist and three metal darts in the other. The darts were long enough to have been bought second-hand from Robin Hood, and they had plastic flights with pictures of the Queen Mother on. Duncan was nothing if not patriotic.

I asked the landlord for a pint, pointing at Duncan. He pointed at two full ones lined up at Duncan's elbow but agreed to put one in the barrel for him. I ordered a pint of alcohol-free lager, as I had Armstrong outside and I didn't fancy losing any of my driving licences.

'Come on, the Flying Horse!' somebody yelled behind me. 'Hello, Fitzroy, luv. Joining us?'

I knew without turning that it was Doreen, Duncan's wife – actually 'the wife,' as Duncan always said. She was the official scorer and unofficial cheerleader for Duncan's team.

I waggled a limp wrist at her and said: 'Sorry, luv, but the eyesight's not what it was,' and she hooted with laughter and threw a piece of chalk at me. From the look of the scoreboard, the Flying Horse were getting slaughtered, and the team spent more time looking at their watches than the board.

'So what are you after, young Angel?' said Duncan between deep breaths of beer. I'd bought him a drink, so there was no point in wasting any more time.

'A tool kit. One of the belt jobs that looks professional.'

'Sure. What sort of work?'

'Mostly electrics, laying cables, that sort of thing.'

'Domestic, three-phase, telephone or undersea across the Atlantic?'

Oh, very droll.

'I don't know. Telephone, say.'

'Got something in the back of the car would do you. Planning a job?'

Duncan strode off suddenly, and I thought for a second it was something I'd said, but in fact it was his turn at the dartboard.

'Ninety-eight out, Duncan, luv,' screamed Doreen. 'You can do it. Go on! Give it some welly!' Then, in a rather subdued tone, she announced, 'Twenty-seven,' as she turned to do the chalking. Duncan rejoined me and took out most of another pint in one swallow.

'I've *got* a job, Duncan, I'm not going on one.'

'Well, just tha be careful, laddie.' His Yorkshire accent came on strongest when he was being patronising. 'You could get done for going equipped, with this little lot. The bloke I bought 'em off was, bang to rights.'

'Was he a sparks?'

'No, he was a burglar.'

Oh well, that was all right then. Doreen shrieked as the Flying Horse missed another double, and I knew that if I stayed much longer I'd get roped into the darts match.

'So, what's the hire charge, Duncan?'

Dunc was signalling to the landlord for the pint I'd bought him. He raised an eyebrow at my glass but I shook my head. When he'd got his pint, he said:

'Use of Armstrong one Saturday?'

I winced, but agreed. It was not so much that I minded Duncan driving Armstrong, it was just that when he used it for wedding parties at the weekend, it was a bugger to clean the confetti out.

'Okay. Can we get it now?'

'Wait till I get the double, lad. You're not in a hurry, are you?'

'I had hoped to get it while I was still in my thirties.'

I needn't have worried. The home team finished the game in the next throw, and as it was the beer game, there was a lot of to-ing and fro-ing as the Flying Horse team bought their opposite numbers a drink. I stood back from the bar and avoided Doreen, who, like many Northern women, had a Messiah complex about feeding up anyone with a less than 40-inch waist.

Duncan did the honourable thing and then sidled towards the door, and we sneaked out into the car park, Duncan leading me over to a battered white Thames van.

'I thought you hired a minibus for the team,' I asked, genuinely curious.

'Aye, I do. It'll be back at closing time to pick us up.' That way, the team couldn't leave early. 'This is Doreen's. She went to her evening class earlier.'

The van may not have looked much, but Duncan was a wizard with engines, and if the van had his Barking garage's seal of approval, then it would shift even if the bodywork got left behind at the lights. Duncan opened the rear doors with what looked suspiciously like a metal toothpick and began to rummage around inside.

'Doreen still doing panel-beating at night class?'

'Nah, she's moved on to welding. Here we are.'

He handed me a heavy canvas roll a bit like a cowboy's gunbelt. I unwound it and tried it around my waist. It contained a full arsenal of wire-clippers, screwdrivers, pliers and even a small hammer. There was probably something for removing stones from horses' hooves, if only I knew what it looked like.

It weighed a ton and would probably spoil the line of my chinos, but as camouflage it was perfect.

'It's magic, Duncan,' I said.

CHAPTER FIVE

Camouflage is nine-tenths of success in a sneak attack. If a famous retired general didn't say that, then I'd better write to one. People usually see only what they want to see, so give it to 'em.

I wasn't too sure what Prior, Keen, Baldwin expected from a freelance heating engineer who could re-route computer lines, but then I reckoned you could get away with most anything in the City if you were confident enough. My uniform for the day was: clean jeans; a denim jacket that almost matched; red trainers; a plain-white T-shirt not advertising anything; and a baseball cap supporting the Chicago White Sox. I packed the tool belt and the plans Salome had provided in a sports bag and added a pair of brown leather gloves in case I was called on to get my hands dirty.

There was no way I could roll up in Armstrong, and nowhere to park him for the day anyway, so I took a bus to St Paul's and walked round to Gresham Street for about 10.00 am, which I thought showed I was keen for an early start.

Sergeant Purvis, that Guardian of the

Third Floor, was not impressed.

'Mr MacLean. Welcome. We were expecting you this morning. First parade is seven-thirty.'

I smiled a big smile on the basis that the best way to upset his sort was to be nice to them.

'I'm so sorry I missed it, but you see, I have a medical certificate excusing me from working with asbestos, heavy lifting and the hours of daylight prior to 0900.'

I liked the '0900' touch, but Purvis wasn't impressed. 'I was told about you,' he said, but I could tell he wasn't sure what to make of me.

I leaned over his desk.

'And I've been told you've been briefed by Mr Patterson, so you know this is a delicate matter.'

'Oh yes. Of course. Mr P put me in the picture.' He was bluffing, I knew, but he did it well. Years of experience. 'What do you need ... er ... in terms of...?'

I held up a hand and shook my head. 'Nothing, just the run of the place. If anybody asks, I'm measuring up the heating ducts with a view to running computer cables and phone lines through them. Treat me like a minor nuisance, but take note if anyone asks too many questions about me. Know what I mean?'

He put a finger to the side of his nose and

gave me a long, slow wink. Dead subtle.

'Good. Let's compare notes at lunch-time over a pint. On me.'

'Okay, son.' He was warming to me.

'Catch you later.'

I spent the next two hours sussing the lay-out of the third floor, which was bigger than I'd expected, and generally getting in people's way. There was a thin pencil torch on Duncan's tool belt, and I unscrewed a few heating grilles and shone it around in the holes, and I thought I looked pretty convincing.

None of the dealers noticed me at all as far as I could gather. Being the only one not wearing a suit, you'd have thought I'd have stuck out a mile, but it seemed that because I wasn't a Suit, I wasn't there. Some security. I was tempted to come back as a window-cleaner and rip them off a treat.

Trouble was, I didn't know what was valu-able, information-wise. The stuff on the screens could have been my way to a quick fortune or could have been a laundry list. I have to admit that the computer revolution had left me way behind. Six-year-old kids could hack into a bank account from their kindergarten play-pen these days, but I'd have had more chance on a Japanese Scrabble board. Maybe I should have brought a six-year-old kid with me, but there's never one around when you need one.

I wasn't having any more luck earwigging the hundreds of conversations going on around me. Most of them were over the phone, but occasionally a dealer would stick the receiver into his neck and yell to a colleague in front of another screen further down the room.

The dialogue went something like: 'Can you get me a point on seven hundred Barclays, private sale?'

I'd been there over an hour before I realised that they deliberately missed the last three noughts off everything, so 'seven hundred' was actually seven hundred thousand shares. No wonder they needed computers. I did manage to pick up one or two things, though. I got so that I could tell when the dealers were phoning each other, when they were talking to the 'institutionals' – the big corporate investors (where they sounded patronising and unwilling to brook any argument with the investment managers) – and when they were talking to private customers who were buying (very polite) and those they were trying to get to sell (ultra grovelling).

As with any office environment where 95 percent of the work is on the phone, there were very few private phone calls. Or maybe the dealers actually did have wives, they just talked to them in numbers. It was not uncommon to see guys on two phones at once, and most of them had colour VDU screens in front of them where they could just touch a square and they'd get through to somebody without dialling. I was very impressed with some of the hardware, which looked state of the art – i.e. better than anything British Telecom had. I wondered if one of their computers could get me off the *Reader's Digest* mailing list.

I found a spot halfway down one side of the dealing room where there was a gap in the desks and a heating vent in the wall under a window. No-one gave me a first glance, let alone a second, as I unscrewed the louvred grille and sat cross-legged in front of the vent, shining my torch and occasionally examining wires with the end of a screwdriver.

I knew that videos of the film *Wall Street* had been the 'in' present in the City the previous Christmas. I knew because I'd helped 'import' some of them in advance of the film company's planned release, and one of its side-effects – that there was still a bull market in red braces – was still evident. Some of the dealers even wore 'Greed is Good' lapel badges, and any three of the suits in the room would probably have been taken in part exchange for a decent motor.

At about noon, while I was under a desk trying to make head or tail of a telephone junction box, I spotted my first suspicious character.

He was wearing a lapel badge too, but his said: 'Mild Mannered Guardian Readers Against the Bomb.' Yet it wasn't that so much as the John Lennon glasses and the badly cut suit that gave him away. At a guess, and I was rapidly becoming an expert, the suit was made in Bulgaria, or at least somewhere where they worked to a five-year plan. You know the sort: the jacket fits first time but the trousers are cut round a box and the tailors use a picture of Stalin as their model.

From my vantage point, I watched him walk up and down the dealing room three times. He carried a pile of newspapers and seemed to be collecting more as he went round. Then he disappeared into one of the analysts' offices.

It was nearly lunch-time, so I decided to check him out with Purvis on reception. Fortunately, I was discreet; I didn't come right out and ask who the wally was.

'Oh, that's young Mr Keen,' said the Sergeant. 'He's a bit of a problem child, but harmless enough. He's not interested in the City. Great disappointment to the senior partner, of course. No, young Morris wants to be a journalist, so he comes in every day and collects all the newspapers. He thinks that if he reads them all regularly, he'll get a job on one eventually.'

I'd met people like that. They were the

ones who'd bought Betamax videos and 8-track stereo systems for their Minis.

I asked Purvis if he was ready for a beer, and he said he was and put on his jacket and peaked cap. I had rather hoped he would come in mufti, but he seemed to enjoy looking like a product of a South American junta. On the way down in the lift, I tried to tap him about Morris Keen, but he regarded him with pity rather than suspicion. He held a unique position, though, in that he must have been the only young male under 21 that Purvis did not think would benefit from a reintroduction of national service.

'Oh, yeah, national service. I've read about that,' I said, just to niggle him.

He led me to a pub near the Guildhall and elbowed a space at the bar near a plastic display case of sandwiches; obviously his regular spot, which newcomers strayed onto at their peril. A barman caught his eye, and two pints of bitter appeared, which I was expected to pay for. I didn't mind; I wasn't paying.

'So, young Mr Keen has the run of the place, does he?'

Hardly the most subtle of openings, but with somebody like Purvis, subtlety came dispensed with a hurled half-brick.

Purvis put half the beer down his face, then drew breath.

'Don't even think it,' he said, and went

back to his beer.

I admitted to myself that young Morris Keen was so bloody inept that he couldn't be the leak, but then again, if I pointed out to Patterson that there was a strange bloke wandering around who could get access to almost anything, it would prove I was doing my job.

Despite my best endeavours and several free pints, Purvis didn't let anything slip over lunch – and I use the word loosely, in its non-food connotation. According to him, security at Pretty Keen Bastards was watertight. He'd stake his reputation on it. Well, that would keep the bookies awake nights, I don't think.

After three pints, he mellowed enough to admit that maybe security wasn't watertight, or rather not as watertight as it had been. After four pints, he confided that he put the fact that he couldn't guarantee security any more down to Prior, Keen, Baldwin's employment of women, blacks, people educated at secondary modern schools (which showed how abreast of the times he was), people with degrees in sociology; so forth, so fifth. If we'd stayed for another pint, he would have included gypsies and Jews, and I would probably have had to clout him.

As a source of information, Purvis was a dead loss. As a source of lunch, he was even worse, so I bought him a final pint but declined myself and, saying I had something to do, sneaked out of the pub and called in at a sandwich bar I'd seen down the road.

It was nearly 2.30 by this time, and the girls in the sandwich shop were packing up for the weekend. They left me in no doubt that they were doing me a favour as they stumbled around to find two bits of brown bread in which to squash the teaspoon of scrambled egg and the half anchovy I'd reserved just before they threw them out.

I waited, hopping from one foot to the other because I'd had too much beer and nothing to soak it up with. Through the shop window, I could see the street entrance to the PKB building. There are a lot of offices in that building, I told myself. And they all have lots of visitors – visitors in all shapes and sizes – so why should the hairs on the back of my neck stand up as I saw people come and people go?

Because if the leak wasn't *inside*, it must be bleedin' obviously *outside*.

I hadn't got the details then, of course, but I had grasped the principle. A few judicious inquiries below stairs in the PKB set-up should confirm it. Case cracked. Sherlock Marlowe-Wimsey strikes again. Ele-fucking-mentary, my dear Poirot.

But at this rate of pay, who wanted the case closed? With luck, I could stretch it out for another week or so. Of course I could.

Take it easy, say nothing yet.
Big mistake.

I spent most of the afternoon in the postroom of Pretty Keen, etc.

It wasn't so much an office, more an open space with a table and a franking machine, and was womanned by Gerry, Michelle and Anna, with whom I got on famously, because none of the Suits ever gave them the time of day. That, and my magnetic personality (and the fact that I brought a couple of bottles of Liebfraumilch with me), endeared me to them to the extent that by four o'clock, I knew the ins and outs of every sort of mailing that left PKB.

Gerry explained that all regular mail was enveloped and franked in the postroom, then put into sacks that Purvis collected four times a day for the postman. A menial task that annoyed him intensely. Special circulars and notes to clients were sometimes sent that way, but if they contained anything confidential, they were classed as an 'S' (for sensitive) mailing. One of the executives would bring the address labels already printed out from the computer in Patterson's office and would stand over the girls while they photocopied and stuffed envelopes.

Michelle told me about the hand deliveries; a rapidly expanding part of their work, as nobody actually trusted the post these days.

It was her job to keep a chart of messenger deliveries, who they were authorised by, what time they were collected and which postcode area they were going to. Regular hand deliveries went out every two hours, or rather a messenger looked in every two hours to see if there was any work. For S-rated hand deliveries, Michelle had a number to ring and a bike rider would turn up – 'Usually within five minutes; they're very good' – to be briefed by the executive authorising the mailing. In all cases, the motorbike messenger service was the same company: Airborne PLC.

Gerry added that it had a 'funny number' with a lot of digits, and she'd always assumed it must be a radio phone. I made a note of it on the back of a packet of Sweet Afton, saying that it was always a good idea to keep tabs on useful companies like that. I don't know if they believed me, but they'd certainly been worth the investment of the white wine, and that was going on the expenses. All in all, a very helpful bunch of girls and an afternoon well spent.

The only thing left to work out was where to take Anna for dinner.

By 4.30, PKB's main dealing room was virtually deserted, but the sounds of telephones and typewriters still came from some of the analysts' offices. I saw Salome only briefly, with Alec Reynolds, going

113

through swing doors towards Patterson's office, but she didn't see me. From what I could tell, she seemed cheerful enough.

I gathered my tools together and screwed back the odd duct cover I'd left off. By the time I was putting on my White Sox cap, there was only one dealer left, way down at the end of the room in the last chair.

He was maybe 22, blond and quiffed, and had regulation-issue red stripe shirt, red dot silk tie and red check braces. I watched him for a minute or so as he sat looking at a blank VDU screen. I had the feeling he'd been like that for some time. Then he sniffed loudly, wiped the palms of his hands down the sides of his face and stood up to put his jacket on.

He brought a natty, inch-thick briefcase out from under the desk and opened it on his chair. The only thing he put in it was a carefully folded copy of *The Times;* the 'White' *Times* as we call it in the City, as opposed to the 'Pink' *Financial Times*. Then he snapped the case shut and headed for the door.

I don't think he even saw me, let alone registered my presence.

Maybe it was because I wasn't wearing a suit.

Maybe it was because he was zapped out of his head.

But why worry? It was the weekend and

nothing (Rule of Life No 31) interrupts a weekend. Nothing, that is, except the odd case of murder.

The Friday night went by pleasantly enough. I got back to Stuart Street, showered, changed and was out again by 6.30. I remembered thinking to myself that I hadn't heard Salome or Frank come in, but I just put it down to them working late.

It took me an age to get across north London in the rush-hour traffic. Anna lived in Willesden, and as I crossed Hampstead to get there, every other car seemed to be a Volvo estate with its sidelights permanently on, heading for the M25 and, eventually, a weekend cottage in Suffolk or Norfolk. I'd heard more than one coastal village in East Anglia referred to quite seriously as Hampstead-on-Sea; still, I suppose it was good for somebody's property values.

Anna shared a flat with another girl, who was away for the weekend. That was duly noted. There are some things I don't have to be told twice.

I'd decided to take her to Break for the Border, a Tex-Mex restaurant in Soho, because I thought it would impress her. But I could have settled for a Big Mac and saved money, as the thing that really impressed her was Armstrong. Once she realised that the black cab outside her flat was mine and that it had a four-speaker sound system (and a tape of the new LP from the Christians – a band to watch), she could talk of little else. She stayed off the booze and even showed me her driving licence (and by decoding the licence number I could work out her age, which surprised me, but she didn't look it) to persuade me to let her drive us home. Back to her place? Why not? I've never regretted buying Armstrong, you know.

I got back to Stuart Street on Saturday morning, too late to do a book swoop (checking out all the church jumble sales and charity bashes in the area for first editions to flog to the dealers around Leicester Square; you'd be surprised what I could pick up for 10p and get more than the author did the next day). So, facing the harsh realities of life, I decided to do my laundry round at the local launderette.

On the way there, I did notice that Salome's VW Golf wasn't parked in its usual place. But I paid it no never mind and spent an hour in the company of Mrs Patel, the launderette manager, discussing the Pakistani cricket team and the price of green peppers at Patel's (no relation) round the corner.

On the way back, I picked up a pizza from our local pizzeria. It's a friendly, neighbourhood, family-run little joint that serves drinks all afternoon even if you only look as if you're thinking of ordering food. It had a picture of a different Roman emperor on each wall panel, and I'd often wondered if they knew that they'd all, except Julius, been poisoned. I wondered if they wanted a PR man.

I was balancing the pizza on my knee and holding laundry and trying to find the key to the front door of Stuart Street when it opened suddenly. I lunged forward inadvertently and the pizza was somehow suspended in mid air between my chest and Lisabeth's ample bosom. I didn't give odds on the olives surviving the encounter.

'Angel! Just the person we wanted to see!' she boomed. Maybe she had a thing about being massaged with pizza. The mind boggles.

'Hello, Angel,' said Fenella from somewhere behind her.

'Er ... what can I do for you two?' I said, struggling to recover my balance, and when I realised I was looking down Lisabeth's cleavage, I added 'Ladies' pretty quickly.

'Come and pick us up from Sainsbury's in about an hour,' she said, examining her blouse for leaking tomato paste.

'Make that two hours,' added Fenella, then she prodded Lisabeth in the ribs. 'You know what you're like in supermarkets.'

Lisabeth 'hurrumphed', a noise only she and submerging hippopotami can make, then said cockily: 'We're doing Salome's shopping for her, even though it does mean

117

buying *meat.*'

She said it quietly, like people over 30 say 'condom.'

'That's why I'm going as chaperone,' Fenella chipped in. 'To stop her assaulting the staff at the butchery counter.' Then, with a sideways look: 'Like last time.'

Lisabeth pursed her lips and said: 'All *you* have to do is handle it, dearest. That's all.'

I'll never say that Lisabeth doesn't feed me the good lines, but with my hands full and no obvious route of escape, I bit my tongue and held back on that one. Instead, I asked why they were doing Salome's shopping.

'Because she's away for the weekend,' said Fenella primly. 'On a self-improvement course.'

'A what? Come on, my pizza's congealing.'

'Well, I think it's some sort of a health farm,' said Lisabeth, before Fenella could get another word in. 'Frank's away on business in Edinburgh until Monday at some sort of legal seminar on Scots law, so Sal's taken the opportunity of sneaking off to some health club without telling him. She's left you a note to tell you what to say if Frank rings the house.'

Frank and Sal, being upwardly mobile, had a mobile phone on Sal's PKB expense account, but if Frank couldn't get her on that, then he may well have tried the communal house phone in the hall. If he was out, it usually fell to me or the weird and rather reclusive Mr Goodson in the down-stairs flat to answer it.

'I saw no note,' I said, knowing it sounded stupid.

'Well, she did, because I saw her put it through the cat flap. Which reminds me, Mr Nassim is coming for the rent tomorrow. Do you want me to give him yours so he doesn't see the cat flap, as usual?'

Nassim Nassim was our landlord, and we called him that because when we asked his surname once he said it was too difficult for us to pronounce, let alone spell, so stick to Nassim. Hence, Nassim Nassim. As land-lords went – and let's face it, who likes 'em if they don't run pubs? – he was a diamond.

'Yeah, I'll drop it round,' I said. 'No, on second thoughts, I'll give it to you when I collect you from Sainsbury's. Give me a bell when you're ready.'

They primped off to the bus stop and I struggled upstairs and into my flat.

Salome had pushed a note through the cat flap. It read:

Angel. Frank's away until Monday in Scot-land. I'm going with Alec to follow up our business from the office. We might get something on the Cawthorne end, but say NOTHING to anybody about this. Should Frank get in touch, remember he knows

nothing about anything, OK? Back Sunday
pm. Love Sal.

The reason I hadn't found it earlier was that
Springsteen had hijacked it and half buried
it in his litter tray. It was his way of telling
me he hadn't been fed.

I opened a can of cat food, keeping my
hand over the label so he couldn't see it was
on special offer that week. He's so snobby
it's a pain.

Then I re-read Sal's note. Say nothing, it
said. Well, I was good at that.

Just as well, really, as the police called later
that night.

I'd been out playing with an oppo called
Bunny, who really is a mean sax player and
could be good at it if he laid off the women
(well, you know what I mean), not like me,
who's really only in it for the beer. We'd been
backing a new band making their debut at
Dingwall's at Camden Lock (Saturday's not
a good night because of the poseurs; mid-
week's better), and the gig had gone down
well, though I couldn't for the life of me remember the name of the band. They played
what I call anorak rock, and I always dismiss
bands like that out of hand. I wouldn't have
paid to hear them, but I've said that before
and a few months later found their albums in
the charts. That's why I'll never make it in

the music business; my wallet's not in it.

It was just after 1.30 am when I turned Armstrong into Stuart Street. I was singing along to a pirate tape of (Bruce) Springsteen's Wembley concert the year before and hardly noticed the police car until I'd parked in front of it. I switched off the tape pretty quick. I knew the Boss didn't approve of bootlegged concerts – since he'd made it up with the recording studios, that is – but I didn't think it merited the cops.

The Plod – or Old Bill Street Blues as they were known in some quarters – were represented by a pair of uniforms from Traffic Division. They were half way up the steps to No 9, but they'd stopped way before the doorbell and were watching me park.

I climbed out of Armstrong, confident that the only suspicious thing about me was my trumpet case. I hadn't been drinking and they wouldn't find any naughty substances on me. You see, I'd been to Dingwall's before, and some nights, anyone coming out of there is regarded as a legitimate target.

'Good morning, sir,' said the taller of the two. 'Do you live here, by any chance?'

They were both fresh-faced constables with nothing much to choose between them. Sure they were young, probably younger than me. But I don't worry about when the policemen start looking younger. Only when they start getting closer.

'Certainly do, officers. Anything wrong?'

'Do you know a Ms Asmoyah by any chance?' asked the tall one.

'Mrs Asmoyah, sure.' Then my stomach churned. 'It's not Frank, is it? Has something happened to Frank?'

'Frank who, sir?'

'Frank Asmoyah. Mrs As ... Salome's husband.'

'We'd better go inside, sir.'

As I put the key in the lock, I thought that if there was room for a cop car and Armstrong out front, there wasn't room for Salome's Golf. In the hallway I said: 'Sal ... Mrs Asmoyah's away for the weekend.'

'Which is her ... apartment, sir?' asked the shorter one, and the 'sir' was definitely an afterthought.

'Top one,' I said meekly. 'But...'

They politely pushed by me. Half way up the first flight of stairs, the taller one bent over to scratch Springsteen behind the ear. Springsteen was mouthing a silent howl to warn me that there were cops about. As an early warning system, he was about as much use as Neville Chamberlain. I made a mental note to cut his rations.

I followed them up as far as my door and, as I unlocked it, they were banging on Salome's. I flicked the lights on and put my horn down, then went back to the stairs.

The noise had woken the denizens of Flat

2, and rather than get out of her pit herself, Lisabeth had sent Fenella to see what was going on. From the little of her that she poked around the door, I guessed she was wearing only the green-striped man's shirt with the sleeves cut short that she used as a nightie when her Snoopy pyjamas were in the wash. (I hoped Lisabeth didn't know I knew this kind of stuff.)

I put a finger to my lips when Fenella saw me and shook my head slowly. She got the message and closed her door quietly. The two uniforms started downstairs, and as they drew level, I nodded them inside. They looked at each other before coming in, but then they did and they took off their hats as they came. A good sign – a British policeman never does anything unspeakable (or official) with his hat or his helmet off.

As I showed them into the living-room, Springsteen shot through my legs and into the bedroom. One thing was for sure, his conscience wasn't clear. I wondered if I should offer our boys in blue a drink. But then, my conscience wasn't crystal clear either.

'Have you any idea where Mrs Asmoyah is, sir?' asked the taller one.

'Not exactly where, no,' I said. 'But I know she's away for the weekend.'

'And you are?' The smaller one had his notebook out.

'Angel. A,N,G,E,L.'

'And your relationship to–' he looked back a page – 'Mrs Asmoyah?'

'I'm her neighbour. N,E,I,G,H...'

'Thank you, sir,' said the taller one. 'We had gathered that. Do you know where we can contact Mr Asmoyah?'

'I think he's in Edinburgh, but I don't know exactly where. He's there on ... well, something to do with his firm.'

I gave them the name of Frank's law firm. The taller one seemed impressed.

'What's going on, officers? Come on, I'm practically family.'

Again they exchanged glances. Maybe the police college at Hendon was teaching telepathy these days.

'Do you know a man called Alec Reynolds, sir?'

'I know the name. He works with Mrs Asmoyah. Why?'

'There's been an accident, Mr Angel, down in Kent, around midnight. We don't know the details, but it seems that Mrs Asmoyah and Mr Reynolds were involved in a road traffic accident.'

'What kind of accident?' I asked loudly.

'Seems they ran out of road and drove off a hill near the M20. Pissed as rats, by the sound of things.' This from the smaller one, who was not bucking for community policeman of the year.

'No way. Don't believe it,' I snapped. 'Salome drunk and anywhere near her VW? Not in the realms of possibility, man.'

'We were informed that the car was a VW Golf, sir, registered to Mrs Asmoyah, and she was the driver,' said the taller one. 'But we don't know anything about charges of drunken driving.'

He glared at his partner. Good. He didn't like him either.

'Is Sal okay?'

'She's in hospital in Maidstone, in a coma. I'm afraid her condition is serious.'

'And Alec? You mentioned Alec Reynolds. Was he...?'

'Mr Reynolds was a passenger in the vehicle. He was dead on arrival at the hospital. This is a very serious business, sir.'

You're telling me.

CHAPTER SIX

As I didn't know where Frank was and I couldn't give them Alec Reynolds' address, the Plod soon lost interest in me.

They did give me the name of the hospital Salome was in, and the taller one told me that the accident had happened 'just off the M20 near Wrotham,' but they had no more details, they were just running errands for the Kent police.

And no, I didn't know why Salome was driving around Kent at midnight on a Saturday. As soon as they'd gone, I got on the phone to Directory Enquiries and asked for the number of the Maidstone hospital. I was dialling it when I heard the door of Flat 2 open, and I glanced over my shoulder to see Fenella, who had added pyjama trousers to her stripey shirt, and Lisabeth, in an ankle-length woollen dressing-gown, creeping down the stairs like they were doing a commercial for a new edition of A A Milne books.

I covered the mouthpiece and said: 'Salome's been involved in a car accident. I'm ringing the hospital.'

Lisabeth's mouth dropped open and she swooned slightly against Fenella, who cunningly stepped forward out of the way so Lisabeth had to right herself.

'Is she all right?' Fenella whispered.

I shrugged my shoulders, and then the hospital came on the line.

They told me Mrs Asmoyah was 'critical' – hospitals are only generous with the truth when it's bad – and if I was her husband, father, mother or sole blood relative, I could visit her any time, but preferably after 7.00 am. Ask for Ward 4 – Intensive. Have a good night and try not to worry.

I passed this on to the assembled crowd – Lisabeth in her dressing-gown constituted a crowd by herself – and held up my hands to silence the chorus of 'What'll-we-do-now?'

'We go to the hospital and stay with her. I've told the police the name of Frank's firm, and they'll trace him. Don't worry, the police are good at getting solicitors out of bed on Sundays. But there's no way Frank can be back before tomorrow night, I reckon.'

Lisabeth nodded her agreement and said firmly: 'Quite right. I'll get dressed.'

'Not now,' I said patiently. 'First thing in the morning. We'll leave at nine.'

Fenella's eyebrows shot up.

'Okay, eight,' I conceded. 'But one of you'll have to stay here in case Frank calls.'

'Can I help?' said a voice behind us, almost scaring me to death.

It was the reclusive Mr Goodson from the ground-floor flat, who was something in local government, though nobody knew quite what, and who was never, ever seen at the weekend. He was standing with his flat door open about four inches to preserve his hundred percent record of letting no-one, except presumably Mr Nassim, see inside. From what I could see of him – mostly his spectacles and his left arm around the doorjamb – he appeared to be wearing a red silk kimono. I bet myself it had a dragon on the back.

'Are you doing anything tomorrow?' Lisabeth asked, and for a moment I thought he was going to slam the door on us.

I explained quickly about Sal's hospitalisation and how we wanted someone to keep an eye, or an ear, open for Frank. He said of course he'd do it if I gave him the phone number of the hospital.

I said I'd leave it pinned to the noticeboard above the communal phone, and he said that was probably best and good night.

We all said good night and Fenella added, 'Oh, and thank you,' and ignored Lisabeth's warning glare against fraternising with the enemy.

I pointed up the stairs. 'C'mon. Up the little wooden hill to Bedfordshire.'

Fenella giggled. Lisabeth kept up a barrage of whispered questions. What was Sal doing in Kent? How did the accident happen? Was anyone else involved?

I parried most of them until we got to their door, then I put a finger to my lips and shushed them.

'Tomorrow. I need my beauty sleep, even if you don't. Eight o'clock, on the dot.'

Fenella put a hand on Lisabeth's arm. 'I'll set the alarm for seven,' she said sensibly.

'I'll set mine for five-to. Night-night.'

'Don't let the bedbugs bite,' whispered Fenella as she closed the door.

This was followed by a 'What did you say?' in what, for Lisabeth, passed as a whisper, but probably registered on a seismograph somewhere in California.

Actually, I set my alarm for 7.00 as well, and by quarter past I was standing outside Frank's and Sal's flat with my trusty nail-file doing the business on their Yale lock. It's one of the old-fashioned files with a curly bit on the end for doing your cuticles, and I've always had better results from it than bending any amount of credit cards.

I wasn't too sure what I was looking for, so I wasn't disappointed at not finding anything obvious. The bedroom showed all the signs of Salome throwing some things into a bag in a hurry. The bed was covered in odd stockings, T-shirts and stuff not wanted on voyage, so to speak.

A wardrobe door was jammed open by the sleeve of a dress, as if Sal had kicked it shut on her way out. I opened it out of curiosity more than anything and there, in between the high-heeled shoes, was Sal's executive briefcase. It was a real leather one, the clasps held by two sets of combination tumblers each with three digits.

A real thief would have taken a screwdriver and levered off the clasps. I didn't want to do anything so drastic, so I flipped the combination until it read Salome's birthdate. (Rule of Life No 8: Never disregard the obvious.) Then I slid the catches sideways and – nothing happened. (Rule of Life No 9: No Rule of Life is inviolate.)

Most people would have keyed in their birthday as one of the few six-digit numbers – if you put a zero in front of single figures and for the months up to October and just the last two digits of the year – they can remember apart from their telephone number. I'd ruled that out, because London numbers are seven-digit and Sal's and Frank's private radio phone had something like 27. So if it wasn't Sal's birthdate, how about Frank's?

I knew the day and the month and made a stab at the year. The catches snapped open, and I was left feeling annoyed that Frank really was that much younger than me.

The case contained one office file and a brochure. The file was a standard office file with a Prior, Keen, Baldwin label stuck in the top right corner. Written on the label in felt tip was: 'CAWTHORNE – CONFIDEN-TIAL.' The brochure, a coloured affair of four A4 pages, looked at first like a holiday advertisement. But I knew there was some-thing unusual about it. The cover photograph was of three guys in full army kit – camouflage dress, boots, black berets, black make-up and all waving rifles – jumping off a wooden bridge that appeared to be under shellfire.

The brochure had a splash title: 'THE EXHILARATOR – TRY IT.' Club 18-30 it was not.

I stuffed it inside the file, closed the brief-case and put that back in the wardrobe. There wasn't time to read anything then, so I nipped back to my flat and found a Virgin Records plastic bag to hide them in. Then I told Springsteen not to invite any strangers in, or any of his friends for a party, put my flying jacket on and jogged downstairs to wind up Armstrong.

Fenella must have heard me, as she appeared at her door as I reached the first landing.

'We'll be with you in one minute pre-cisely,' she said precisely.

'Holy God, you mean the Kraken is awake?'

I don't know if Fenella knew what the Kraken was, but she knew who I meant.

'Up and dressed. She's just cutting some flowers from the window-box in the kitchen – to take to Salome.'

I had a sudden pang of conscience that I really ought to tell them that the funny-looking herb on the left of their kitchen garden was not really an obscure form of ivy and on no account must they attempt to smoke its leaves. But that could wait.

Armstrong started up first go and I dialled around the local radio stations to try and catch if anyone was doing anything stupid on the roads. There were no warnings of fun runs, protest marches, street carnivals or charity pram races, so it seemed safe to cut through the City and head for Kent direct, rather than heading east and using the Dartford Tunnel.

Lisabeth agreed with my navigating for once, but then she and Fenella were sat in the back like royalty, ready to wave to the crowds, the deserted Houses of Parliament and so on. But as it was Sunday morning, there were few admiring fans about.

I slipped an old Eurythmics tape into the cassette deck I have installed where Armstrong's meter used to be and adjusted the speakers so the full effect came in the front rather than the back. I spent most of the journey wondering why Annie Lennox could make 'girl' rhyme with 'thrill' but nobody else could. The last thing I wanted to do was debate the horrific possibilities of Salome's condition with Les Girls.

It was only as we came into Maidstone and I started looking for hospital signs that I began to suffer the nervous whirling pits way down in my stomach.

The hospital had a flower shop inside its main entrance and I subbed Fenella a tenner to get a decent bunch of flowers (I knew I should have told them about their pot plant) while I tried to chat up the nurse on reception.

Normally, I'm pretty good with nurses, although that's a terribly chauvinist thing to say. It's not meant that way. All I mean is you have to accept that they really have heard it all before – the jokes about taking samples, wearing black stockings, so forth, so fifth. (Though I do have a friend – Bunny – who always insists on a female doctor or nurse if he has anything wrong of a private nature. But then Bunny's idea of a subtle chat-up is a sock full of sand.) In my experience, most female nurses' idea of an erotic evening is sitting in front of the TV with their shoes off and an endless supply of cups of tea. So I try not to try it on, even though I could get mileage out of being an Angel myself.

'Good morning, Sister,' I said. Well, it never hurts to promote people.

'Staff Nurse,' she said, without looking up from the notes she was writing.

'I'm so sorry. We'd like to see Mrs Asmoyah if that's possible.'

She looked up and smiled. She reached for a pair of glasses, but I didn't think it was because she was dazzled by my teeth.

'Are you her husband?' she asked, consulting a clip-board.

'No, just a friend,' I said too quickly, before I realised that she had almost certainly not been on duty when Sal was brought in.

'Then I'm afraid you can't see her. She's in Intensive Care.'

Just then, Lisabeth and Fenella appeared, looking suitably subdued and carrying a huge bouquet.

'But these are her sisters,' I said, thinking on my feet.

Lisabeth and Fenella did a double take between themselves, but fortunately kept quiet.

'Well, I suppose you can wait in the IC reception area,' she said doubtfully.

I jerked my head towards the stairs, having already clocked the sign saying 'Intensive Care 4th Floor,' and Les Girls followed me without breaking step.

'You'll have to check in with the police-man,' the Staff Nurse yelled after us.

I held the staircase door open for Lisabeth and said: 'You first.'

Lisabeth held back and then handed the bouquet to Fenella. 'After you, Binky.' Then, aside to me, she said: 'She's got a way with policemen,' as if confiding some dark secret.

We tramped up the stairs and enjoyed a mutual moan about why hospitals always put the sickest people in the most inaccessible places. On the fourth floor, we opened the fire doors and let Fenella go into the corridor first.

There were more double doors at the end, and in front of them on a tubular chair sat a uniformed constable reading the *Sunday Express*. Under the chair, between his legs, were his helmet and an empty cup and saucer. He folded the paper away as we approached, but he didn't stand up.

'We'd like to see Salome, please,' said Fenella with a smile.

'Mrs Asmoyah,' added Lisabeth politely, and she pointed to the flowers as if they explained everything.

'Sorry, my love,' said the PC, in a soft Kentish drawl. 'No visitors.'

'Oh dear,' said Fenella, 'and we've come such a long way.'

'Out of my hands, my dear. Doctor's orders.'

Fenella pouted. She does it rather well.

'You can have a look, though, but you can't go in. Okay?'

All three of us nodded in unison and we stood in line as he pushed open the double doors for us. I felt as if I was back at school, not that even my school had pupils like F and L.

Another set of swing doors greeted us. These had a big sign saying 'NO UNAUTH-ORISED ENTRY' and various instructions about hospital waste disposal, from which I averted my sensitive gaze.

The doors also had two round glass windows in them, and our neighbourhood policeman stood aside to let us press our noses against them. Lisabeth and Fenella took the left one ('Fenella, you're steaming up the glass!') and I took the right.

Salome was in a metal frame bed with about half a ton of bits and pieces surrounding it so it didn't escape. There was some sort of monitor with dials that I couldn't make head nor tail of, two drip stands with tubes – one lot going up her nose, the other into her arm – and her right leg was coated in plaster and suspended in mid air by a pulley contraption on which the Spanish Inquisition probably held the patent. I made a mental note to myself that if the doctor on her case set that beautiful leg anything other than back the way it should be, then he had better start looking for a good dentist.

Lisabeth and Fenella were coo-ing sympathetic noises and tut-tutting a lot and were riveted to the porthole window like two old men sharing a What the Butler Saw machine. I took the opportunity to have a word with the Kentish Constabulary's finest.

'I hear the passenger with her is a goner,' I said knowledgeably.

'Yeah.' He nodded. 'But she don't know that yet, of course.'

Of course she doesn't; she's unconscious, you chucklehead. But I didn't say it. Still, at least he'd confirmed Salome was driving.

'I can't believe she'd been drinking. It's not like her at all,' I said quietly.

'Well, they've taken a blood sample, so I understand, on account of her not being able to give a breath specimen, but I've not heard one way or the other. You a relative?'

I think I flinched at that. Well, I mean, you just can't trust policemen, can you? One minute nice as pie and the next – asking questions.

'Business colleague. She's quite something in the City, you know.' Then I felt I'd better add: 'The Stock Exchange.'

I wondered if I should add 'in London,' but I didn't want to appear too pushy.

'Where did it happen?' I asked casually.

''Bout eight or nine miles from here off the A227. Place called Blackberry Hill. Bloody dangerous piece of road, between you and me,' he confided. 'We get a lot of day trippers motoring around the Downs, and they see the signs for Brands Hatch and they automatically put their foot down thinking they're bleedin' Formula One drivers.'

I filed that away and asked if it was all right for the girls to stay until the doctors had done their rounds.

He said he supposed it was and offered to show them into the Intensive Care room, which had a hot drinks machine. By this time, Lisabeth was sniffing dramatically into a wad of Kleenex and Fenella had an arm round her (well, half around – her arms aren't that long) for comfort.

I gave Fenella a handful of loose change for cups of tea and told her I was just popping out to 'see to Armstrong' and I'd be back in an hour. She knew me well enough not ask what I was up to in front of a policeman.

Back in Armstrong, I dug out a road atlas from under the driver's seat and turned to the page covering south-east London and north Kent. I found the A227, which fed into the M20 motorway near Wrotham, easily enough, but the scale of the map was too small to identify anything called Blackberry Hill. From what the copper had said, though, it was somewhere between the North Downs Way country park and Brands Hatch. It was worth a looksee anyway, and there was bound to be somebody around to ask; a poacher or an itinerant hop-picker or whatever sort of person wandered the countryside these days.

I zipped back along the M20, letting Armstrong have his head as I thought it made a nice change for him not to plod through heavy traffic at ten miles an hour. At the A227 turn-off, I switched off the cassette-player so I could concentrate on the terrain.

The road wound gradually upwards towards the Downs – only the English could call uplands downs – until I was clear of the motorways that cut through Kent like the prongs of a carving fork stabbing at France.

The scenery was lush and the home values just as high as in London. I even passed a couple of oast houses where hops used to be dried after being picked by families of East Enders for a pittance and a daily beer ration. Nowadays, the graphic designers who'd converted the oast houses into very bijou residences all commuted to their dockland offices in the East End. It's a funny world.

At a petrol station near Vigo, I got directions to Blackberry Hill, proving yet again that taxi-drivers are the only people who can get service at a garage without buying anything.

A few miles further on, I took a left on to a B road that curved up even higher. It didn't say Blackberry Hill anywhere, there was just an old-fashioned road sign saying Broughton Street was four miles away. The hill was a switchback, and at the top of the first rise, I stopped and got out to have a look around.

There was no traffic at that time in the morning; it was too late for the milkman and too early for the lunch-time pubbers. So I climbed onto Armstrong's bonnet for a better view.

Blackberry Hill curled down then to my right and up again. From my vantage-point, I could see exactly where the accident had happened – about 60 yards from the summit – as the cops had left a portable barrier with yellow flashing lights on top to mark the spot.

I got back into Armstrong and wound him up again. I couldn't see anything from road level because of the hedgerow, but as I started up the second switch of the hill, I noticed an Escort estate car parked on the left, opposite the police barrier. I parked behind it and prepared some sarky backchat in case the owners turned out to be sight-seers. Then I saw that it had a light on the top and the crest of Kent Fire Brigade on the driver's door.

I couldn't see anyone around, so I sauntered over to the barrier.

About a hundred and fifty feet down the side of the hill was Sal's VW Golf, lying on its roof waving its wheels at the sky. The body shell had been crushed in, and any-body in there could only have come out through the windscreen.

I climbed the barrier and scuttered down towards the wreck, dislodging bits of chalk underfoot. As I drew nearer, a man stepped out from behind the Golf. He was wearing a peaked cap and pullover with epaulettes and elbow pads and carrying a clipboard.

'There's very little worth nicking, son,' he said straight off. Some people are dead suspicious.

'I'm here on behalf of the owner,' I said,

nodding at the Golf.

'And who would that be?' he asked, narrowing his eyes.

'Mrs Salome Asmoyah,' I said politely, and offered to spell it.

He looked down at his clipboard.

'That's okay, then. We have to be careful, you know; there are so many rubber-neckers and bloody souvenir-hunters, you wouldn't believe. 'Specially on Sundays. They make a fucking day out of it if they hear of a prang as nasty as this.'

I tut-tutted sympathetically.

'What do you reckon happened?' I knew he couldn't resist being asked his professional opinion.

'For my money, she just came over the top of the hill from the Broughton side too fast. It's straight up that side–' he waved his clipboard at the hill– 'but it twists this side. She didn't correct enough or she lost control or maybe she'd had a few bevvies. Who knows? Anyway, she hit the hedge, which is only about an inch thick, and found there was nothing this side. I think maybe she jammed the anchors on, because the car didn't sail out into space or anything.'

He made a motion with his clipboard like an aircraft taking off.

'It hit the hedge sideways and just kept rolling. There are faint traces of tyre on the road, but no serious skidding. Could have been just carelessness or inexperience or the booze.'

'That's not like her,' I said, putting on the concern.

'But tearing about the countryside late at night with a man not her husband is par for the course, eh?' He saw my expression change. 'I know, I know. That's none of my business. That's for the cops now, but they don't seem to be worried. The poor cow'll have to live with it.'

'Brakes okay?' I pointed at the car.

'Yeah, as far as I can tell.'

I walked around the wreck with him.

'No fire?'

'Nah.' He dismissed the idea. 'It's only in American movies where they catch fire. The petrol tank split open as it rolled, and most of the gas spilled out over the hill.'

We'd come full circle round the Golf, our feet crunching bits of windscreen.

'She was a lucky lady, your friend,' he said thoughtfully.

I agreed, and we stood in silence for a minute, gazing at the pile of crumpled metal.

'If you'd brought a brush and shovel with you, you could have taken it home,' he said, slapping his clipboard against a thigh.

'Yeah. I reckon even the insurance company will accept this one as a write-off. What'll happen to it?'

The Fire Officer shrugged his shoulders.

'Probably stay here till it rots. It ain't on the road, and this isn't exactly prime farming land.'

'Would there be any objection to me shifting it?' I asked on a hunch. 'It would be easier to get this back to London than to get an insurance assessor out here,' I added on the spur of the moment.

'Don't see why not. I've finished with it, but you'll have to check with the boys in blue. Here.' He reached into a back pocket and produced an official-looking business card, which said his name was Davis. 'Clear it with Inspector Ball in Maidstone first, but it should be all right. The police photographers were down here first thing this morning.'

I thanked him. Then I asked what time it had happened.

'Just before midnight – well, before then maybe. It was reported by a bloke down the hill coming back from the pub. He heard a crunch or two and saw the headlights where he knew there wasn't a road. Road Traffic were here within ten minutes, and the ambulance almost straight after. We brought a rescue team and an appliance–' I realised he meant a fire engine – 'but we were able to get the girl through the windscreen. She was lucky not to be trapped; nine out of ten would be. Of course, there was no rush with the bloke.'

'You were here?'

'Yes.' He nodded. 'I'm on three days' leave, but I wanted to get my report done. It's best. When there's a death.'

I bent down to try and look in the back of the Golf. 'All the luggage has gone to the hospital,' said Davis.

I straightened up.

'She'll probably ask for her clothes as soon as she comes round,' I said, just for the sake of something to say.

Davis and I climbed back up to the road together. 'She wasn't showing much dress sense last night,' he said over his shoulder to me.

'What?'

'Your lady friend, the black girl.'

'I don't follow.' I stopped but he didn't and I wheezed after him.

'Dressed like a fucking commando she was, last night. You know, battle fatigues – camouflage gear. If it hadn't been for the long hair and the high heels, we'd have thought we had a squaddie on our hands. In fact, one of the Road Traffic boys thought she was a Libyan terrorist at first. God knows where she'd been last night.'

I was beginning to think I might have an idea about that. But Salome had said to say nothing, so nothing was what I said.

By the time I got back to the hospital, I'd

missed the doctors' rounds. The policeman on duty was a different one, but he seemed to have already struck up a friendship with Fenella. Lisabeth was sitting apart from them reading a newspaper and eating a bar of chocolate. They vied with each other to fill me in on the gruesome details.

'Salome's got a brain clod,' said Lisabeth.

'Clot, you idiot,' said Fenella. 'A blood clot on the brain.'

'They're going to operate tonight.'

'They've done the operation hundreds of times, though.'

'And they won't have to shave *all* her hair...'

'And it'll grow back anyway...'

'And they don't know if it's affected her brain ... her memory...'

'Or her eyesight...'

'Or sense of smell. That happens too sometimes.'

'Well, thanks, ladies, now I'm really depressed. Still, who comes to a hospital to be cheered up, eh?' I put an arm round them both.

'Pregnant women,' said Fenella.

'Pardon?'

'Pregnant women. They come to hospital and are cheered up.'

'Oh yes, I forgot. Sorry.' Sometimes you just couldn't open your mouth with those two.

'Ignore her, Angel. I think the smell of this place has gone to her head. Or maybe it's that nice policeman,' she hinted, emphasizing the last syllable.

Fenella blushed, and I changed subjects quick.

'Any word on Frank?'

'Ooh yes,' cooed Lisabeth. 'Fenella's policeman told us. They've found him in Edinburgh and he's on his way to Heathrow or Gatwick, I forget which. But anyway, he's hiring a car.'

'You'd have thought the police would have sent a car,' said Fenella loudly.

'Who for, miss?' asked the policeman.

'Salome's husband. He must be worried sick.'

'Sorry, miss. You heard the doctors. There's not likely to be any change until they operate, and that probably won't be until late this evening. We just haven't got the manpower to play at taxis.' He was gentle enough about it, but of course Lisabeth got the hump.

'Well, what are you doing here?' she snapped.

I moved between her and the constable. That way he might live to make sergeant.

'He's waiting to give her a breathalyser if she comes round,' I said under my breath. 'He's only doing his job, and pretty soon he'll give up and go away. It doesn't sound like she is going to come round, so he won't have to do anything.'

Lisabeth fumed but I went on.

'Now make up your minds where to go for lunch. I've got something to do. Oh, and remember, this is the countryside, not the big city, and it's Sunday, so your choice is limited.'

I approached the copper and held out Davis the Fire Chief's card.

'Hi there. I've seen the Fire guys and they told me to ask for an Inspector Ball. It's about the car Sal – Mrs Asmoyah – was driving. I wondered if I could arrange for the wreck to be taken back – er – back home. Where can I find him?'

'Down the Shop, I 'spect. You a relative of...' He jerked a thumb at the Intensive Care doors.

'We all live together.' Did I lie?

His eyebrows would have disappeared if he'd been wearing his helmet.

'I could get him on the radio and ask for you if you like.' He tapped his collar radio – his 'talking brooch'.

'That's decent of you,' I said, and I meant it.

He moved down the corridor nearer to the window to get better reception.

'Fenella says there's a vegetarian café down the High Street, which does Sunday lunches, or so her policeman friend tells her.'

'Okay, we'll find it.'

Lisabeth's vegetarianism made it difficult to take her into pubs at lunch-time. Her temper made it inadvisable at other times.

'It's expensive, so Clive says,' said Fenella.

Behind her, Lisabeth mimicked 'Clive says' silently.

'Don't worry, this is on expenses.' I peeled off 40 quid from the wad in my back pocket. 'But keep the bill.'

Clive the Constable came back with as much of a smile on his face as uniformed coppers ever allow themselves.

'I got through to Mr Ball. He's quite happy if you want to move the car; we've finished with it. In fact, he reckons you'll save us and Kent County Council a few quid by doing so.'

'That's magic. Great. It's ... er ... something to do instead of hanging round.'

'Yer, I know what you mean.'

I was warming to young Clive.

'Any idea what's going to go down over this?' I asked, making sure we were not overheard by Les Girls.

'Depends. Could be drunken driving, manslaughter, who knows? Did the chap who copped it have family?'

'I don't know. Would it make a difference?'

'It might. Mothers Against Drunk Driving, that sort of thing, though usually it's the mums of young daughters who beat the drum. The present Chief Constable's very keen on causes like that. I'd line up a brief if I were you.'

'Her husband's a solicitor,' I said, which wasn't strictly true, but he was in the legal profession, and they're all thick as thieves as far as I'm concerned. (Rule of Life No 24: If you ever find yourself needing a solicitor, it's too late.)

I looked at my watch. There were 15 minutes to opening time, which meant I might just be able to head Duncan the Drunken off at the pass.

'Look,' I said to Clive. 'Er ... thanks for everything, but I've got to get these ladies some food. See you later, eh?'

'I'm off at two. I don't think there's much point in hanging around.'

'No, I'm sure you're right.'

He came closer and bent towards my ear.

'Tell me something. Are those two really her sisters?' He nodded towards where Salome lay in traction.

Well, they were Sisters, if not sisters, but I didn't know if he'd get that. So I said:

'Oh yes. And that one–' I pointed discreetly at Fenella – 'is the black sheep of the family.'

CHAPTER SEVEN

I rang Duncan from the phones on the wall in the hospital entrance as time was running out. As it was, I got Doreen, because Duncan was halfway down the garden path (all three feet of it) on his way to the pub. I told her I had a job for Duncan and there was money in it, and that was enough for her to yell 'Duncan!' so loud I felt I heard it without the need of the phone.

Duncan took some persuading – £250 and the scrap option on the VW, to be exact – but agreed to meet me at Blackberry Hill with his wrecker truck (there isn't a vehicle known to man he can't get hold of) in two hours. He told me I should be grateful, as this was the first Sunday lunch-time down his local that he'd missed in five years. I promised to buy shares in the brewery to make up for it.

I drove the girls around the suburbs until we found a newsagent big enough to sell maps, and stuffed behind a wad of yellowing, unfunny birthday cards, I found an Ordnance Survey map of the Blackberry Hill region. I wedged it in the carrier bag with the papers I'd taken from Salome's briefcase, and then we went in search of the veggie noshery recommended by Fenella's nice policeman.

We found it easily enough, and it was open for business – at least it was when they went in. I said I'd pick them up in an hour, and then drove until I found a pub with a bar food sign and a quiet corner. I bought myself a pint of shandy and something called a French banger, which turned out to be a six-inch sausage served in a nine-inch piece of French bread. In a crisis, it could have doubled as a draught excluder or, if the pub got rough, as a cosh.

I had my bag of reading material with me, and before the pub got too crowded, I spread the map, the Exhilarator brochure and the file marked 'Cawthorne' over a metal-legged table and got down to it. By the time the pub had filled enough so that the punters were giving me dirty looks for taking up so much room, I felt I had discovered enough to put two and two together and make five if not six.

The Exhilarator bumph advertised the latest in executive pastimes – dressing up as soldiers and running round the countryside shooting each other with paint pellets from air guns – a sort of hide-and-seek directed by Sam Peckinpah. The address on the brochure was Pegasus Farm, Blackberry Hill, Broughton Street, Kent, but there was no name to it. Yet Werewolf's new friend Sorrel had said 'Cawthorne' and 'assault courses' virtually in the same delicately-taken breath, and surely there couldn't be two of them? But then, how come Sorrel knew about things like that? Cawthorne's file from Prior, Keen, Baldwin didn't actually mention the Exhilarator; it was mostly financial stuff about his holdings and interests in the City. There was a lot of stuff in there I didn't understand, such as 'MM' and 'TF' and 'JS', mostly in the form of cryptic notes after a company name, though even I worked out that 'BB' meant Big Bang, when the City had been deregulated two years earlier.

On the personal side, there was very little about Cawthorne, except that he was the son of a Colonel in the Parachute Regiment now retired to darkest Wiltshire.

To my mind, that clinched the connection with Pegasus Farm, the Winged Pegasus being the emblem of the Parachute Regiment, which used to be called the Red Berets (when Richard Todd was making films) but nowadays (since American Football and Rambo) referred to itself as the Maroon Machine. I've always said that all those games of Trivial Pursuit wouldn't be wasted.

I sat back and treated myself to a cigarette, determined to make it the first and last of the day. I dug out the packet of Sweet Afton I'd managed to make last most of the week and lit up.

On the back of the packet was the phone number of Prior, Keen, Baldwin's motorbike messenger service, which I'd jotted down while snooping in their postroom on Friday afternoon. I remembered Gerry saying she thought it must be a radio phone as it had so many digits. It wasn't; it was a country STD code, and it matched the number printed on the Exhilarator leaflet for Pegasus Farm.

I should have made the connection sooner, given that the company was called Airborne PLC, but nobody's perfect.

Lisabeth and Fenella were waiting on the pavement outside the Spring Onion when I arrived to pick them up. The restaurant was still standing, but I suspected some unpleasantness had taken place as neither of them said a word until we arrived at the hospital again. I did ask if they'd had a nice meal, but Lisabeth just 'harrumphed,' so I dropped the subject and told them instead that I was going to meet Duncan and collect Salome's car. As they hopped out of Armstrong, Fenella leaned in through the meter window as if paying off a real cab. She handed me a bill from the Spring Onion and mouthed 'Sorry,' before skipping off to catch up with Lisabeth. Puzzled, I scanned the receipt to find, at the bottom after the VAT, an added amount of £7.50 just listed as 'Breakages.' I made a mental note to ask about that. One day.

I got to Blackberry Hill before Duncan showed, and cruised by the barrier that marked the scene of the accident. A few yards up the hill, on my left, was a turning that at first I thought was just the entrance to a field. I pulled in there as it seemed a good place to get Armstrong off the road, and it was only then I saw that it was in fact an unmade road curving away round the back of the hill.

I snuffed Armstrong's engine and dug out the OS map I'd bought. I opened it out, knowing straight off that I'd never get it re-folded properly, and found Blackberry Hill. The track I was parked on was a back way into the village of Broughton Street and, as the crow flew, a quicker way than coming around by Blackberry Hill. Broughton Street was a collection of grey boxes on the map with nothing to distinguish it from loads of other small Kentish villages. Near the village end of the track, a 'Fisher's Farm' was marked, and behind it, a green rectangle with the legend 'Fisher's Wood'. There was nothing saying Pegasus or Exhilarator.

A motor horn sounded off behind me and scared me silly. It was Duncan reversing a flat-back wrecking truck complete with winch and hook gear. On the doors of the truck was stencilled 'Ron's Recks of Romford.' Obviously Duncan was calling in a few debts.

We wotchered each other as I led him across the road.

'Wotcha, Angel.'

'Wotcha, Dunc. Thanks for turning out.'

'No problem. It's double time for Sundays.'

'Never forget you're Yorkshire. It's over here.'

We looked down over the police barrier at the upside-down Golf below us.

'Got enough rope?'

'Should have. If the wheels turn and we can tip it rightside up between us – should be a doddle.' He rattled the yellow and black barrier with both hands. 'This'll shift easy enough.'

For the second time that day, I scrambled down the slope of the hill towards the sad little car. I hadn't done this amount of countryside rambling since I was drummed out of the Boy Scouts.

Duncan tested the wheels and then indicated the old heave-ho motion. The slope of the hill helped us, and the Golf flipped over after three or four big rocking pushes. When it stopped bouncing on what were left of its shock absorbers, I tried to get the driver's door open, but it, and the passenger

155

door, were jammed shut. As there was no windscreen left, I stuck my head in, but there was nothing to see, not even blood, thank goodness.

Duncan got behind the Golf and pushed it to prove it would move, then set off back up the slope to get the truck.

'That's a tough little motor,' said Duncan as we climbed. 'There's not many would have stayed in one piece like that. I'm impressed. I think I'll get Doreen one.'

Back at the top, I helped Duncan carry the police barrier across the road so that it blocked traffic coming up. Duncan then marched over to the Ron's Recks truck and opened the passenger-side door. He took out two large plastic orange cones – the sort you get on motorway hold-ups – and gave them to me, telling me to put them the other side of the bend to slow the traffic coming down. The lad had come prepared.

He reversed the truck so that its winch poked over the edge of the drop. Then he attached a rope to it and scuttered down to tie the other end onto the front axle of the Golf. While he was getting ready, I wandered back to the turning where I'd left Armstrong and looked back across the road.

It wasn't exactly square on to the place where Sal's Golf had gone for a roll, but it wasn't far off.

I waited until Duncan had winched up the

Golf to the road and exchanged the rope for the winch hook, which lifted the front of the VW off the ground so it could be towed. I bet myself he had professional 'On Tow' plates in the truck, and he had, along with a seemingly authentic 'Police Aware' sticker, which he stuck on the rear windscreen. Then I asked him if he had any thoughts on how it had happened.

'Pissed?' he tried for openers.

'Doubtful.'

'Bit of nookie that got out of hand?'

'Not a chance.'

'Speed job?'

'What do you mean?'

'Either. Pedal-to-the-metal or naughty substances.'

'Wouldn't give you odds on either.'

'Then I'm buggered if I know, but I'll check the mechanics for you. I might have to unbend a few things, though.'

'Don't unbend too much – not until the insurance people have seen it.'

We replaced the police barrier to prevent a repetition of Sal's sudden decision to travel sideways, although I hadn't seen another car on the hill either time I'd been there. Which, of course, would just make it that much safer a place to do the business, if business had needed doing.

I asked Duncan to come over the road and look at the unmade road where I'd left

Armstrong. Some civic-minded soul had attempted to lay gravel at some point, but the track was pretty soft, and there were tyre marks, showing somebody had been down there pretty recently.

'What do you make of them, Dunc?'

Duncan looked at the ground then at me.

'I'm supposed to be fucking Tonto all of a sudden, am I?'

'Not if that makes me the Lone Ranger, son.'

And I meant it. My idea of a truth-and-justice lone avenger never appears in less than platoon strength, preferably nuclear-armed.

'Well, I nivver said I could read Indian signs, but them's some make of jeep thing. You know, one of the flash four-wheel-drive jobs.'

'You mean a Range-Rover? Something like that?'

'Nah, too small. More like a Shogun or one of the other smaller Jap 4Ws, or maybe a South Korean. I don't keep up with the names any more.'

'Duncan, you're supposed to be a car mechanic. You're supposed to know these things.'

'All I know is the bastard things are good enough not to need much repair, and there's no real second-hand market in them. People with loadsamoney–' he said it as one word, just to prove he had learned something living in London – 'buy them to play with and throw them away when they're bored with 'em. Nobody wants secondhand toys.'

What he really meant was there wasn't a market in nicked ones. Yet. He'd work on that and probably end up getting a Queen's Award for Industry.

'Just what're you getting at, young Angel?' he asked, narrowing his eyes the same way he did when he had a cigarette going and he was looking in a petrol tank.

'It was just a thought, Duncan,' I said casually. 'Lemme give you af'rinstance. What if you wanted to push that there VW Golf off this 'ere road, through that there hedge...'

'And down that there hill?' He scratched his chin. 'I'd probably wait here in my 4 by 4 with the lights off and then charge out so they have to swerve, only there ain't anywhere to swerve to.'

'What about hitting them side on?'

'Possible. It would be difficult to prove anything from the VW – it got pretty crumpled going down the hill. And you'd expect some broken headlights or something here on the road. Look. Nuffing.'

He was right. There wasn't really any trace of another vehicle, and neither the cops nor the Fire Officer had mentioned anything.

'You're not happy about this, are you?'

said Duncan.

'No. I'm not. Take the Golf back to Barking and stash it somewhere. Don't do any work on it till you hear from me, okay?' Duncan nodded. 'And don't worry if you don't hear from me for a few days. I think I'm going to be busy.'

Even then, I knew roughly what I was going to try and do, although I had no idea how to go about it. But first things first, and while Duncan headed back to town with the VW riding piggyback on his truck, I turned back towards Maidstone and the hospital.

The corridor outside Intensive Care was about as organised as Euston Station on a Friday night when I got there. Our friendly policeman had gone, but there were nurses there for the first time that I'd seen, and even the odd doctor. Maybe all that stuff about cuts in the health service wasn't true.

Lisabeth and Fenella were being moved out of the way and generally harried from pillar to post. Fenella told me, breathily and all excited, that they were going to operate and we'd all have to leave, but it was all right really because Salome's mum (who was ever so nice) had turned up, having been called by Frank, and was in there talking to the surgeons. Oh, and yes, Frank was on his way.

I told them there was nothing much more

we could usefully do there and we'd better leave before we were ejected. Truth was, I wasn't that keen on meeting Salome's mother again. Not because she doesn't approve of me (few mothers do), but she was bound to have a lot of questions I had no intention of answering.

Lisabeth reluctantly agreed after I put her in charge of phoning the hospital for twice-daily reports, which was exactly the sort of thing she liked to take charge of. Fenella was easily bribed with the promise of an ice-cream on the way home, and Lisabeth kept her company by devouring a couple of choc ices, which meant I had to wash down the upholstery of Armstrong's back seat that evening. I thought about the real taxi-drivers in London who took parties of kids to the seaside on day trips each year, and realised just what courage was.

The next morning, I was up and on my way to work by eight o'clock. Not bad for a Monday, I thought. For me, that wasn't bad for any day with a 'y' in it. Even so, the over-bearing Purvis looked at his watch when he saw me and said 'Good afternoon.'

'I need to see Mr Patterson,' I said, as if I was letting him in on a big secret. 'It's urgent. I was told I could get him on 2001.' I nodded to the phone on the reception desk.

'No chance,' Purvis said with a smile. Saying no seemed to suit him. 'He's in the Monday morning conference with the dealers, and that'll go on till nine, then he's got a policeman waiting to see him. You'll have to join the queue.'

'Thanks, but no thanks. I'll wait. Catch him later.'

I sneaked into the main dealing room and found a heating vent near the skirting-board at one end, which I could unscrew and look as if I was doing something professional. Only two or three of the terminals were occupied, by guys who looked as if they'd been up all night and who were already on to their second pack of cigarettes.

Shortly before 9.00 there was a general hubbub down the corridor and the Suits began to appear from their conferences, most of them holding styrofoam cups of coffee. Patterson was one of the last out, but it seemed he'd got the message about his visitor, as he hurried towards his office without a sideways glance.

I decided to join Anna and the girls in the postroom and scrounge some coffee. I think Anna was pleased to see me, despite the knowing looks from the other two, and none of them seemed to have heard about Salome, so I stayed tight-lipped. I did drop a bit of business into the pleasantries, like asking if there were likely to be any hand deliveries that morning. When they said it was almost a certainty, I made an excuse and nipped out to see Purvis.

'Mr P wants you to do something for him, Sergeant,' I whispered.

'Oh yes? Seen him, have you?'

'Yes, as he came out of the conference,' I said without a word of a lie.

'What?'

'If a motorbike messenger turns up today–'

'Do you mean a Don/R?'

'Yes, a despatch rider. If it's an Airborne guy, ask him for some ID.' He liked the idea of 'ID'. He would. 'And see if you can get his name. But be discreet.'

He looked offended, but I guessed his idea of discretion was swapping his length of lead pipe for a rubber truncheon.

I was back in the dealing room looking vacantly into an empty conduit when Patterson emerged from the end office and escorted a guy to the lobby. The visitor was wearing a suit, but you could tell he wasn't in the City as it was double-breasted.

On his way back to his office, Patterson caught my eye and, without breaking his stride, he tapped his wristwatch (I put odds on a Rolex) and held up five fingers. I nodded my White Sox cap in his direction and bent down to start screwing back the vent cover.

As on Friday, no-one seemed to notice me and certainly no-one challenged me as I walked through to Patterson's office whistling cheerfully (a Tommy Smith riff that I wished I could transfer from his tenor sax to my battered trumpet) and holding a plan of the air-conditioning system out in front of me. It was only as I rapped on the open door of his office that I realised the plan was upside down.

Tel-boy was a worried man. I could see that from the way his knuckles whitened around the telephone. He wasn't saying much; mostly 'yessir' and 'certainly,' and he ended with the words 'Very well, Mr Prior' and hung up.

He looked at me as if I had trodden in something on the way in.

'You've heard,' he said.

'Yeah, and I think we'd better talk.' I closed the door and sat down in the one chair this side of his desk. From his reaction, that was probably A First.

He narrowed his eyes.

'What do you want?'

'I want to know what Salome and Alec Reynolds were doing down in Kent on Saturday.'

'How should I know?' He avoided eye contact immediately. 'Husband away, cats will play. Alec and Salome were very close.'

'Is that what you told the copper who just left?'

Patterson reached for a paperclip to fiddle with.

'That's none of your business.'

'Who was he? Road Traffic?' Patterson's eyes flickered as if I'd given him a straw to grasp, but I pressed on. 'Or was he City Squad?'

Even I knew about the CS, which had been set up the year before in the wake of a couple of real humdinger scandals in the Square Mile. They were a cross between the most intelligent members of CID and the hardest cases in the Fraud Squad. They were computerised, all young enough to be looking for promotion and supposedly as mean as hell. They had replaced private wheelclamp units as the bogeymen of middle-class London.

'That's certainly none of your business,' he said, but his heart wasn't in it.

'Come on, Tel. Don't play hard to get, I'm on the payroll – remember?'

'Not any more you're not.'

He reached into a drawer down to his left and produced a chequebook, one of the big fat jobs that meant it was a company one, not a personal account.

'I think a thousand should cover it. After all, you haven't been here anywhere near a week and you don't seem to be getting anywhere.'

'That's where you're wrong,' I said as he reached for a pen. 'Leave the payee line blank, will you?'

'Just what do you want?' he asked, his pen poised above the signature space.

I sat back and crossed my legs.

'I want to know what you told the copper, what he told you, why you sent Sal down to Cawthorne's place at the weekend, what you're going to do about her now, what you intend doing about Alec Reynolds now that he's dead, and why you're trying to give me the bum's rush. Though that's pretty obvious: you're trying to sweep shit under the carpet, and that's never a good idea.'

Patterson blinked a couple of times. It was to clear the sweat from his eyelids. I noticed that he had pressed his elbows into the desk to stop his hands shaking.

'You don't know anything,' he snarled. 'You were a mistake.'

'I know how you're losing information.'

'How?'

'Your motorbike messenger service. I'll lay you odds that leak has come from something hand delivered.'

'You think we haven't checked that? You think we haven't timed the deliveries? You think we haven't sent a bike off and asked the receivers to phone us on arrival? Not one delivery–' he held up one finger –'was more than six minutes later than we estimated, taking account of the traffic, and we checked every delivery over a period of two weeks.'

Well, after all, he was supposed to be in charge of security.

'All the same messenger service?' I said confidently.

'Yes, as it happens.'

'Airborne?'

He thought for a second then said: 'Yes, that's the name. So?'

'Oh, nothing. If you've checked them out to your satisfaction, then fair enough. I just thought that them being owned by Simon Cawthorne would...'

'What?'

I think it was fair to say I had his attention, though the fountain pen he was strangling would never be the same again.

'Didn't you know? Didn't you even check that far? Didn't you make the connection with Pegasus Farm? Or am I way off base thinking that's Cawthorne's little war-gaming place down in Kent? Maybe Sal and Alec really were having a dirty weekend down there with the hedgehogs among the cow-pats?'

'You're sure about this?'

'Fairly.'

'That's not good enough.'

'Hey, hey, José, that's your department – finding out who owns who. I'm just the hired help, and if I'm still hired, I'll find out how they're doing it.'

His pen moved away from the cheque-book. Bad sign. He was getting his confidence back.

'We've gone through that procedure. There's no way it can be the bike riders. How are you going to find out?'

'Ever followed one?'

'Christ, no.'

'I can, without being spotted. If we know where he's supposed to be heading, even easier. Rig a delivery for this afternoon. It doesn't have to be anything important.'

'How did you rumble them? It was more or less the first thing we checked.'

'After Salome, that is.'

'How did you know *that*?'

'She's female and black. I'm surprised you didn't have her shot out of hand.'

He looked down at the cheque-book.

'You don't think much of us, do you?'

'Not a lot.'

'Except her.'

'That's right, and I want two things. First, is Salome covered by BUPA or some company medical scheme?'

'Naturally.'

'Good. Get her moved up to town ASAP. Private room, whatever it takes.'

He blanched at that, but it wasn't the insurance premiums he was worried about.

'You think she's in danger?' He wasn't as daft as he looked.

'Let's just say she's too near to Cawthorne

at the moment, which brings us, mystery lovers everywhere, to this week's request on Desert Island Discs. Tell me, Tel, which eight records and which book other than Shakespeare and the Bible, would Mr Cawthorne choose?'

'What the hell are you talking about?'

'The second thing. I need to know all you know about Cawthorne.'

In a split second he made his mind up and decided to be decisive.

'No.' He began writing on the cheque again. 'The moving of Salome, yes, we'll do that. We're covered for it anyway. But the rest – forget it. Take this and we'll call it quits.' He handed me the cheque and looked at his watch. It was a Rolex.

'Not bad for one and a half days' work,' he said smugly.

I took the cheque, folded it and put it in the back pocket of my jeans.

'Orders from Mr Prior, was it?' I slipped into my Humphrey Bogart, but it came out more like George C Scott. '"Get that fella Angel's ass off this case, Patterson." Something like that?'

'How...?'

'Oh, come on, you were on the phone to him when I came in. Reporting on what the copper said.'

He tried to get angry.

'I don't have to listen to you. Get out or

I'll have you ejected.'

I liked that. In the City you get ejected, in a pub it's chucked out.

'No you don't.' I didn't stand up. 'You talk to Mr Prior, I'll have a word with Mr Keen. Is there a Mr Baldwin, by the way? I wouldn't want him to feel left out.'

'Why do you want to talk to Mr Keen?' he snapped.

'To tell him that his son Morris is the office pusher, and I don't mean the tea-trolley.'

Patterson's mouth fell open. I thought I was getting to him.

'Wha ... wha...?'

'Young Mr Morris Keen is your friendly coke machine. Deliveries at least every Friday, probably mid-week too, I'd guess, direct to your door. Well, your desk anyway. I could even put a tag on a few customers. They're all out there beavering away at their terminals right now.'

'Cocaine?' he said loudly.

'Look me in the eye and tell me you never suspected.'

'Just exactly what do you want to know?' he said carefully.

'That's more like it.'

I gave him my full smile. I've got good teeth, so why not show them? And I always like doing business with a man who knows he's over a barrel.

170

I spent just over an hour with Patterson, which, I found out later, turned out to be another first. Time is money in the City, and few people are worth an hour unless it's over lunch and only then if you're involved in a takeover bid. It was also, I learned, one of the few occasions anyone at PKB could remember that Patterson had a meeting with his door shut and nobody got fired.

Even Purvis treated me with more respect as I sauntered out. Well, at least he toned down his sneer a notch or two.

'Have we used a Don/R at all?' I asked, remembering to slip into the Purvis jargon.

'Just the one.' He slipped a sheet of paper out from under the blotting-pad on his desk, then put on a pair of spectacles to read from it. 'Lewis Luther; that's Lewis with a "w." Lives at 23 Marlowe Road – that's Marlowe with an "e"–'

'As in Philip.' He looked blank. 'Or Christopher?' I tried. Double blank.

'London SW2,' he completed.

'Brixton. Would Mr Luther by any chance be a coloured gentleman?'

'Dark as pitch. Not that I noticed, of course.'

Not bloody likely you didn't, I thought, but bit my tongue.

'Good work, Sergeant. How did you find out?'

'Asked to see his driving licence.'

'Did he clock you – did he notice you copying it out?'

Purvis bristled. 'Of course not. I've got a photographic memory for some things. Wrote it out soon as he'd gone.'

'Excellent.' I took the sheet of paper from him. 'Good initiative there, Mr Purvis. I'll make sure it's mentioned in the right quarters.'

As I went down in the lift, I thought it pretty clever of Purvis to get the bike rider's licence. I was impressed. But I was also glad he'd never asked to see any of mine.

I bus-hopped down to Covent Garden to start putting the feelers out for Werewolf. The City is one of the few places left with the old London buses you can jump on and off. With most punters having travel passes with those twee colour pictures on their identity cards, the conductors rarely bother to come upstairs to collect fares any more, so you get a fair amount of free rides in if you're prepared to keep moving. The new, one-man buses that are everywhere these days are not only designed by maniacs who've never heard of the aged or disabled, but you can't get on one without flashing the cash. Sometimes I think all the fun's going out of London.

Sorrel was on duty at her stall on the corner of the flea market, so that was my first port of call.

She was wearing biker leathers and cowboy boots, which all looked as if they'd been applied with the aid of a shoehorn. The jacket had 'Those Whom the Gods Love' picked out in brass studs across the back, and the trousers had parallel lines of matching studs down the side seams. The boots had fake spurs. She was carrying more rivets than the average U-Boat and would probably have turned a compass away from Magnetic North.

The antiques business looked slack. Sorrel couldn't have made more than a grand so far that morning.

'Hi. Remember me?' I smiled at her.

'Sure. It's Gabriel, isn't it?'

'Close, but no cigar.'

'What?'

'A Transatlantic expression meaning–' I paused and looked in the air for inspiration – 'meaning "almost," I suppose.'

She studied me for about half a minute, then rearranged some of the knick-knacks on her stall.

'The Wolfman was right,' she said, as if to herself. 'You are a weird person.'

'Werewolf said that? About me? About anybody?'

'Yeah, I know what you mean. Don't worry, I'm not convinced. Not totally, anyway. What can I do for you?'

'Loyalty to Werewolf, and the fact that he's bigger than me, rule out answers 1 to 100, so I'll settle for knowing where the lad is.'

She picked up a book from her stall and browsed. She browsed beautifully. It was an 1875 edition of *Villette* by Charlotte Bronte. I'd never read it, but I knew how much I could have sold it for.

'The lad, as you call him,' she said, still reading, 'or the Mad Irish Git as I prefer to call him, is in my flat nursing a Full Metal Hangover. If there's any justice in the world, that is.'

'Good night last night?'

She shook her blonde hair. She shook her hair wonderfully. I'd better stop looking at her, I decided.

'You could say that,' she said in a sing-song sort of way. 'I never knew there were so many different types of stout. I never knew there were so many Irish pubs in London. And I've never been carol-singing in April before. Yes, you could say it was a good night.'

'Is he in a state to receive visitors?'

'The Pope and maybe a Guinness sales-man, but otherwise I'd have to say probably not. But since it's you...' She looked at me suspiciously. 'He seems to think a lot of you.'

'There's no accounting for taste,' I quipped, but she took it seriously.

'No, I suppose not. I'll give you the

address if you want, but I'm heading back there with some lunch for him in an hour or so.'

'That'll do. Just ask him to ring me this evening, would you? Tell you what, let's go out and eat tonight. On me.'

'Okay. He knows where to get you?'

'Yeah. Tell him to ring about seven, and we'll fix a place for eats. Italian food okay with you?'

'Sometimes I could kill for fresh pasta.'

'Good. But you'd better give me your number just in case.'

I like to think there aren't many tricks I miss, but I have to credit Sorrel in that she did write it down on a scrap of newspaper without saying 'In case of what?' I filed it away in my wallet.

'Are you sure you want me along?' she asked. 'I mean, it's not boys' night out or anything, is it?'

'Oh no. It's purely for the pleasure of your company. The two of you, that is.' She didn't believe a word of it. 'Well, I do want to pick your brains, just slightly.'

'What about?'

She turned half away from me as she had, rightly, detected a brace of customers approaching down the aisle of tables. They were a couple in their mid-fifties, I'd say, but dressed like they thought they were 20 years younger. The man carried a bulging leatherette wrist bag. I put them down as Dutch, and everybody knows the Dutch buy antiques by the lorry-load.

'The other day,' I said quickly, 'you mentioned a guy called Cawthorne. Simon Cawthorne.'

'Uh-huh,' she said, busying herself with miners' lamps, old spectacle cases and various china oddments that had 'A souvenir of Cromer' stamped on the bottom.

The Dutch couple stopped and began to inspect the merchandise. Out of the corner of her mouth – and she did it with great flair – Sorrel said:

'Sure I'll come along. You're going to need all the help you can get.'

CHAPTER EIGHT

By 2.30, I was having lunch at the wheel of Armstrong, parked on the edge of the pavement in Gresham Street about 60 feet from the Prior, Keen, Baldwin entrance. I had disguised myself with an old cardigan with faded leather elbow patches and a copy of the *Daily Express*. Lunch was an avocado and prawn sandwich and a carton of mango juice, which I admit were a bit out of character, but otherwise I looked for all the world like a real musher. I must have done, as not only did the Old Bill and the Ritas (as in meter maids) ignore me, but a real cabbie parked nearby came over to pass the time of day.

He told me how he'd been conned three times that week by people who took ten-quid rides, then said they hadn't any cash but offered to leave a watch with him while they went inside (usually a block of flats) to get some dosh. Of course they never came out, and he was left with three digital watches that, in the cold light of day, turned out to be worth approximately 99p each retail, 30p wholesale. I sympathised and threw in a few choice obscenities and 'Hanging's too good for 'ems,' but made a note to pick up a few watches next time I was down the Brick Lane midnight market.

He wandered back to his cab eventually. It was one of the newish, two-litre Metrocabs, and it was painted red. How gross. As a staunch supporter of the traditional FX4S design in any colour you like as long as it's black, I suppose I shouldn't have even talked to him, let alone been friendly.

At 2.40, a motorbike rider appeared on Gresham Street, parked outside the PKB building and disappeared inside. I couldn't tell much about him, as he was covered from head to toe in red crash helmet with black visor, red riding leathers and red boots. The bike, a medium sized Kawasaki, had rigid saddle-bags with 'AIRBORNE' stencilled on them, so even if it wasn't Lewis Luther, it was the right company.

I started Armstrong up as he emerged from the building with a large jiffy bag under his arm. Like most of the City messengers these days, even the ones in the dinky shorts on BMX bikes, he was radio-controlled and, like a copper, he had his radio tacked on to his collar. Before he got on the Kawasaki, he spoke into it and then tilted his helmet to hear the response. Then he was mounted and off.

It's almost impossible to tail a bike in London unless you're on a bike yourself, and that's a definite if it's rush-hour. But the next best thing is a taxi, which can always bend the odd rule and rewrite bits of the Highway Code without attracting too much attention. And of course it helps if you know where your target is going.

Patterson had arranged for the hand delivery to a firm of corporate solicitors who had an office in Bloomsbury round the back of the British Museum. The contents of the jiffy bag weren't important, but they were genuine and the solicitors were well known for handling City problems. Even I'd read about them. The idea was that the package might be tempting enough to follow all the other leaks down whatever conduit somebody was using.

I'd picked the Bloomsbury address, from a handful of alternatives Patterson had offered for the set-up, as the easiest route, and also the time, early afternoon, though in town these days the traffic was a matter of pot luck with the odds stacked on it being bad. If it rained, I'd be in trouble. Despite the number of golfing umbrellas you see around, advertising everything from building societies to aftershave, nobody ever uses them; they jump into cabs when it rains. I'm convinced half of them don't actually open, they're just designed as offensive weapons for use by psychopaths fed up with not getting a seat on the tube.

The Kawasaki cut through to St Paul's as I'd expected and accelerated up towards Holborn. So far, so good. I didn't bother with keeping a car or two between us like they do in the movies. If he looked behind him (he didn't have a mirror), all he'd see would be a black cab. So what? And how many despatch riders ever look over their shoulders?

Having said that, the bugger nearly threw me at Holborn Circus.

He turned left down an alley without indicating, and I had to carve up a Volvo with Swedish number plates in order to follow him. I felt a wee bit sorry for the driver – reindeer probably don't drive like that – but this was London, and if you can't

179

stand the heat, leave the wheels at home.

The Kawasaki disappeared to the right up ahead of me and I followed slowly. He seemed to be working his way round the back of the *Daily Mirror* building, though I couldn't think why. There were loads of light vans in the Mirror livery parked on both sides of the street, and the pubs down one side were doing a roaring end-of-shift trade – or maybe pre-shift. It was difficult to tell, but since Fleet Street had more or less stopped producing newspapers, this area was now the journalism centre of town, which meant the pubs would be doing some sort of trade.

I slowed some more, and it was just as well or I would have missed him.

He'd pulled up behind one of the news-paper vans, except it wasn't a newspaper van. It was a red Transit, one of the new designs that look like they've been punched in the nose, but there were no markings on it and the rear windows had been painted out.

The rider parked the bike nose-in to the pavement and killed the engine. I swung Armstrong to the right and mounted the pavement on my side, not more than 20 feet from him. I took down the battered, broken-spined *A-Z* I keep taped to the driver's sun visor and pretended to be looking some-thing up.

The Don/R spread his legs so he was holding the bike up, then he rapped on the back door of the Transit with a gauntleted hand.

The door opened and he handed in the jiffy bag.

I timed the operation on my Seastar. Three minutes and ten seconds later, the door opened and the jiffy bag was handed out. Mr Luther, if it was he, stuffed it into one of his saddlebags and freewheeled the bike back on to the road, kick-started and was away.

Patterson had arranged for the solicitors in Bloomsbury to ring him immediately the jiffy bag arrived, so that end was covered, and I was pretty sure that's where the Airborne messenger was heading without further interruptions. I decided to stay where I was and watch the van. I even took the number just to prove how professional I was, not that I had any idea how it could help.

I kept one eagle eye out for wardens and policemen with nothing better to do than harass taxi-drivers, but I didn't have to wait long.

After about five minutes, the rear doors of the Transit opened and a guy hopped down. He scanned the street as he looked up, but true to form, he didn't pay Armstrong the compliment of a second glance.

He pulled on a pair of folding sunglasses (the sort you pay an extra load for to have 'Porsche' stamped across your field of vision) as he made for the driver's door, but even with them and the soft brown leather blouson jacket, which made him look a bit like an off-duty copper (they get them cheap down Brick Lane), I still recognised him.

He was the one who had asked Werewolf if he played in a band, and the one I'd seen being ticked off by Cawthorne.

Werewolf had called him Robin Redbreast because of the striped shirt and red tie. I'd called him Chinless Wonder on the same basis that regular enlisted men in the Army call Sandhurst graduates 'Ruperts.' Maybe we'd both misjudged him. Maybe he was the sort of guy who pushes VW Golfs off hills in the middle of the night. Just for fun, of course.

I followed the van for an hour, and dead boring it was too. I was certain he didn't know I was following him, but he led me a pretty dance almost as if he was trying to lose me, As the traffic thickened towards the rush hour it got easier, but more boring, to stay fairly close behind him. Only once did he stop, having looped back towards the City, in Finsbury Circus. He had to double park there – doesn't everyone? – so he put the warning indicators on as he climbed in the back of the red Transit.

Sure enough, Lewis Luther, or whoever, turned up in full Airborne rig – I was pretty sure it was the same bike and made a note of its number this time – and they did business as they had at Holborn. This time, it was an ordinary letter by the looks of things, and it took, again, just over three minutes.

This time, though, Chinless Wonder stuck his head out of the van and said something to the rider before he went. The rider nodded and pushed off on the Kawasaki. Chinless looked up again and got back into the driver's seat and headed east.

I followed him out of the City until I was convinced he was packing up for the day. My guess was he would head for the Dartford Tunnel and then Kent. There was no way I could hope to keep up with him through the tunnel (a route I highly recommend if you want to lose a tail) as there were just too many imponderable lane changes and toll booth stops, so I turned where I shouldn't and headed back. Turning around brought a couple of angry hoots from the odd civilian driver – taxis and buses never blow their horns at taxis or buses – but I was now going away from the traffic flow, and I was back outside PKB by 5.00. I even found a legal parking space. Things were looking up.

Patterson listened to me in silence, then said, 'I just don't believe it,' a couple of times to himself.

'My guess is they've got a photocopier in the back of the van, and a typewriter and a selection of envelopes. They photocopy what you send out and then repackage it pronto. Takes a coupla minutes, and the people getting it at the other end don't notice anything wrong. Still sealed up, addressed to them. You ring up and say, "Did you get a jiffy bag five minutes ago?" and they say, "Sure, one jiffy bag, containing one letter, just arrived." So maybe it took one minute more than it should as the crow flies. We ain't talking crows. We can allow for traffic, bike breakdown, rider can't find the right doorway, whatever. All the things you take for granted that are going to screw you up in London. It's pretty ingenious.'

'It's diabolical,' said Patterson with feeling. 'But we could put them out of business if we, say, used sealing wax, or special security envelopes...'

I shook my head slowly in disappointment with him. 'I was thinking of something more permanent.'

'Not in that,' I said emphatically. 'No way, not ever. Not even in daylight.'

'What's the matter with you now?' Patterson yelled at me.

I don't think he meant to yell, it was just that his voice echoed a lot in the underground car park. I hadn't known before that

184

there was an underground car park to the building, but as the building was shared, only about eight spaces were reserved for Prior, Keen, Baldwin bigwigs. Therefore, Patterson was a bigger wig than I'd had him down as. I still thought he was a dickhead.

'You are a right dickhead–' I broke it to him gently – 'if you think we are driving down to Brixton in that.'

'What in Christ's wrong with it?' Patterson screamed. I have to admit that on a good day I find little at all wrong with the prospect of a ride in a new BMW, and Patterson was obviously well-pleased with his material rewards of Yuppiedom.

'Look, Tel, here in the City, it's a very nice status symbol, and a fine example of German craftsmanship, but in Brixton it's a Bob and therefore a legitimate target for any kid big enough to keep a tyre wrench in his nappy.'

'A Bob? What are you talking about?'

'Bob Marley and the Wailers. BMW.' I could see it sinking in. 'Shall we take mine?'

He was somewhat mollified to find that Armstrong was a cab and he could ride in the back and scowl at me, but he knew I thought it was a lousy idea going down to Brixton to track down Lewis Luther.

'Do you know where Marlowe Street is?'

'I'll find it,' I yelled back at him, then slipped an old Simply Red tape into the cassette just to annoy him, although it had the added advantage that I couldn't hear him any more.

I'd told him in his office it would do no good, but he'd insisted. So I'd used his phone to ring Sorrel's number and got an answerphone. I'd told it to come to the Vecchio Reccione in Leicester Square at 9.30, then I'd rung the restaurant and made a booking, using my PKB Amex card to confirm it. That'd also annoyed Patterson, as he'd forgotten about the card.

Round about the Elephant and Castle, I decided to call a truce and talk to him. I told him I reckoned Marlowe Road to be one of the 'poets' run of streets off Railton Road, all named after Shakespeare, Milton, Spenser with an 's' and so on.

'What's the plan, then?' I asked. 'Go up to the front door and ask if Lewis is coming out to play?'

'At least we could see if there's an Airborne motorbike parked outside. That would be a start.'

'You think he'll leave his bike outside round here?'

I was winding him up some because I thought he deserved it. He'd probably never been to Brixton before – I could tell that from the way he was sinking down in the back of Armstrong the further along Effra Road we got. Mind you, I was a bit out of touch myself. In fact, I hadn't lived south of the river for nearly five years, and that had been further over in Southwark until a small matter of an exploding terrace house had persuaded me to go flat-hunting. Not that that little affair had anything to do with the riots on Brixton's Front Line. No, that was a purely personal piece of business.

So I didn't know the area like I should. But, as they say in the ads on the telly, I knew a man who did.

'I've got an idea,' I yelled over my shoulder. 'I've a friend lives near here in Jonson Road.' But he wasn't the sort to have actually read *The Alchemist,* and probably thought his street was named after an American President.

'What good does that do us?' Patterson moved onto the jump seat just behind mine. I think it made him feel more secure.

'My man in Brixton knows everybody worth knowing and a sackful of those you wouldn't want your enemies to know. I think we should check in with him. It's just down here on the left.'

'Well, okay,' said Patterson nervously. I knew Lloyd Allen was at home as soon as I turned into Jonson Road, because nobody else would have a pink (yes, pink) 1964 Ford Zephyr – the nearest the British ever got to a car with fins – parked outside. Well, in Brixton they might, but only Lloyd would have had a tenor saxophone painted in gold on its bonnet. The year before, he'd been into the whole Absolute Beginners scene, and everything around him had to date from the late '50s, early '60s. Now he was into jazz, because he'd heard that the Yuppies had hijacked it after Clint Eastwood's film on Charlie Parker, and had moved back a decade to the late '40s. It was only a matter of time before my more traditional sort of jazz became popular again and I'd have to think of a new image.

I parked Armstrong in front of the Zephyr, reversing until the bumpers almost touched. A couple of black kids no more than about nine years old appeared from nowhere, hands in pockets, just sauntering by. They would be the official minders for the street.

They stopped and examined the half-inch gap between Armstrong and the pink Zephyr. I think they were impressed.

'Lloyd in?' I asked, not expecting an answer.

I didn't get one. They just shrugged their shoulders. I opened the door for Patterson and then locked the cab up after he'd stepped gingerly onto the pavement.

Lloyd's house was a three-bedroom semi-detached in a street that about 60 years ago would have been classed as a greenfield development. The front door was open and at least two sorts of music were oozing out onto the street. I recognised some pirated recordings of Sade in cabaret coming from the upper floor and, louder, some mid-period John Coltrane from the living-room. I knocked on the open door and strode into the front room, trusting that Patterson was right behind me. He was. I could smell his after-shave.

The room had stripped pine flooring and white walls. All the lights were white golfball shapes on stands about four feet off the floor. The furniture was expensive wood and leather and probably Danish. There were two cases of Red Stripe lager in the middle of the floor, roughly a couple of thousand record covers in various piles, and about six people in the room. One of them stood up and took off his sunglasses.

'Angel! Hey, my main man. Where've you been for the last six star signs?'

'Hello, Lloyd, you cooking?'

'I'm gettin' by, but you – you just disappeared off my screen, man. What's going down?'

Lloyd was wearing the bottom half of a pale grey pinstripe suit with turn-ups that probably took on board water when it rained. His braces were vivid blue and yellow zigzags, and were button fasteners not clips, worn over a see-through white shirt that didn't have a collar. He almost certainly had a pearl fedora to go with the image, and brown and white two-tone shoes, if he'd been wearing any.

'Low profile, Lloyd, that's me.' We shook hands. Both of us were too old to 'slap skin.' We left that to the teenyboppers with personal stereos and skateboards.

'Man, I ain't heard you play since the days of the old Mimosa Club,' said Lloyd with a thoughtful expression.

In the past, I'd seen a fair bit of Lloyd. I'd played at a club in Soho, even backed a few rock bands Lloyd had claimed to manage, and he'd run a string of female mud wrestlers, mainly in the clip joint next door.

'And are you still into mud – or is the record business paying off?'

'I get by, Angel baby, I get by.' He grinned. 'Meet the guys – and the next superstar I'm grooming.'

He put an arm around my shoulder and steered me to one of the leather sofas, which had a girl where other sofas have cushions. She was wearing a plain white T-shirt. Oh yes, and sunglasses.

'Hi, Mr Angel,' she said, stretching her legs together just enough to produce static electricity.

'Hello, Beeby,' I smiled.

'You know each other?'

'Mr Angel sort of put me on to you, Lloyd,' she purred. 'And I've never looked back.'

The kid was going to make it.

'Well that's just wicked, man, really wicked. Mr A, I'm in your debt.' Lloyd slapped my shoulder.

'Good,' I said.

'I thought so,' Lloyd said, grinning. 'But first, meet the Dennison brothers.'

The three black guys didn't get up or anything – I was pretty sure two of them couldn't – they just nodded as Lloyd reeled off their names.

'That's Derek, Selwyn and Melvin, and I know what you're thinking.' He prodded me playfully in the chest. 'And you'd be right. Del, Sel and Mel. Would you credit it? Your ma had a weird sense of humour, boys.'

The boys took this all in good heart, as they probably had all their lives.

''Nother coincidence,' I said. 'Meet my mate Tel.'

'Hey! Welcome! Del, Sel, Mel and now Tel. Beeby, get the *Guinness Book of Records* on the horn. Pull up a beer, you guys, and utilise the accommodation.'

Lloyd picked up a beer can, lifted Beeby's legs up with one hand, sat down on the sofa and let her legs fall across his lap.

I sat down on the cases of beer, and Patterson perched on the edge of an armchair.

'Tel here works in the City,' I opened. 'He's got a problem.'

'I can relate to that, Angel my man. No decent food, no place to park and almost zero women. Good street prices for Jaws though, gotta admit that.'

'Jaws–' I explained to Tel – 'otherwise known as the Great White Powder. Very naughty substances.'

He made an O with his mouth. I turned back to Lloyd and tried not to look at Beeby's legs.

'Tel's problem's a wee bit more specific than that. It involves a Brother, a local one. Thought you might know him.'

'He got a name or am I psychic suddenly?'

'Lewis Luther. Rides a Kawasaki 125. Know him?'

'Maybe.'

'Lives round the corner in Marlowe Road.'

'So does my tailor.' Lloyd beamed, and a couple of the Dennison brothers laughed dutifully at the in-joke, which went over me.

'If I were your tailor, so would I, but I wouldn't tell anyone.'

Beeby laughed at that until Lloyd lifted one of her legs and sank his teeth into her inner thigh until she squealed.

'Know your place, woman!' shouted Lloyd, and Beeby wriggled more into his lap, laughing like a drain.

Patterson coughed to cover his embarrassment.

'So what's this Loo-is been a-doing then,

Mr A?'

'That's what we want to ask him, Lloyd. It may be that Lewis doesn't know he's doing anything out of order, but some of the messages Lewis is delivering ain't getting through, or at least not in one piece.'

'What sort of messages?' Lloyd ran his fingers up Beeby's legs, like a concert pianist warming up.

'Mostly financial stuff.'

'Any firm in particular?' Lloyd was concentrating on miming what looked to me like Mozart's 'Turkish March'.

'Tel's company.'

'Which is?'

'Prior, Keen, Baldwin,' Patterson said nervously.

Lloyd stopped tuning up Beeby's legs and looked up in genuine surprise and then disgust.

'Shit! Has that little jerker Lewis been messing with my brokers? I'll kill him.'

If I was surprised to hear that Lloyd had a stockbroker, Patterson was dumbfounded. But a client is a client, and he perked up no end as we walked round to Marlowe Road, Lloyd between us and one of the Dennison boys about ten feet ahead acting as an outrider.

I'd been right about Lloyd's two-tone shoes, though I had expected him to put socks on, and I was wrong about the hat – it was a white Panama. I was glad he chose to wear it, for otherwise, in his shirtsleeves and braces walking between us, it could have been mistaken for an arrest or at least a 'helping with enquiries,' and the last thing I wanted was a street riot.

By the time we were out of Jonson Road, Lloyd and Tel were getting on famously, talking 'fundamentals,' 'half yearly growths' and 'sell options.' The Dennison lad had pulled ahead of us and disappeared round a corner. He emerged giving Lloyd the thumbs-up sign, and Lloyd jerked his head without pausing in his conversation on the future of the British economy. Dennison crossed the road and disappeared again. He would be covering the back door of No 24 if I knew Lloyd.

The front door of No 24 was a yard back from the pavement. Lloyd didn't knock; in fact he didn't stop talking to Tel. He pulled a key from his trouser pocket and slipped it into the lock.

'You do know Lewis, then,' I said, looking at the key.

Lloyd pushed the door open and showed me his teeth. ''Course I do. He's one of my tenants.'

'This is your house?' asked Patterson, impressed.

'One of 'em,' said Lloyd modestly. I

wondered if he had just the one broker. 'This way, gentlemen. Ground-floor ap-art-ment if my memory serves me well. And we know he's home.'

I followed his gaze down the hallway to where a Kawasaki was parked on a spread-out copy of the *Evening Standard*. The number plate told me it was the same one I'd followed earlier.

Lloyd rapped his fist on a badly-stripped fake pine door with a metal numeral 1 nailed to it. Further down the corridor was a kitchen, and across it I could see young Dennison loitering with intent outside the window.

'Looo-ees,' Lloyd cooed. 'It's your friendly landlord. Social call.'

The door opened an inch and a yellow and brown eye looked out.

'Do I lie?' said Lloyd, pushing the door.

Lewis Luther was about 19 in age years but a lot older in street-time. He backed across the room, keeping pieces of furniture between himself and the three of us. Not that there was much furniture in the room: a table, covered with copies of *Motor Cycle News*, two dining chairs, a bed with a duvet cover illustrating a big Honda bike, and a chest of drawers with a midi stereo cassette unit on it. The whole place had an odour of long-gone take-away curries and engine oil.

'What can I do for you, Mr Allen?' said

Lewis suspiciously, rubbing the palms of his hands down his red leathers. He'd lost the leather jacket and the boots, but maybe he slept in the trousers.

'You happy in your work, Lewis?' Lloyd put a foot up on one of the chairs and flicked imaginary dust from the toecap with his fingertips.

'Sure, Mr Allen. It's a good job. Regular pay.'

'Your mum keeping well?'

'Yeah.'

'Still giving her housekeeping?'

'Every week.'

'Good boy.' Lloyd turned to me. 'His ma's got six other Luthers and an Episcopalian church to support, but she's a good lady. Would break her heart to hear of Lewis in trouble.'

'What trouble? I ain't done nuffink.' But he was looking worried.

'That's for these gentlemen to decide.' Lloyd waved a hand, giving me the floor.

'Who's they?'

'We're financial advisers to Mr Allen,' I said, and Patterson nodded enthusiastically.

'What's that to me?' Lewis spread his arms.

'Your job with Airborne—'

'Yeah, what about it?'

'Do you always do pick-ups from Prior, Keen, Baldwin?'

'What's that when it's at home?'

Patterson grabbed Lloyd's arm and said excitedly: 'But he was there twice today and...'

'Leave it out, Tel,' I said without looking at him. 'Gresham Street, in the City.'

'Oh, them.' Lewis looked relieved. Like most delivery riders, he never looked at the name, just the address. 'Yeah, I was covering them today and–' he thought about it for a second – 'twice last week.'

'How do you get your instructions?'

'Radio. The despatcher just tells us where to pick up and where to go.'

'What about the Transit van? Why did you take the Gresham Street stuff there first?'

Lewis didn't bat an eyelid.

'Take everything to the van and check it with Mr Sorley. The van's the office, man, that way they keep the overheads down.'

Lewis found himself looking at three puzzled faces. He tried to explain.

'Look, man, Airborne doesn't have a base in town. The whole operation is run from the van. There are six or seven riders and we split the shifts. We rendezvous every morning near Blackfriars Bridge and get the first jobs over the radio. We do a pick-up, then check in with the van. Everything gets registered by Mr Sorley so he knows how much work we've done and how much to bill the clients. Where's the harm in that?'

'You doing this self-employed, Lewis?' asked Lloyd. He was either concerned for the lad or thinking up a scheme of his own.

'Yeah. So?'

'Paying tax, are you? National Insurance?'

'I will, I will.'

'How long have you worked for them?' I asked.

'Three months.'

'Know any of the other riders?'

'One dude, Lenny Emerson.' He looked at Lloyd when he said this.

'Lenny's only been out of the jug five, maybe six weeks,' said Lloyd.

'Ever seen any other Airborne riders?' I tried.

'No.'

'Ever drawn a night shift?'

'No, I'm lucky.'

'Weekend work?'

'Nah. Like I said, I'm lucky.'

I looked at Patterson and Lloyd looked at me. 'Conference?'

I said yes and Lloyd told Lewis to go and make a pot of tea and invite the Dennison kid in. Lewis said he hadn't got five cups. Lloyd looked at him, then at the ceiling, sighing as he did so, and Lewis got the message. Lloyd shut the door after him and pulled up one of the chairs, straddling it.

'Is the boy in trouble?'

I shook my head. 'He's no idea what's

going on,' I said. 'But he'll probably be needing a new job soon.'

Lloyd scratched the underside of his chin.

'What have we got?' Patterson asked me.

'A very sensitive operation. I think they're targeting one or two City firms and getting the inside track by reading their mail. Airborne gets a reputation for quick service from the companies they're interested in because the bikes are cruising round outside just waiting for a call. They probably have three riders on call in case one goes sick or gets delayed or is already on a job, but I'll bet they never deal with more than two companies at a time. It sure as hell ain't a full-time job for Mr Sorley, if that's his name.'

'It is,' said Patterson thoughtfully.

'Go on,' I prompted.

'Jeremy Sorley-Smith to be exact. Long-time gopher to Simon Cawthorne. I think they were at school together.'

'Cawthorne, eh?' Lloyd let out a low whistle. 'Bad news baby if ever there was.'

'How come you know of Cawthorne?' I was getting annoyed about everybody knowing more than me.

'Just because you don't read the financial pages, Angel-face...'

'Later,' said Patterson, looking at his Rolex. I hoped he remembered to pull his cuff down over it when we got out in to the street. 'What do we do now?'

'Well, I'd like to get a look inside that van,' I said. 'So maybe tomorrow we arrange for me to do one of Lewis's runs. Think he'll agree?'

'It'll cost,' said Lloyd, weighing up Tel's wallet with his X-ray vision.

'Can he be bought?' asked Tel.

Lloyd and I just looked at him. (Rule of Life No 28: Everybody can be bought. The trick is to make them think you're buying them from Harrods, not Woolworth's at sale time.)

'Okay. Negotiate what you want,' he said with a defeated air.

'As Lewis's agent–' began Lloyd, then he saw my face – 'recently appointed, I'll handle that. Just give me a bell as to when and where you want him. He'll be all yours.'

Tel and I didn't stay for tea.

Lloyd had the Dennison lad escort us back to Jonson Road while he had a word with young Lewis, who seemed remarkably nonplussed by the whole affair.

Armstrong was still there and in one piece, though I walked around him to check that all four wheels were in place before we got in. Beeby came to the door of Lloyd's house and waved us goodbye. She was fully dressed; she had her sunglasses on. I still didn't know why she was called Beeby.

'How did you know it was the motorbike service?' Patterson asked over my shoulder as we left Brixton. 'You were convinced that was where the leak was from the start. Why?'

'Because that's the way I would have done it, Tel-boy.'

I dropped Patterson back at the PKB office so he could pick up his BMW and, though he didn't say it, I think he was glad he'd left it behind. At least he had something to drive home in.

I made it back to Stuart Street just before 8.00. I needed a shower and a change of clothes, and if I was meeting Werewolf and Sorrel in Vecchio Reccione's it was wisest to leave Armstrong behind.

Besides, there were my domestic duties to perform, such as getting updated on Salome's condition from Lisabeth at mission control, and feeding Springsteen.

Lisabeth was out of her flat before I'd closed the front door behind me.

'Frank's been back but he's gone again,' she said, quivering with importance. 'Salome's had her operation but there's no change in her condition which is a good sign rather than a bad one...'

'Stable!' Fenella shouted from inside their flat. 'Don't forget to tell him she's stable.'

'Thank you, Binky,' Lisabeth said, in a voice that would have sliced vegetables. 'Don't have a dog and bark yourself, dearest. Concentrate on your macramé.'

She said it the way judges passed sentence at Nuremberg.

'Salome's condition is described as stable. We'll know more tomorrow night.'

I was almost up the stairs level with her by this time. 'How's Frank taking it?' I asked.

'Quietly,' said Lisabeth. 'Very restrained. He's gone back to spend the night near the hospital.'

I have to admit I was relieved. I dread having to go through the sympathetic ear act, even when it's merited. I'm no good at it, and I hate doing things I'm no good at.

'Anything he wants doing?'

'No, I don't think so.' Lisabeth frowned for a second. 'Oh – he did say to tell you he'd fed Springsteen. In case you were late back.'

'He didn't have to do that,' I said, squeezing past her and on to the next flight of stairs to my flat. Then I did a double take.

'How did he get into my place to get the cat food?'

'He didn't. He microwaved some steak out of the freezer. The poor little beast...' And this from someone who firmly believed all cats had 666 tattooed on them somewhere under their fur! 'Just like Salome does when you're out.'

I found Springsteen lying in the middle of my bed. He didn't look up when I entered the bedroom, he just put a paw on the end of the sirloin steak he was chewing to make sure I didn't grab it.

I shook my head at him in disgust.

'You're an animal,' I said.

CHAPTER NINE

'You're an animal!' Sorrel shrieked in delight. Then she grabbed a handful of ice cubes from a nearby wine cooler and stuffed them down the front of her partner's trousers. She stood back and acknowledged the applause of the crowd as the lights came on again and we were able to concentrate on our dessert.

I suppose I'd better explain. If you want an Italian restaurant where the waiters bring you menus instead of shouting at you, where they leave the lights on instead of turning them off every 20 minutes, and where they make you get up and dance before they'll turn them on again, then don't try the Vecchio Reccione, however convenient it is for Stringfellows.

I only eat at the Vetch-Retch these days when someone else is paying, which is much the same as saying when England wins at cricket. However, this was on PKB's Amex card, the pasta had been delicious, the

Frascati had flowed, the zabaglione was on its way and all was right with the world. Though I couldn't go so far as to say that service was included, as all the waiters seemed interested in was getting the lights off so they could dance with Sorrel. Little Gino, whose ambition had always been to be taller than four foot ten, had got a little too interested when it was his turn, and even in the candlelight we could all see that he'd *deliberately* got his charm bracelet tangled in one of Sorrel's suspenders. The miniature St Christopher on it had a brief treat before Sorrel cooled him off in no uncertain terms.

The blue-rinsed grandmother from Iowa – 'just passing through Lunnun to catch a few shows' (like anglers collect trout) – I had drawn as a dancing partner clapped louder than anybody.

'I've always wanted to do something like that,' she confided to me. Then to herself, she said: 'Never got the excuse.'

I thanked her for the dance, and Werewolf bowed deeply to her 'girlfriend' (Oxnard, California), which made her day, as they say in those parts.

Back at our table with the promise of at least a half-hour's respite while Gino dried his trousers, I brought Sorrel and Werewolf up to date.

'Why are you telling us all this?' asked Sorrel. She was direct, I'll give her that.

'Because I thought it was more interesting than the weather, the rattle on Armstrong's exhaust pipe, the situation in the Lebanon, additives in food, the price of...'

'What do you want us to do?' asked Werewolf, scraping the last of the zabaglione out of his glass.

'There you are,' I said to Sorrel. 'He understands every word I say.'

'So what's the deal?' She raised her spoon to her mouth then sent her tongue out to meet it.

I averted my eyes.

'All you have to do, Sorrel dear, is fill me in on the gossip about Simon Cawthorne. You, Rambo, come and play soldiers with me down on Jollity Farm. Cawthorne calls it the Exhilarator. It's in Kent; one of these paintball guns and combat trousers action games for bored executives. They run over cross-country courses and pay through the nose for it. In fact, they pay for the sort of thing they used to skive out of when they were at school.'

'I nivver did games at school,' mused Werewolf.

'Lack of coordination,' Sorrel said to me.

'Bad attitude?' I asked.

'Yeah, that's right,' said Werewolf, genuinely surprised. 'How did you know? That's exactly what the priest put on my report. Not just for games either, come to think of it. Still, the pompous bugger wrote it in Latin, so my Dad never understood. Thank God. So when do we go yomping over south-east England?'

'Tomorrow if I can fix it, Wednesday if not.'

'Today Kent, tomorrow the world!'

'Somebody must have seen that before now,' sighed Sorrel. Then, seriously: 'The Exhilarator can be rough, you know. I've played it.'

Werewolf and I looked suitably impressed.

'They don't like women there,' she offered, playing with the froth on her coffee with a fingertip. I found it disturbingly moving. 'And they don't make concessions, and it's not just air pistols firing paint blobules. They have the whole works – thunderflashes, booby-traps, smoke grenades, the lot. That's why he charges top whack and it's a nice little earner for him.'

'If it's such a nice little earner, why does he go round prying into other people's mail?' asked Werewolf.

'Nice little earners are even nicer when they grow into big earners,' said Sorrel philosophically.

'Is he greedy?'

'Greed is everything in the City.'

I'd heard that before.

'What exactly *is* Cawthorne? Somebody told me something like he was "of the City" but not "in it." Does that make sense?'

'That's very astute.' She nodded. 'Sums him up nicely. He was a real bright boy in the pre-Big Bang "golden hello" stakes. Built himself a shit-hot reputation and moved firms three, maybe four times, before the Bang. You've got to remember that at the time, deregulation was looked on as an open cash-register. The firms with the best teams – analysts, jobbers, corporate lawyers, financial PR men, whatever – those were the firms that were going to set the going rate and get it. And for a while – the Golden Time – they hired anybody, giving six-figure "golden hellos" to anyone willing to break a contract. At one point, I think Cawthorne was actually getting paid by three brokering houses.

'Anyway, soon after Big Bang, things settle down and eventually start to tighten up.'

She flicked a finger at her empty glass and Werewolf added some more white wine.

'The writing on the wall for the Yuppies, eh?' he asked her.

'You could say that, but few saw it. The spray-painting on the wall came with the big double M in '87 – Meltdown in the Market, which started on Wall Street – but some of the bigger houses and the banks were already letting people go–'

'I love that,' I said, '"Letting people go." I have this vision of a Biblical stockbroker

207

standing in the Red Sea shouting "Let my people go."'

'It was a bit like that,' Sorrel said, smiling. 'I know one jobber who spent his twentieth birthday in the slammer for throwing his VDU through a fifth-floor window onto the street.'

Werewolf whistled low and slow. 'Did it hit anybody?'

'Worse than that. It bounced off the roof of another jobber's Porsche. *He* got bound over to keep the peace for punching the guy who got fired.'

'Was Cawthorne let go?' I asked.

Sorrel shook her head, and her hair stayed wondrously in place. I realised that a haircut like that was no Saturday-morning trim and blow-dry. Come to think of it, the little party frock number she was wearing (and I'm so glad hemlines are on the up) didn't come from Oxfam either.

'No. He jumped, but only just before he was pushed. He was dealing himself in too much. It becomes obvious, even to the Stock Exchange. You could say he was an insider trader before it became fashionable. Nothing was ever proved, of course. That was still before people went to chokey for dodgy dealings, but he soured his own patch. The DTI – the Department of Trade and Industry – started to check up on one or two deals, and at the first whiff of them he was away on his toes. Couldn't get a job in the City scooping dog poop nowadays.'

'So how does he earn his daily?' Werewolf leaned over and pinched a Sweet Afton from the packet on the table in front of me. He rolled it between two fingers and tapped it on a thumbnail and generally fondled it, as I knew he would for a good five minutes before lighting it.

Sorrel watched him for a few seconds, then snatched it out of his hands and stuck it in her mouth. Two waiters clashed wrists getting a light to her. She blew smoke out, coughed, and handed him the cigarette, and he took it without a word. She'd known him less than a week and was already on to his annoying habits.

'He panders to people's whims,' she said pointedly, still looking at Werewolf. Then to me, as if she heard my brain going click-whirr. 'No, not drugs. I don't think he deals. It's the other things, like the Exhilarator – a playground for young executives. And he has a small ticket business, you know, last-minute box at the opera or hospitality suites at Wembley for a Springsteen concert, or Centre Court at Wimbledon, that sort of thing. You pay, of course, but that's rarely a problem for his clientele. And there's his latest venture – Le Tube.'

'I have to ask...' I said.

'It's what we – they – in the City call the

Channel Tunnel and the opening up of the full Common Market in Europe in 1992 and '93. Well, the market integration comes in '92 and the Tunnel is supposedly the following year. The two together are referred to as Le Tube, though the papers sometimes call it the French Connection.'

'It's the houses, isn't it,' said Werewolf, nodding wisely.

'What houses?' I had to ask.

'Property prices in rural France are a joke compared to this country. Near where the Tunnel comes out on their side...'

'*Le* coast,' said Werewolf, interrupting her. She ignored him.

'...you can pick up an old farmhouse with barns and stables, so forth, so fifth, for less than a terraced house in Bolton at the moment.'

'*Le* snip,' grinned Werewolf.

'And there's sod-all planning permissions needed over there. Ideal for doing up into dinky Yuppie holiday homes or even regular homes. With the Tunnel, you can commute to the City from France faster than from, say, Wiltshire or Dorset – which are the in places to live at the moment. Or you could live there, rig up your personal computer and play the Stock Exchange and the Bourse at the same time and then nip over to the West End for a show.'

'*Le* life *du vin et* roses.'

'Ignore him,' I told Sorrel. 'He tripped over a volume of Proust when he was a kid. So Cawthorne is doing up houses in France?'

Sorrel shook her head. 'No, buying up, not doing up. Pure speculation. It's been said he's got a bigger investment in bricks and mortar in the Pas de Calais than Hitler had. Once the Tunnel opens – or maybe just before it does and before the French realise what's going on and think up a way to stop it – he'll sell them for maybe a thousand times what he's paying for them now.'

'Is it *le* con?' asked Werewolf.

Sorrel shrugged. 'That seems a legit business, though knowing Cawthorne, a few corners will have been trimmed. But the idea seems a decent punt – that means a bet to us city slickers, Wolfman–' she smiled sarcastically – 'not a cockeyed Irish pound note.'

Werewolf narrowed his eyes and pursed his lips at her, making a face that would have worried an exorcist.

'It's the way he's financing it that's dodgy,' Sorrel went on. 'He's into cash businesses. Like the Exhilarator. And he owns leases on half a dozen pubs in the new Docklands, and he does a bit of importing – high value stuff like furs or cars. They're all cash deals. No extended lines of credit, no invoicing 30 days later, and all designed to be quick in-and-out operations before the tax man or the VAT man has twigged there's anything going on at all.

'From what you've said about Airborne, he's also into some dodgy share dealings. That's a dangerous business these days, so he's being clever – if he's being successful.'

'What do you mean?' I asked, before Werewolf could say anything.

'Look, insider dealing is regarded as the downside of legal nowadays. A coupla years ago, it meant you had good contacts and you used them well. Now it's naughty with a capital N. So you don't do it, or you don't do it in the normal way, which is relying on somebody inside a company to tell you things. Cawthorne seems to have cut out the middleman. He just reads their mail without them knowing it, and the thing that would really appeal to him is that the companies he sets his sights on are actually paying him for delivering it!' She smiled and shook her head some more. 'Yes. He'd like that,' she said to herself.

I caught Werewolf's eye and knew it had to be me who had to ask.

'How do you know all this, Sorrel, love?'

'Simon used to work for my father a few years ago, but he...'

'Had to let him go?'

'You're catching on, Angel. It's a small world in the City, though, so...'

'Speaking of small worlds...' Werewolf nodded towards the restaurant's kitchens, from where Gino had appeared zipping up the flies on a new pair of jeans.

'Your father is ... in the City?' I asked innocently.

'Oh yes,' she admitted. 'Well, he's a businessman, but he has a lot of dealings in the City.'

'Okay, blue-eyes,' I drawled, even though they were green, 'be difficult and make me twist the information from you until you scream for my kisses...'

'Oooh, I love it when you talk dirty!'

'Not you, you Fenian oik, her!' I turned back to Sorrel and leaned forward so we eyeballed each other. 'Now listen very carefully...'

'I shall say this only once,' she completed, moving closer so our noses almost touched. She had good teeth too, I noticed.

'What – and think carefully before you answer – is your surname?'

'McInnes,' she said, dead straight. 'Big M, small C, big I.'

'So your father is called–' I paused dramatically – 'Mister McInnes.'

'Correct!' she squealed, and leaned over a millimetre and kissed me quickly. 'Go to the top of the class.'

'You get any closer to him, my lass, and he'll have to stand in the corner till he cools down,' said Werewolf, draining the last of his wine.

'Oh, is that a salami in his pocket?' she said, all innocent, with eyes as wide as a Volvo's sidelights. 'And I thought he was just pleased to see me.'

'Now, now,' I said soothingly. 'It'll end in tears. I want to get one thing straight before this conversation finally goes down the drain and before he orders liqueurs.'

Sorrel and Werewolf sat up straight in their seats like schoolkids at morning assembly. Their faces were studies of faked interest.

'So your father is...'

'Innes McInnes,' said Sorrel primly.

'*The* Innes McInnes?' I asked stupidly.

'The rich Innes McInnes,' said Werewolf. 'As in company takeover McInnes, company chairman McInnes, seat-on-a-thousand-boards of directors McInnes and so on.'

'Oh, that Innes McInnes.' I nodded, hamming it up. 'I thought you meant the Innes McInnes who runs the bookmakers on the Goldhawk Road.'

'Nah,' Werewolf joined in. 'That McInnes is McInnes with two "M"s and a silent "q". Any anyway, he's Jewish.'

'I don't think you two,' said Sorrel, sniffing loudly, 'are in any position to take the mick out of people's names. I mean to say, Fitzroy Maclean Angel! Would you believe it?'

'No,' I agreed, 'but it happens to be true.'

From the corner of my eye, I saw little Gino make his way over to the restaurant's background music system.

'What sort of a name is it?'

'My father was a great reader,' I explained, as I have a million times. 'And when I was born, he'd just finished reading *Eastern Approaches* by Fitzroy Maclean. Hence the name. Lucky, really.'

I noticed Gino reaching for the volume control on the amplifier with one hand and the restaurant light-switch with the other.

'Why lucky?' she asked, as I knew she would.

'The following week he read *Mein Kampf.*'

The restaurant was plunged into darkness and the music boomed out as Gino dived across the table at her.

I got home, eventually, via a minicab and two large malt whiskies at Sorrel's flat in the Barbican – or the Barbarian, as Werewolf insisted on calling it. It was a nice flat with a good view, and as I let myself into Stuart Street, I wished I could remember how to find it again.

No 9 had long since gone to bed, so I crept up the stairs as quietly as I could. I did put the landing light on, though, as I'd been ambushed in the dark on those stairs before, barely escaping with my life. But Springsteen wouldn't catch me napping again.

There was a note from Lisabeth Sellotaped to my door telling me that Frank had phoned and that Salome was 'comfortable,' which was heaps better than 'stable,' and he'd talked about her being moved to town. Oh, and Frank wanted to see me about the car.

There was also a PS:

A Man rang this evening (Lisabeth always used capital M for the enemy) and asked how Salome was. Wouldn't say who he was, just said he was a friend. Very posh voice. Don't forget to tell Frank if you see him before I do. L.

Underneath, in purple ink, had been added: 'And love, Fenella,' with a capital X as a kiss. I might have known Lisabeth wouldn't have walked up the stairs herself to leave the note. She was convinced Springsteen would come out of the cat flap like a bullet and zip up her trouser-leg. Though, to be honest, there was hardly room for her leg in there.

With such idle thoughts, I repaired to my virginal couch to stack up some zeds in the sleep bank. But even as I engaged in the ritual unarmed combat with Springsteen (well, I was unarmed) over possession of the duvet, I had a nasty feeling that I wasn't taking this whole thing seriously enough.

My brain went some way up through the gear-box next morning as I padded down-

216

stairs to collect my pint of gold top. Frank usually left it outside my flat door on his way back from his morning jog. I was missing him already.

Lisabeth appeared in her doorway as she heard me coming back up.

'Did you get the message?'

'Loud and clear, and good morning to you too.'

'Hrumph.'

'You look worried.'

'Well, I don't like Men phoning who won't give their name,' she said as I drew level.

I shook my head to dislodge some of the dead grey cells that were clogging things up.

'What are you on about?'

'The posh voice last night who kept asking where he could send flowers to for Salome.'

'You didn't say that in your note,' I said accusingly.

'But I said he wouldn't leave his name.' She'd also said it was a Man with a capital M, and you don't get much lower in Lisabeth's book. In her dictionary, Men came between Sewer and Slime. I never said she could spell.

'What's this about flowers?'

'He kept asking where he could send flowers and whether it would be better to send them to the hospital or to here if she was coming home.'

'So what did you say, Lisabeth? *Exactly.*'

'Well, *exactly*–' she hrumphed some more – 'I said she was still going to be in Maidstone for a few days though we were thinking of moving her to a private hospital. And that's *exactly* what Frank said yesterday except you weren't here, of course...'

By then she was talking to my back as I headed downstairs again to the communal phone on the wall.

Salome's hospital number was still pinned up on the noticeboard alongside the little red book where we are supposed to log our calls. I checked my watch as I dialled: 9.15, which meant the admin shift should be into their first tea-break by now. It was worth a try.

'Hello. Administration, please. Hello, can I speak to whoever handles press inquiries, please. Yes. My name is Fitzroy.' Do I lie? 'Yes, from Radio Invicta.' Well, occasionally.

A male voice came on the line.

'Hello, I'm trying to clarify a rather confused report we've picked up – I think from the local police – about an incident at the hospital last night, or it could have been early this morning. We don't like to broadcast things unless we're absolutely sure, of course, so...'

'But the police told us there was nothing worth reporting,' said the voice impatiently. 'We were worried, naturally.'

'Well, of course,' I agreed quickly, without

the faintest idea of what I was agreeing to.

'*They* couldn't find anybody outside and there was certainly no-one in the wards unaccounted for,' he went on bossily. 'So they put it down to a prowler, probably a junkie after drugs. We have a one hundred percent record on security as regards drugs, I don't mind telling you.'

'I'm sure you do, sir. Now this incident was around midnight, wasn't it?' Well it was a fair guess.

'No.' There was a rustle of paperwork. 'It was probably 2.06 am when the forced window was noticed.'

Oh how I love a bureaucrat.

'So someone actually got into the hospital?'

'No. The police think that the prowler – that's what *they* called him, not me – was disturbed and made off across the car park.'

'There doesn't seem to be much in it, sir. Just as well I checked.'

'Yes it is... Just who did you say...?'

'Thank you. Goodbye.'

I hung up, feeling vindicated in my analysis of human nature. (Rule of Life No 83: Approached in the right way, anyone will tell you anything, and it will usually be true.)

I was smug for only about half a minute. Then I moved into worried.

By eleven o'clock I was standing in front of Patterson's desk laying down the law. I was dressed in red leather riding gear and red boots and sweating a lot despite the air-conditioning. That may have ruined the image a bit; after all, not even Prior, Keen, Baldwin could have had that many motor-bike-riding clients. Mind you, if they had Lloyd Allen as a client, they should have been used to anything.

'I want her moved now, Tel. Today. Before end of play this afternoon. Make a window in your Filofax for the downside of this afternoon or whatever the fuck you have to do, but get it organised. Okay?'

I thumped his desk with a gauntleted fist and the telephone rattled in its handset.

'You really think...'

'I know, Tel. As long as Sal is in that hospital, she's in danger. There's been one pretty definite go at her, and you can ask Alec Reynolds if you doubt that – if you've got a ouija board, that is.'

He fluttered his fingers as if he'd picked up something hot.

'All right, okay, relax. It's done. There's a BUPA clinic up West, somewhere near Paddington, I think. Well get her in there by tonight.'

'Good man, Tel, you're a diamond. And don't worry, it must be deductible from something.'

His eyes lit up for a moment at that.

'Then what?' he asked.

'Well, I thought I'd go and sell ice-cream outside the Stock Exchange, which is why I dressed like this.'

'Did anyone ever tell you you had a smart mouth?'

'When they could get a word in.'

'So you're going out with the black kid, the messenger?'

'No, I'm going out instead of Luther, although Luther doesn't know it yet, and if it isn't Luther who comes when you ring for a rider, then we're in trouble. But the plan is for me to get a look in that van without, for the moment, the driver noticing anything wrong.'

Tel, I have to say, looked sceptical.

'Won't he notice that you are somewhat less tinted than our friend Luther?'

'I'm banking on him being colour blind,' I came back, but it was getting too easy to wind him up. 'With this gear on and his helmet with the visor down... And remember, it's for about three minutes only, and the driver will be busy doing whatever it is inside the van.'

Tel reached into a desk drawer, confirming his reputation as the fastest cheque-book east of Chancery Lane.

'How much will Luther want?' he asked, going for a pen from his inside suit pocket.

'Luther will want cash, and 50 should do it.'

He got on to the internal phone and asked for petty cash, not specifying any amount. Maybe petty cash only came in fifties these days. It was brought in almost immediately by Anna from the postroom, who smiled at me, but it was one of those you-haven't-phoned smiles that are supposed to make you feel guilty and usually do.

As soon as she'd gone, Patterson flipped the five ten-pound notes across the desk. I scooped them up before he could think of asking for a receipt, and zippered them into a jacket pocket.

'Where did you get the Hell's Angels outfit?' he asked, then he realised what he'd said. 'Hey – Hell's Angel.'

'I rented it, so I'll be putting in an expense claim.'

I hadn't, I'd borrowed it from Duncan, but I'd heard the Hell's Angel crack so many times before that I suddenly decided to charge him for it. And there'd be a drink in it for Duncan, so he'd be happy.

'Now I want you to call a courier and sort out a couple of juicy documents to somebody not too far away, but it doesn't matter who. But make the stuff kosher, top grade. We don't want them thinking they've been sold short or rumbled.'

'Okay,' he said slowly. 'But it goes against the grain.'

'All in a good cause, Tel, all in a good cause.

Now, any comeback on Alec Reynolds?'

Patterson consulted a notepad on his desk.

'Alec was an only child, brought up by an aunt, an unmarried aunt, in Preston, would you believe. His parents died in a car accident while he was still at school. No other relatives, nobody asking questions. The aunt gets his insurance and pension – both generous – and the police reckon the body can be released more or less any time. I've talked to the aunt and she's taken it well. She's talking about a funeral next Monday or Tuesday up in Bolton. Nobody's asked any nasty questions, not even the cops. Lucky, really.'

'Not for Alec,' I said.

'No. Oh, there's one other thing. Salome's blood sample showed no trace of alcohol. She would have passed a hundred breathalysers.'

'That's good news. How did you find out?'

'I got on to the hospital and then the local police lab and said I was from her insurance company and we operated a no pay clause if drink-driving was involved.'

'That's very good, Tel,' I said, genuinely impressed. 'That's just what I would have done.'

The one thing that had bothered me was having to borrow Lewis Luther's helmet. I'd got the riding gear from Duncan, but he'd been unable to come up with a red helmet with black visor. So when Lewis turned up, I decided to show him the money straight away.

Patterson had prepared an envelope addressed to the secretary of a small, but well-known, wine and spirits shipper that had offices in City Road. It was a draft of PKB's analysis of their half-year results to be announced the next day. Not high-grade stuff, Patterson had said, but bloody useful to get the figures in advance if you held shares. I had to take him on trust on that. Maybe I should have consulted Lloyd. He probably had the company in his portfolio of holdings. Knowing Lloyd, he probably owned it.

I told Patterson to follow normal procedure, and he got one of the girls in the postroom to ring Airborne and say there was a package for delivery ASAP and give them just the district, EC1, where it was going.

Lewis Luther was there within five minutes, and I was waiting for him in the foyer by Purvis's desk.

Purvis had even stood up, maybe in the expectation of aggro, so I was glad to disappoint him by greeting Lewis like a soul brother and flashing 50 quid at him.

'Mr Allen said you might want to do something wicked,' he said.

'I'll need your helmet,' I said.

He balked slightly at that, then he tucked the tenners down his gauntlet and handed it over. I tried it on and it fitted well enough.

'You'll need this too,' said Lewis, tapping his collar radio.

'Good point, but you call it in first.'

'Have to do that outside, man. Can't get no reception inside.'

'The lad's got a point there,' said Purvis, as if somebody had asked him.

'Where's Sorley likely to be with the van?' I asked.

'Never know till I call,' Lewis shrugged. 'But I've never known him closer than a mile to a pick-up. He's careful that way.'

I bet he was.

'Okay, let's risk it,' I said and called the lift.

Lewis stood by my side and eyed me up and down.

'You think he ain't gonna notice a difference?'

'With this gear on, he wouldn't know if I was yellow and green striped,' I said.

'No man, I didn't mean that,' said Lewis as the lift doors opened. 'I meant one of us so handsome and cool and the other...'

There are some people you can go off real quick, aren't there?

In the foyer of the PKB building, Lewis got

on the radio and called up 'Airborne One.'

'Airborne Two, what is your destination?'

'City Road, Airborne One,' said Lewis.

There was pause, then some static crackle and then:

'Rendezvous is Barbican Centre, White-cross Street entrance. Confirm.'

'Confirmed,' said Lewis.

He flipped a switch, then took the radio off and slung it round my neck.

'He won't call again unless something goes wrong, like he gets clamped or stuck in traffic or sumfink like that. If he does, you're Airborne Two, and he likes you to say "Confirmed" instead of "Roger and out" or "Over" or "Piss off," suchlike.'

'Thanks. You stay here and keep out of sight. Is there any signal when I get to the van?'

Lewis stuck out his bottom lip and shook his head. 'Not really, I just kick the back door and he sticks his head out.'

'You ever been inside?'

'Nope.'

'Okay. I'll do the business with Sorley and I'll come straight back here so you can do the run proper. Go back upstairs and ask Sergeant Purvis to get you a coffee,' I added maliciously.

'I'll squat here, man. Less aggro.'

He unzipped his jacket and took out a scrunched-up copy of *Motor Cycle News*, opened it out, leaned against the wall of the lobby and began to read. People got in and out of the lifts and didn't give him a second glance. He could have been put there by the interior decorators.

I slid Lewis's helmet on and cut myself off from the world.

It was a bit unnerving at first, and the lining stank of old aftershave. I put the visor down before I got out on to Gresham Street and almost walked into the edge of a glass door, but by the time I got to the Kawasaki, my eyes had adjusted themselves. I fumbled Lewis's key into the ignition, the gauntlets handicapping my fingers and adding to the impression that I felt like a spaceman dropped into molasses for gravity training.

The bike started sweetly and proved easier to handle than I'd expected. It had been a few years since I'd ridden a bike, but it's like sex: provided you don't fall off, you soon get back into the swing of it.

I cut round the Guildhall, almost taking out a couple of early-season French tourists who hadn't got the hang of looking left first before they crossed the road, and through on to Moorgate.

If I'd been doing a pukka delivery, I could just have carried straight on virtually due north and come to City Road. To give him his due, Sorley had picked a good place for his sneak preview of Patterson's mail.

Unlike the residences bit of the Barbican, where Sorrel had a flat, the entrance to the Arts Centre part is off Chiswell Street, which was an easy left turn for me just after Finsbury Circus.

Chiswell Street is quiet and sedate nowadays, but two hundred years ago it was the powerhouse for the Whitbread brewery, which churned out Porter, the dark beer named after the London market porters who knocked it back at a fearsome rate early in the morning. Nowadays they get sales like that only if one of the Philharmonic Orchestras is in residence round the corner at the Barbican.

Left again, after the brewery (where they still have the Porter Tun Rooms, a tun being a big barrel not a weight, though not many people know that) is Whitecross Street and the Barbican entrance, where many tourists go in and some actually find the theatre or gallery they're supposed to be going to.

I found the red Transit easily enough; it was the only one in the street and it had the same number plate as the day before. I parked snug in behind its rear doors, at an angle, straddling the bike like Lewis had done. I was about to knock when the door opened.

The Chinless Wonder stuck his head out and said something which was probably 'You're late' but I couldn't hear because of the helmet and the idling bike engine.

I took the envelope out of the left-hand saddle-bag and held it across my chest. This meant Sorley had to lean further out of the van to grab it, and as the door opened wider I got a good look inside.

One side of the van's interior had been kitted out with shelving. The higher shelves held plastic containers of the sort a do-it-yourself handyman would keep screws and nails in so the effect was of a dozen or so pigeonholes. Each hole was stuffed with envelopes; brown ones, manila, white and jiffy bags. The bottom shelf was wider and it held a square white machine that looked like a document shredder.

Then Sorley's arm, the envelope and the rest of him disappeared inside and the door closed.

It couldn't be a shredder; that was just plain daft. Yet it didn't look like a photo-copying machine. I decided to chance it and killed the bike's engine and took off the helmet.

If anyone had seen me bent over a motor-bike with my ear pressed to the back of a Transit van outside the Barbican that morning, probably they wouldn't have looked twice. They would have put it down to an alfresco commercial for one of the shows.

I could hear Sorley thumping around inside and then a distinctive whine and a sort of humming stutter. It could be only one thing, a fax machine. The cheeky buggers were faxing the stuff to save time.

I had the bike revved up and the helmet and visor back in place by the time Sorley opened the door and thrust the letter at me. It was a new envelope and address label, so he must have had a typewriter in there too, but unless you were looking for it, you would hardly have spotted the swap.

I turned around and pulled away. I was confident that Sorley hadn't rumbled me, but I didn't look back. I turned into Chiswell Street and then risked a look. There was no sign of the Transit, so I hung a right back the way I'd come.

So now I knew how the Sorley/Cawthorne private intelligence line worked, and I was willing to bet that there was another fax machine at Pegasus Farm currently on 'receive.'

Doing that had been easy. Now came the difficult part: telling Patterson I was borrowing his car.

CHAPTER TEN

'A fax? A fucking fax machine?'

'Deep breaths, Tel, keep calm.'

'It's not possible.' He was beginning to look like a man who wished he smoked. 'We don't use fax to send stuff like that, because they're not secure.'

'What do you mean, secure?'

Patterson waved away my stupid question.

'Oh, not the machines themselves; they're bloody useful. It's just that most offices put them in the open near the coffee machine or the Ladies loo and anybody can see what's coming over. So you send only non-confidential stuff that way. Eyes Only material goes by hand.'

'By Airborne,' I said smugly, crossing my feet on the edge of his desk.

He gave me a look that made me wonder if the leather riding gear was knife-proof, then he sprang at the internal phone and pressed two buttons.

'Ask Howard to get in here,' he said into the mouthpiece. Then he stared at the phone rather than me for about a minute until the door opened.

'This is Howard Golding,' he said to me,

but made no effort to tell Howard who I was. 'He's our analyst for electronics and the communications sector.'

Howard was wearing regulation red-striped shirt and braces but his glasses were the trend-setting steel octagon design rather than the circular, coloured owl frames that were on their way out. He leaned against the wall of Tel's office as there wasn't another chair, and folded his arms. 'How can I help?' he asked with a faint American or Canadian twang.

'Fax machines,' said Patterson. 'What do you know about them?'

Howard raised an eyebrow and took a deep breath.

'Facsimile transmission of hard copy documentation began in this country just after World War II but was not really exploited until the late '60s, and even then very limited in numbers and versatility. Breakthrough came in the '80s with digital technology and speeds of sub-one-minute per page transmission and greatly enhanced copy quality. I reckon there are now more faxes around than telex machines, say 100K in this country. Something like two dozen brand names, biggest player probably NEC Business Systems with their Nefax machines. On the horizon, laser printing and faster transmission times as telephones improve. Growth market, good potential. I'd flag the whole area as a "buy" without a worry.'

I blinked at Patterson, but he seemed to have understood most of it.

'What about a mobile unit?' he asked.

'You mean in a car or something?' Howard considered for about a micro second. 'Sure. If you can have a car phone, in theory you can have a fax machine to go with it. There's certainly one mobile unit on the market at the moment, though not many people realise it. All you need is an interface from the car phone and an inverter from the battery to supply the power. No problem. Want me to check it out?'

'No, never mind,' said Tel, looking at me.

'Can you have an ex-directory fax number?' I asked Howard. 'They have their own phone lines, don't they?'

'Sure,' Howard said. 'I don't see why you can't have a private line, though it defeats the object of getting people to send you things you need in a hurry.' He looked at Patterson and said, 'Anything else, boss?'

Tel shook his head and Howard closed the door on his way out.

'So where are we?' He looked at his watch. 'Apart from late for a lunch meeting.'

I'd taken my feet off his desk while Howard had been in. It wouldn't have been good for staff morale. I replaced them.

'We know how your leaks happened and we have a good idea where the information

233

ends up. Salome and Alec weren't doing the Exhilarator for their health, were they?'

He looked uncomfortable at that. I wondered if it had been his bright idea that had sent them there.

'My guess is that one of them found the other end of the conduit, maybe the fax machine at Pegasus or evidence of Cawthorne acting on information he shouldn't have had. Whatever it was, he felt he had to get rid of them.'

'Are you sure about that?' He was definitely uncomfortable now. 'I mean, you are talking serious crime here.'

'Yes, Tel, it's called murder, and the last I heard it was certainly against the law. I believe the expression round here is "downside of legal."'

'You can't prove a thing.'

'Get me a camera, and if we repeat this morning's little exercise, we'll be able to prove the leak end of things. But I want to look round Pegasus Farm and see if we can dig up anything there. If we blow Sorley, he'll just sell the van and do a runner.'

'The Exhilarator only does night exercises – don't look at me like that, that's what they call them – on Friday and Saturday. That's why Alec and Salome went then, so they could look around. They knew what they were looking for. Think you can do better?'

'I can't do worse, can I?'

He thought about this.

'When?'

'Tomorrow maybe. From the brochures, you can book the day before. I'll need some cash. Expenses.'

He automatically reached for the cheque-book. 'I'll make it for cash. I don't want any comebacks on the company.'

'Sure.'

'Are you any good at these war game things?'

'Never been on one. But I have to look the part. You know, bored City whiz-kid. I'll have to borrow your BMW.'

'What?'

'Well, I can't turn up on the bus, can I?'

'Haven't you got a car?'

'Sort of, but it wouldn't create the right impression.'

'Are you insured?'

'Up to the hilt, Tel. Don't worry.'

He scratched his head, then tweaked his nose before fishing in a pocket for the BMW's keys.

'I'm taking one hell of a chance on you.'

'What are the options?' I picked up the keys before he could change his mind. 'Go to the police? With what? Maybe we've got enough to get them interested, but the word'll be out that Prior, Keen, Baldwin leaks like a sieve. Want that?'

'Of course not.' He narrowed his eyes and

235

tried to look tough. 'But what are you getting out of it? Are you doing this because you think he hurt Salome?'

'I'm sure he did, Tel. I think he waited on Blackberry Hill in the dark until Sal and Alec came round the corner and then he bumped their car off the road and into space. I didn't know Alec, but Salome's virtually family, so I'm after Cawthorne for that, yeah. But also–' I flipped the keys a couple of times as I stood up– 'because I think he enjoyed doing it.'

I rang Sorrel's flat from Sergeant Purvis's desk, and as he was out to lunch, I sat on it and rearranged his pencils in a petty and thoroughly satisfying bit of vandalism.

Werewolf answered and said he was in the middle of cooking lunch as Sorrel was out. I hoped she knew to expect that her kitchen would look like a nuclear test site when she returned.

I told him I had planned to take him to lunch. He said he couldn't wait, as he had some business to attend to, but he'd be in a pub called the Banker if I could pick him up about 3.00.

I asked him if he'd misheard the name of the pub, and he said gosh how original, he bet nobody had thought of that before and he'd be sure to tell the landlord.

After he'd hung up, I phoned an OADF(F)

– old and distinguished friend (female) – called Fly. I'm sure her mother called her something else, Eunice I think, but most people called her Fly, though I've no idea why. I can be terribly innocent in some things.

Fly ran the Hackney branch of a chain-store optician's, and we went back quite a long way together, as OADFs go. She told me she didn't eat lunch any more as it had become a bourgeois meal, but I could call in for a cup of decaf and con her into whatever it was I wanted. Fly knew me well. It's frightening sometimes.

Never having been one to look an un-guarded telephone in the mouth, I made another call, to the number on the Exhilar-ator brochure I'd taken from Salome's case.

A woman answered with: 'The Exhilar-ator. How can I help?'

'Good afternoon. A friend and I have come across your brochure and we'd like to give your course a try. Would there be a chance, say, tomorrow?'

'We have a shoot scheduled for ten a.m., sir. We do not call them assault courses.'

'I'm so sorry.' I can crawl when I have to. 'Could I book?'

'Certainly, sir. Briefing is ten a.m. sharp. How will you be paying?'

'Cash.'

'Could I have the names, please.'

'Maclean and ... er...' Come on, think fast. '...Chaney.'

Well, Lon Chancy had played the Wolf-man, hadn't he? And I didn't think that was bad at such short notice.

'Fine, sir. Booking confirmed. We'll see you on parade. Everything is provided, but you might wish to bring your own action footwear.'

Action footwear? Christ.

That little bridge would have to be crossed later. For the moment, I had two vehicles in PKB's underground car park: Armstrong and Tel's BMW.

Much as I was itching to play with the Bob Marley, I knew I would have more chance of parking Armstrong illegally when I collected Werewolf. And I had a change of clothing in Armstrong's boot, so the faithful old retainer won out over the flash German status symbol.

The garage attendant, who'd almost called in a SWAT team when he'd seen me arrive that morning, had a few more palpitations when he watched me climb in the back seat and start peeling off my biker's gear. God knows what he thought when I emerged in jeans and Roar of Disapproval T-shirt (I've no objection to advertising good causes) and got in the driving seat. I tooted Armstrong's horn as I passed him, but he didn't wave.

One of the many advantages of a de-licensed black cab is that unless the cops know it's de-licensed, the chances of getting pulled for not wearing a seat-belt are fairly remote. This means you can eat a Big Mac, suck on a vanilla shake and drive in relative comfort, though I don't recommend it for anyone who hasn't done at least two combat tours driving in Central London.

I cut up back towards Hackney and Fly's optician's, judging I could still make the Banker by three, though I wondered why I was worrying about leaving Werewolf wait-ing in a pub.

Fly is a tall, skinny, short-haired, very independent lady who dresses and swears like a Vietnam veteran. (North Vietnam, that is.) I'd once helped her break a habit. No, that's going too far. She hadn't actually caught the dragon's tail, but she was reach-ing. To my surprise, she'd taken a regular job selling frames and contact lenses, and had stuck at it and was now boss of the shop. Her gimmick was that she wore a different pair of glasses every day, and somehow they all seemed to suit her. She'd even been on the local TV news for it, and it had done wonders for business. Her eye-sight, of course, was 20/20 straight arrow.

I parked Armstrong on double yellow lines outside her shop and dived in. Fly broke off from a customer and headed me off.

'You really come for a cup of decaf, Angel?
I hear you're a city slicker these days.'

'Is nothing secret in this town?'

'Village, Angel. This city is just a collection
of villages that happen to share the same
map reference.'

'You've been reading too many Sunday
supplements.'

'You could be right. What're you after?'

I put on my all-innocent, how-could-you-
think-it-of-me expression. After two seconds,
I dropped the pretence.

'I want a pair of glasses. The sort we city
slickers wear, but with clear glass in the
frames.'

Fly tapped a pencil against her teeth.
'Would that be regular workaday frames, sir,
or for dress wear?'

She was serious.

I picked some black, carbon fibre frames
that had been signed by an Italian designer,
made in Japan and retailed in England for
over a hundred quid. Fly produced an aero-
sol spray and cleaned the clear glass lenses
for me. Then she made me promise to get
them back to her in one piece within a week
and sold me two tickets to a Ward Bond
Retrospective at her film club in Ponder's
End. I'd have to go. She'd ask questions
later.

I wore my new glasses as I drove south to
pick up Werewolf. The Banker is a riverside

pub, converted from a warehouse or something at the end of Cousin Lane, a cul-de-sac tucked under the armpit of Cannon Street station. There's no way draymen in London deliver after lunchtime, so I felt fairly safe there, even though I had to rearrange the kegs around Armstrong.

It's a great barn of a pub, with a high ceiling, a balcony area and lots of glass in the south wall so you can drink and look at the Thames without having to smell it. The bar had a headbanging range of Fuller's beers, but I decided I'd better be in training for the Exhilarator, so I opted for an alcohol-free lager, turned my back to the bar and its temptations and scouted for Werewolf.

The lunch trade had mostly disappeared, so he wasn't hard to spot. He was at a window table, but he was ignoring the river, being deep in conversation with a middle-aged man wearing a suit and a short, sheepskin car coat with matching, brown suede shoes. Even from this distance, you could guess the guy's tailor was based in Dublin. And Werewolf was drinking tomato juice. Another bad sign.

I left them to it, but didn't have to wait long. Within five minutes, the older guy got up and left. I replaced him at the table opposite Werewolf, who was staring into his tomato juice. He looked up and saw the glasses.

'Bloody hell. I always said you'd go blind.'

'Pardon?' I said, cupping a hand to an ear because I knew the routine.

'And deaf.'

'Done the business?'

He made a see-saw gesture with his right hand. 'Gotta go see a man about a dog at the weekend. In Dublin. Go on Saturday, back Sunday. I'm not stopping.'

'Family trouble?' I asked diplomatically.

'You don't wanna know,' he said. Then, looking at me: 'It's just an errand I have to run for ... somebody. Nothing heavy, trust me. You know I don't tangle with the looney politico fringe. Just don't ask, okay?'

'Don't forget to bring me some poteen,' I said, and left it at that. From the look in his eyes, there wouldn't be a result in pressing it unless I was really keen on acquiring a broken nose.

'Sorrel's cooking for us tonight,' he said, apropos absolutely nothing.

'Great. I've booked us to play soldiers tomorrow.'

He shrugged, then linked his fingers and made his knuckles crack. 'Good.'

I made a mental note to make sure I got put on his side.

'She's keen for you to meet her old man,' he said, then drained the last of his juice.

'She's not thinking of proposing, is she?'

'I think she's up to something,' he said.

'But she's a good cook, and if I don't get some decent wine in, she'll skin me.'

'Okay, let's go shopping.'

I reached into my wallet and flashed my PKB Amex card at him. His face lit up.

'I feel suddenly invigorated beyond measure,' he said with a grin.

'Good. I think we should go in character tomorrow,' I explained, moving the Amex card out of his reach. 'Hence the glasses. We're supposed to be bored Yuppies, you know.'

'So we'll need some clothes...' He was catching on.

'A suit at least...'

'Or two...'

'And some action footwear. They specified that.'

'Some *designer* action footwear...'

'And we have to turn up in style.'

'Meaning?'

I flipped Patterson's keys on to the table.

'Do you want to play with a new BMW?'

I had to run to catch up.

I'll gloss over the afternoon's shopping expedition. Suffice it to say there is now a branch of Suit & Co I dare not go to again, but there is a Tie Rack where Werewolf and I are on a promise with the girls serving there. We also managed to find a couple of bottles of Chilean Chardonnay (trust me, it's great) in a very posh wine merchant's where the staff were halfway to calling the cops as we walked in.

At the end of our shopping spree, we collected Tel's BMW from Prior, Keen, Baldwin's garage. This time, the garage attendant just shook his head and walked away, not wanting to know. I think the thing that really upset him was seeing Werewolf slide across the BMW's bonnet to get to the driver's door.

I knew it would be a race back to Stuart Street, and I was pleased that it ended in an honourable draw. The BMW had the power – too much for the traffic conditions, if truth were known – but Armstrong knew the side roads better. I parked outside No 9 just as Werewolf reversed into a space two millimetres longer than the BMW across the road.

As was traditional, the race didn't finish until we were both out of our vehicles, leaning on the engines (to prove they'd cooled down) with our arms folded. It was only as we were doing this and grinning inanely at each other that I noticed the red Transit van turning out of the other end of the street.

I didn't exactly run up the steps to No 9, but I didn't hang about either. At that time of the afternoon, I knew only Lisabeth would be home, so I wasn't too worried. Lisabeth could look after herself. Muggers went around in threes when she was out.

As soon as she opened her flat door to my hammering knock, I knew something was wrong. Her mouth had fallen open and her eyes popped even more than usual.

'What's happened?' I almost shook her. 'What's the matter?'

'I didn't know you wore glasses,' she said.

I took them off.

'There. Now what's been going down?'

'Nothing.' Lisabeth relaxed. She obviously just had a thing about men who wore glasses. 'Except the delivery man with the flowers.'

'The man in the Transit van.' This from Werewolf, who had come up the stairs behind me, his arms loaded with parcels.

'Sorley,' I said.

'What is a Sorley?' asked Lisabeth.

'The man with the flowers,' I said slowly, 'said what, exactly?'

'What's with this "exactly" business? He said he had a bunch of flowers – and he really had – for Mrs Asmoyah. When I said she wasn't here, he asked where she was, and I said Maidstone, and he said she'd moved, and I said then I didn't know but he could leave the flowers here for Frank, but he wouldn't. Where's the harm in that?'

I assured her there wasn't any harm and that she'd done nothing wrong. Telling her not to speak to strange men would be like asking if the Pope was free on Sunday.

Halfway up the stairs to my flat, Werewolf said quietly:

'They're on the bloody ball, aren't they?'

'Christ! I thought you were Mormons!'

You couldn't blame Sorrel, I suppose. She'd never seen either of us in a suit before – we were running them in, checking for labels we'd missed and so on – and we had stood on her doorstep as if we were about to launch into the 'Have you heard the Good News...' routine.

Mind you, not many Mormons would turn up at a Barbican flat at 7.30 clutching two bottles of wine. Fewer still would be dressed as Werewolf was. He'd bought a red-striped shirt to go with his charcoal double-breasted, but back at Stuart Street he'd remembered that that was the only shirt he had for the next day. As a consequence, the overall effect of the smart suit was marred by the Miami Dolphins T-shirt and the fact that his brand-new, red-and-black-squared silk tie was in a bow knot around his right wrist.

That was the first thing to go. Without a word, she untied it and stuffed it into Werewolf's lapel pocket until it looked like a dress handkerchief, then she moved behind him and pulled the sleeves of his jacket up to the elbows. She looked me up and down and adjusted my tie an inch or so (I'd gone for green silk, and I now had two ties), then said:

'You'll have to do. My father's here, so behave yourselves.'

And she said it like she meant it.

Innes McInnes was taller than I'd expected, but then how tall should a millionaire be? If he was Sorrel's father, then he must have been around his mid-forties at least, but he'd worn well. The skin was healthily tanned and the hair thin but not receding, and slicked back from the front. He wore a pencil moustache, above which his nose twitched like a rabbit's as he sniffed the wine glass he was holding.

'Franzia,' he said, and there was just a hint of Scottish burr. 'A very nice Cabernet Sauvignon from California. Try some.'

Sorrel busied herself fetching glasses while she yelled the introductions. 'Daddy, this is Roy and Francis.'

Francis?

Werewolf avoided my gaze as he sipped wine.

'Very good, Innes,' he said politely. 'Have you bought the winery yet?'

McInnes laughed. 'It wouldn't make it taste better if I owned it.'

'But at the moment, you're drinking somebody else into house and home,' argued Werewolf. Sorry; Francis.

'He's Irish,' I explained. 'It's the Ballymurphy school of economics.'

'We used to call it living out of the shop. It never works. The best publican is the one who buys you a drink but puts the money in the till.'

'Publicans usually buy us a drink to go somewhere else,' I pointed out, and Innes McInnes smiled to show us he had all his own teeth.

'Let's eat,' said Sorrel, handing over a second, opened bottle of Franzia. 'It'll be ready by the time you've worked out which cutlery to use.'

We three males looked at each other, then meekly trooped to the circular dining table laid out near the window. Below us, the lights of the City did what they were good at; they just sat there and twinkled.

Sorrel excelled herself with the meal, although her father never mentioned it. Maybe he ate like that all the time. Maybe he'd had his taste buds removed by surgery.

Starters were bowls of a rich stock soup with julienne of vegetables (if that's what they're called when they're chopped into sticks) and the earthenware bowls had puff pastry hats on, which kept the soup scalding hot. Then she served a carbonnade of large cubes of beef and triangles of wholemeal bread spread with French mustard, the gravy tasting largely of Guinness. (I suspected Werewolf's influence here.) Another bottle of

Franzia appeared then and a big piece of Stilton to round things off. Innes McInnes was obviously a soup-meat-cheese man from way back, but had come up in the world.

He asked a lot of questions about my interest in Cawthorne, and I answered honestly. (Rule of Life No 5: Always tell the truth; not necessarily all of it, though, and not all at once.) Yet as we talked and ate, he looked mostly at Werewolf and then at his daughter, and occasionally you could see him thinking that maybe he ought to change his will. I hadn't asked, but I just knew she was his only offspring, and I'd lay odds there wasn't a Mrs McInnes any more.

Over the cheese, he picked up on something I'd said about the PKB file on Cawthorne's dealings.

'I don't pretend to know what it all meant,' I said. 'But some of the references I've picked up since, like Meltdown in the Market, Inter-Broker Dealing and so on. I haven't found out what TT means, though.'

'I can help you there,' said McInnes, reaching inside his jacket for a pen. 'Pass me the back of an envelope, Sorrel my dear.'

Sorrel couldn't run to the back of an envelope, but found instead a spare section of Filofax pages; just about the most expensive scribble pad you could get, short of using ten-pound notes.

'It means The Touch,' said McInnes, 'and

it goes like this.'

He began to jot down figures in two columns, and he talked as he wrote.

'Since Big Bang, all the market prices are flashed up on the electronic screens.'

'The Topic system,' I threw in.

'That's right. More screens than the Odeon at Leicester Square.'

I could relate to that.

'And most of the shows are X-rated, but the naughty boys can alter the programme.' He finished scribbling and held the Filofax sheet up so we could see it. 'A company's prices are shown by dealer, with the median across the top. So, let's say the company is called Bloggs International.' He'd written:

Bloggs 'A' Shares: BCF 294-6 E

```
A 293-8  25x25  E 291-6  1x1
B 294-9  25x25  F 294-7  25x25
C 294-9  50x50  G 292-7 50x50
D 293-8  50x50  H 293-8 50x50
```

'The letters are the firms, the numbers are the prices in pence of a typical Alpha stock, and the volumes they are prepared to deal in at a particular time. Now, the trick of course is to buy at the cheapest price or sell at the most expensive. Best execution, they call it. Let's say you were buying a particular stock...'

'Because you've found something out about them that nobody else knows?' I tried.

'You're catching on.' McInnes winked at me. Werewolf looked impressed too.

'The Touch indicates who has what stock. This top line here–' he pointed with his pen – 'comes up in a yellow strip, and this is the best bid, best offer line. Each of the dealing firms has a different amount of stock, but you can work out who has what by how keenly the prices compare with the best bid, best offer. Remember, these volumes of stock are in thousands, so one by one is one thousand shares.

'Market-makers may be prepared to offer stock in larger sizes at less attractive prices. Look at this example. Firm A is dealing in 25s at 293-8, that's 293 pence or 298 pence, buy/sell. Now, he may be willing to buy large at, say, 292, or offer larger than 25 at, say, 299. To get the stock, of course, he has to trade with the other firms.'

'Inter-Broker Dealing,' I said knowledgeably.

'Very good,' nodded McInnes.

'So you can use one dealer to trade with the rest and get control of a company?'

'No. In theory, if you buy over five percent of a company, you have to declare it on the Stock Exchange. You must also remember that whatever deal you do, it's reflected for all to see on the Ticker page of the Topic system.'

'And all the deals will add to the price, especially if other dealers see something going on and have a punt themselves.' Even Werewolf was interested.

'Absolutely, Francis.'

I did a double take to see who this Francis was, but McInnes was in his stride.

'So if you want to get as big a share of, say, Bloggs's stock, as quickly as you can, you take out all the firms offering stock at once, before they can deal among themselves.'

'Taking out the market-makers,' I said, more or less to myself.

'That's right,' said McInnes. 'Mean anything?'

'It explains a reference on Cawthorne's file at Pretty Keen...' I realised what I was saying.

'...Bastards,' McInnes completed, without batting a manicured eyelid.

'But how do you take out–' I looked at the Filofax page and did a quick count – 'eight market-makers at once?'

'You get several colleagues and the latest British Telecom touch dial screen technology with all the market-makers' numbers pre-programmed, and you ring 'em up at exactly the same time. If you've spare people or even just another pair of hands, you ring their second numbers as well just to block the lines, and it never hurts to put a few idiot inquiries through to the dealing house main switchboard.'

'So you stop the market-makers dealing with each other.'

'Exactly. I think I will, if you don't mind.' McInnes reached out and took one of Werewolf's Sweet Afton. He lit it with the air of a man considering big moves in the Irish tobacco market.

I noticed Sorrel's expression. Her eyes could not have bulged further if Werewolf had told her he only wanted her for her mind.

'I've never seen you smoke before, Daddy. What's this?'

McInnes blushed slightly. 'I only indulge on special occasions, darling.'

'It's my influence, I'm afraid,' said Werewolf, straight-faced. 'The last time I went to Confession, the priest called for a packet of green Rizlas and an ounce of Lebanese Gold.'

'The last time you went to Confession,' I stirred it, 'they still allowed smoking on the underground.'

'Really?' said Sorrel, joining in wide-eyed. 'I've read about that.'

'The point,' said McInnes, drawing the meeting to order, 'is that there is little change in basic share prices, unless a real story hits the wires. Of course, it doesn't have to be true. It can cover any number of things. Expectation of good results, mergers, a takeover of a competitor or by one, changes in top management, rumour, innuendo, boredom among the market-makers or sheer bloody-mindedness.'

'So speculation pushes up the price based on rumour. Is that what you're saying?' I asked to give him a lead.

'Of course, though I think Karl Marx put it better.'

'He was more long-winded,' I conceded.

'Agreed. But you see now why Salome's job is vital. The backroom analysts provide "the story–" or they refute someone else's story – on which the jobbers make a market. They need to be able to convince the big players – the pension fund managers, the insurance companies...'

'The institutionals,' I offered.

'...the institutionals, that's right. They have to be persuaded to buy a stock, or indeed, sell it. If Cawthorne has been accessing the research material of somebody like PKB – and who knows who else? – then he knows in advance, or can at least have a damn good guess, which way the market-makers are going to go.

'So, if you get wind of a rumour from Salome on, say, Bloggs International, which says that tomorrow they're going to be taken over on very generous cash terms, then you buy as much Bloggs stock as you can. If money or credit is no problem, you buy as many as there are on the market, and there is always a market unless the stock is suspended.'

McInnes put out his cigarette and looked at his daughter. 'Is there any coffee, petal?'

'Only if you promise not to talk Man's Talk when I'm in the kitchen making gagging noises so that you think I've got an Espresso machine,' said Sorrel, eyeing him suspiciously.

'Promise. And I've got the message. One coffee-machine added to the birthday list.'

'Oh Daddy!'

She flushed and stamped into the kitchen.

'It never fails,' said McInnes quietly.

Werewolf looked puzzled.

'It always pays to spoil the child, if female, but not in front of her friends. Unless you want her out of the way,' I explained.

Werewolf mouthed an innocent O. Well, about as innocent as he was capable of. He could make Satan standing at the Gates of Hell shouting 'Come on down!' look innocent.

'She'll expect us to be plotting among ourselves, then,' he said.

'So let's do it,' said McInnes, putting his elbows on the table. 'What did you have in mind?'

'You said that as if *you* have something in

mind.' It was my turn to narrow my eyes. I realised that was how people got migraines.

'I might have, but you go first.'

'Why?'

'I'm paying for the booze.'

'Fair enough. Francis and I–' Werewolf looked at his fingernails; anything to avoid my smug look – 'are going down to Kent tomorrow to do the Exhilarator. Or rather, Francis is actually going to play soldiers, I'm going to be sneaking around the place to see what I can see and maybe take a few incriminating photos with my trusty Box Brownie.'

'Of what?' McInnes came back sharpish.

'First off,' I said, thinking as I spoke, 'I'm looking for a four-by-four. A four-wheel drive vehicle of some sort with a cow-catcher fitted to the front. Hopefully, it will be a cow-catcher with some paint missing, or even better, a cow-catcher with smears of paint on it that belong to a VW Golf of my acquaintance. Then there's a fax machine to check out – the other end of the Cawthorne conduit.'

'That's good, I like that,' said McInnes.

'And if what you've said is kosher, then somewhere there'll be a bank of phones for him to do his dirty dealing on. I've got Tel – Terry – Patterson lined up at PKB to send a hand delivery via Airborne at eleven-thirty a.m. tomorrow, when we'll be there to see how it's received.'

'It sounds as if *you* will,' said Werewolf, looking around for something else to drink. 'It looks like I'll be doing my famous General Custer impersonation. You haven't mentioned any of this up till now.'

'A good general only briefs his troops the morning of the battle. Before the pubs open.'

'Rule of Life?' asked Werewolf, out of the corner of his beard.

'It will be.'

If it worked.

'Then what?' McInnes asked anxiously, one eye on the kitchen door.

'Then I thought we'd set up the nice Mr Sorley and his mobile fax van and photograph him in the act of reading other people's mail.'

I didn't think that was bad, considering I'd just thought of it.

'Then what?' He was beginning to irritate me.

'Then we threaten to hand over the negatives to the City Squad or the Stock Exchange or its watchdog committee – it's bound to have one. I don't think for a minute we'll have to.'

'And you think Cawthorne will just sit back and take this?'

'He'll have to.'

Werewolf offered McInnes another

cigarette and said: 'Won't he?'

McInnes shook his head slowly. 'You're not hitting him where it hurts.'

'We're showing up his operation so he'll never be able to use it again.'

'He'll think of another one.'

'He won't like being bested by friends of a black lady,' said Werewolf seriously.

'You're right there,' said McInnes ruefully. 'He was always a bit twisted that way. Flirted with the National Front at one time.'

'So we hurt his pride,' I said, hoping that clinched what was sounding to be a very skimpy argument.

'But you're still not hitting him where it really hurts.'

'In the wallet?' suggested Werewolf.

'Exactly,' said McInnes with the sort of grin Colonel Sanders gave when he saw a 'Free Range Eggs' sign. 'And I think I can help you there.'

He punched Werewolf gently on the shoulder.

Oh God, he was warming to him.

After coffee, Werewolf offered to wash up. Sorrel, fearing for her crockery, offered to help him. I don't think she was fooled for a minute by Werewolf's professional decoy act, but she went along with it. After five minutes of running water, scraping plates and chinking glass type noises, it went very quiet in the kitchen, but I don't think her old man noticed. Not even that low humming sound, which I knew sure as hell wasn't the thermostat on the fridge. If the kitchen had had a serving hatch, I could have scared the living daylights out of them. No, scrub that. Knowing Werewolf, he would have sold tickets.

McInnes was keen to press his thoughts on me.

'You need to turn the tables on Cawthorne if you really want to stitch him up.'

'You mean go for the jugular – his bank balance?'

'Correct. What we need is a terminal with a thin spread.' He jabbed a finger into the table-top to emphasise his point.

I poured myself some more coffee from the jug Sorrel had left on the table. I felt I needed a drink, but was determined to keep a clear head for the next day.

'Could I have that in English, please?' I asked him.

He took a deep breath. 'We need a company that has come to the end of its natural life. A "terminal." Its products are no longer in demand, it hasn't the capital or the rating to expand or diversify; its management is moribund. The company is, shall we say, clapped out.'

'Knackered,' I offered.

'Flushed down the pan,' he countered.

'Belly up and shat upon.'

'Buggered.'

I thought for a moment. 'I'll see your "buggered" and raise you a "shagged out."'

'You get the picture,' he said, not wanting to play any more. After all, this was business.

'So we find a terminally sick company with – what was it?'

'A thin spread – of shares.' He saw I was little wiser and slowed his breathing down. 'A company where only a few outside interests own the shares. Say, a family where 55 percent of shares are owned by family members and the rest are spread between maybe ten or 12 others, either institutionals or individual punters. It could be a company where only two or three brokers can make markets in the shares.'

'Something tells me you have one in mind,' I said shrewdly.

'I might have.'

'And what do we do with it?'

'*We* do nothing, except make sure that it is drawn to friend Cawthorne's attention.'

'For entirely the wrong reasons, of course.'

'That depends on your point of view.'

'And Cawthorne buys loadsashares and ends up with a bum company.'

'And he can't complain to anyone, because he would have to admit what made him buy the shares.'

'A confidential report of some kind that

only PKB customers should have seen.'

'Exactly. Up the garden path good and proper – if you can fix it with PKB, that is.'

I almost felt sorry for Cawthorne, and I must have shown it.

'Don't worry, Cawthorne deserves everything that's coming to him,' said McInnes in a tone I bet he'd never used on Sorrel.

I agreed with his sentiment, of course. Though in view of what eventually happened, I did regret thinking that.

But not enough to lose sleep.

CHAPTER ELEVEN

'I just do not believe it,' said Werewolf. 'This car has adjustable *thigh supports*. I simply cannot go another mile until my thighs are suitably adjusted.'

'And supported,' I said. 'Don't forget that.'

'Can it massage them as well?'

'I'll ask the onboard computer. No, sorry, massager is an optional extra. Obviously Patterson couldn't run to that.'

'Mean bastard. What's his taste in music?'

Werewolf had been reading the owner's handbook of Patterson's BMW and experimenting with the passenger seat, having achieved what seemed like a dozen different positions before we got south of the river. He was in a filthy mood, first because I'd suggested he sleep on my floor instead of at Sorrel's so we could get an early start, then because I'd made him wear a suit and tie to go with our Yuppie cover (and because I'd insisted on the shirt as well). Finally, I'd won the toss and got to drive the Bob Marley down to Kent. His cornflakes had probably gone soggy at breakfast too.

Tel's BMW was one of the new Series 3, two-door jobs. After years of bullnosing Armstrong through the London traffic, it was an awesome driving experience. I felt like Von Richtofen joyriding Concorde for a day.

Werewolf had one foot on the dashboard and was sorting through Tel's selection of tapes, grunting disapproval at most of the titles.

'Find anything worth damaging the ear-holes with?' I asked, while cutting up a British Telecom van – rather niftily I thought.

'Nah, what you'd expect. Mostly dead hedgehog.'

Dead hedgehog – middle-of-the road music – was one of Werewolf's lowest class-ifications of taste.

'I never thought he'd be into acid house, but there must be something.'

Acid house was all the rage; multirhythmed electronic stuff popular on the disco circuit but comprehensible only when taken with the designer drugs now supplied as openly as condoms in some of the smarter venues.

'There's an old Huey Lewis.'

'Somebody must've left it by mistake. Stick it on.'

Werewolf proceeded to try and blow all four stereo speakers, and by the time he had the volume where he wanted it, and was playing along on his air guitar we were through Sidcup and heading for the motorway.

'Tell me again, what's my name?' he asked between tracks.

'Chaney. Don't look at me like that, it was the best I could do on the spur of the moment.'

'First name?'

'Up to you.'

'Jerome G Chaney,' he mused.

'What does the G stand for?' I asked, knowing I shouldn't.

'Gobsmacked – at having such a daft name. What's yours?'

'Roylance Maclean. I know it is, because that's what it says on my Amex card.'

'I'm surprised that hasn't self-destructed after the damage you gave it yesterday. Remember, he who...'

'...acetates is lost.' We finished together. The old ones are the best.

'How did they get Roylance Maclean?'

'You know how people screw up my name. I don't know why they do, but they just can't accept it.'

'That's okay, Butch.' He grinned.

'Butch?'

'You be Butch Cassidy and I'll be the Sundance Kid.'

'Fair enough.'

I didn't mind. I'm still convinced they got away at the end of the movie. Mind you, I've never met anyone else who is.

I eased the BMW off the M20 at Wrotham so that by the time we got to the A227 our speed was almost legal. At Blackberry Hill, I slowed down and explained to Werewolf how I guessed that Salome, coming the other way, down the hill, had been bumped into space. The yellow and black police barrier was still there as a warning to other drivers coming over the crest of the hill.

Over the top, the road curved around to the left, and a roadside milestone said it was two miles to Broughton Street. I told Werewolf my theory of the track leading from Blackberry Hill to Pegasus Farm, roughly parallel to us but the other side of the Down. He unfolded the map I'd brought and agreed with me.

'The place marked "Fisher's Farm"; you reckon that's it?'

'Yep – and there you are.'

Ahead, on a right-hand bend, was the farm, but it had been a long time since a chicken had shat in that yard.

A discreet wooden sign said: 'EXHILAR-ATOR ACTION COURSE – APPOINT-MENT ONLY – ALL VISITORS REPORT TO HEADQUARTERS.' There was a white wooden-arrow sign below it, pointing to the farmhouse, and that had 'HQ' stencilled on it in Ministry of Defence style.

I pulled into the farmyard and bounced the BMW over the cobbles to where half a dozen cars were parked in front of the farm-house, a long, low stone building probably about a century old. Its oak front door was propped open by what looked like a How-itzer shell, and there was another arrow sign saying 'HQ' hung over it, pointing inside.

I parked the BMW by reversing between a Mercedes and a sleek Volvo 410 until I was pointing directly towards the yard entrance (Rule No 277). Bringing the Bob Marley had been a good idea; there wasn't a cheaper car in the yard, it seemed, except maybe the white Vauxhall Astra with the shirt-button wheels, a car Duncan the Drunken, in a rare lucid moment, had described as a jet-propelled tennis shoe. I bet myself that was Sorley's, as I'd had him pegged as the boy racer type and I was glad the insurance companies were uprating them. Next to it was a red Porsche 944 with a bumper sticker that read: 'My other car's a Porsche as well.' How gross. That one I wanted to be Cawthorne's.

We dismounted from the BMW and Werewolf slipped on a pair of gold-rimmed shades, which reminded me to put on the plain glass Yuppie specs I'd borrowed from Fly. I thought we both looked pretty good: rich enough to have all the trappings, oiky enough to want to come on an Action Man course. I unloaded our holdalls from the boot. Mine advertised Marlboro; Werewolf's had a discreet gold plate in one corner saying Mappin & Webb. I wondered if Sorrel had missed it yet.

The holdalls contained only towels, shampoo and the 'action footwear' we'd bought yesterday. Except mine, that is. I'd stuffed an Olympus Trip camera into one of my Reeboks and some spare film into the other. I was using the very fast, 12-shot per roll film that estate agents use to make houses look good in the rain. If you didn't mind a grainy look, you could slam it through any of the while-u-wait colour processing shops and get reasonable black-and-white prints in an hour. Proper black-and-white processing takes weeks these days, unless you have your own darkroom, and sometimes the photokiosks think they've cocked it up when the pictures come out sepia, and so they don't charge.

As I locked the BMW, Werewolf turned slowly through a circle, scanning the farm's outbuildings with his shades. I asked him what was the matter.

'Just checking for snipers,' he answered, and for a second or two he had me doing it as well.

'Come on,' I said, jerking my head towards the HQ sign. 'Let's be careless in there.'

The interior of the farmhouse had been opened out into a reception office, though it still had the original stone floor and a pretty impressive fireplace in the middle of one wall. The effect was somewhat marred, though, in that the fireplace didn't have a grate or anything, but was filled with what I hoped was a model of a two-inch mortar. And then I began to notice that the pictures on the walls were all prints of cavalry regiments, and a hat-stand in a corner wasn't really a hat-stand but another empty shell case with a clutch of regimental flags standing in it.

The desk that was the focus of the room was probably authentic War Office surplus stock. It even had a 1940s bakelite telephone that seemed to work, but the typewriter was state of the art and so, probably, was the young lady behind it.

Werewolf and I presented our suits to her. I wondered if we should salute.

'Yes, gentlemen?'

'The name is Maclean. We have a booking for the ten o'clock shoot.'

She consulted a large desk diary.

'Ah yes. That will be £115, inclusive of VAT. Would you like a receipt?'

'No,' I said. 'That won't be necessary.'

I could almost hear Werewolf's eyebrows go up as I counted out the cash. I'd decided to pay cash rather than use the PKB Amex card as that would have given the game away as to why we were there. Paying cash had the added benefit of leaving no record of our visit except a pencilled telephone booking under two untraceable names.

The receptionist took my money and locked it in a drawer of the desk, then stood up. She was taller than me, which isn't saying a lot. Her jet-black hair had been precision-cut into a circular mop, shaved high at the back and fringed at the front, about half an inch above eye level. She wore one-piece khaki overalls buttoned to the throat, complete with epaulettes and button-down breast pockets, the left one of which had a name tag saying 'Boyd.' It was a good job she wasn't called Ramsbottom or anything like that, as the material wouldn't have stretched far enough.

'Have you played the Exhilarator before, gentlemen?' she asked.

'No, not this particular game,' I said

268

quickly, before Werewolf could smart-mouth her. She'd almost certainly heard them all before.

'We tend not to use the word "game," sir. Sergeant Waters will be briefing combatants today. There are only six of you this morning. That will be at ten sharp.' She looked at a Swatch watch that she wore upside down on her right wrist. It was a quarter to ten. 'So you've time to get changed. Please follow me.'

She led us to an unmarked oak door that opened into a short corridor, obviously a modern extension to the farmhouse. We trooped after her, watching the sway of her buttocks through the khaki coveralls.

'I dig the action footwear,' whispered Werewolf.

So did I. Ms Boyd was wearing bright red trainers that were certainly against regulations for any decent regiment of the line, despite what one hears about the Guards these days.

'The library,' she said, indicating a door to her left, 'where the briefing takes place.'

The next door had a universal woman sign on it, which presumably meant the Ladies changing-rooms, then another door had 'NO ENTRY' in military style print and a padlock and hasp.

'That's the armoury where we stock our equipment,' said Ms Boyd. 'Weapons issue is immediately after briefing.'

We had reached the last door.

'And this is the male changing-room.'

Ms Boyd opened the door and took a pace inside.

It was like the changing-rooms of a thousand football clubs, or schools for that matter. Rows of benches with wire baskets underneath for shoes, clothes pegs above, and at the end, a bank of showers and toilet cubicles. Down one wall were full-length metal lockers with keys in their locks on the end of long, thin chains so they looked like dog-tags.

Oh yes, and there were two naked men in the room.

Well, only one was really half naked. He was wearing a long, woolly pullover with hedgehogs all over it; nothing else. His companion was zipping up a pair of the khaki overalls.

The man in just the pullover put his hands on his hips and faced us in all his glory.

'Really, Sandy, you ought to knock or you never know what you'll find,' he said in a plummy voice.

'Don't fret, Mr Jenkins, I never let the little things in life bother me,' said Ms Boyd, totally unfazed. 'Everything's in the lockers,' she said to us, 'so get changed and come to the library.'

The door closed and she was probably

back at her desk before Jenkins moved, having abandoned his search for a good comeback. It was probably as well. He would have been fighting out of his class.

The library turned out to be a small lecture room with about 20 hard chairs facing an overhead projector and screen. There were bookshelves along one wall, with titles ranging from John Keegan's *Six Armies in Normandy* and Richard Holmes's *Firing Line*, which I'd read, to anonymous pulp volumes called *A Social History of the Hand Grenade* or similar, which I'd no intention of reading.

There was a coffee machine and a pile of styrofoam cups, and we helped ourselves.

Dead on 10.00, there were six of us on chairs and 'Sergeant' Waters standing by the overhead. We were all dressed in the regulation-issue khaki overalls, but Waters had three stripes on his sleeves in case we didn't know what a sergeant was. He also wore metal-frame square glasses because someone had told him he looked tough in them. In fact, they made him look like a schoolboy showing off his Cadet uniform to a schoolgirl who was really more into sending her underwear to Prince or Dave Lee Roth. Or maybe both, if she had spares.

'Good morning, gentlemen,' he addressed us.

'Bring back the receptionist,' whispered Werewolf.

'As we are only six, this morning's shoot will be an exercise in individual pennants,' said Waters, flicking on the projector.

The screen lit up and showed two pennants crudely drawn on the acetate, one yellow and the other red. They looked like they could have been pinched from a golf course.

'The object of the exercise is to secure one of these pennants and return it to base. For this exercise, home base will be the end of the changing-room block. For those unfamiliar with our operation here, this is the terrain.'

He changed overlays and a schematic map came on the screen. Waters produced a light pointer and began to explain the topography as if conducting a band.

The farm buildings formed three sides of a square in the south-eastern corner of the property, which was bounded to the right by a shaded area. Waters zapped his torch on it.

'First, you should note this area, which runs the entire depth of the Exhilarator course. This is agricultural land leased to a local farmer and is out of bounds.'

He moved the pointer back to the HQ buildings.

'Behind us, immediately outside, is what we refer to as the Paddock. It's open grass with not much cover, and it slopes down to the pond and the stream that bisect the two parts of the battle area.'

The stream was marked with a blue line, and what looked like a child's drawing of a ladder lay across it at one point. To either side, the map had crudely-drawn represent-ations of trees.

'This wooden bridge is the only link between the two wooded zones,' recited Waters. 'It is the only permitted point of crossing of the stream; please bear that in mind.

'The wooded zones are known as the Wood–' he waved his light wand – 'to the north of the stream and, to the south and west of this building, the Orchard. Both are woodland offering good cover and truly exhilarating terrain.'

I exchanged eye contact with Werewolf's shades.

'The Wood and The Orchard are today's combat zones.'

I wondered what they did at weekends. Invade Surrey?

'The red and yellow pennants will be placed in the Wood and Orchard in ten-metre-square cleared areas. We do not tell you the location of these areas, nor do we tell you which pennant is in which combat zone. Your individual objective is to secure one of those pennants and return to base first. You will leave this HQ at one-minute intervals, and that is your minute of grace.

For those 60 seconds, you are not a legitimate target, nor can you fire your own weapon. Questions?'

The guy in front of me – the hedgehog pullover flasher – put a hand up.

'Which pennant do we go for? Or doesn't it matter?'

Sergeant Waters slapped his light torch against his thigh. I got the impression he liked doing that.

'Good question, sir. When you are issued with ammunition pouches immediately after this briefing, you will draw either red or yellow paint shells. Red ammunition aims for red pennant and yellow for yellow. But remember, out there, you have five enemies. Only the first one back wins. There are no other rules. Next question?'

'What happens when you hit somebody?' asked Werewolf.

Sergeant Waters blinked a couple of times. 'Most people say "What happens when I'm hit,"' he said, then looked around to acknowledge the titters of nervous laughter.

Two guys in front of us turned to look at Werewolf, but he stared them down from behind his dark glasses.

'If you are hit at all, you retire immediately to HQ for a penalty of five minutes. Myself, Private Boyd or one of the other staff will be here, and it is up to you to register with them. Your five minutes start only when you make yourself known. Understood?'

We all nodded, and there was some general chatter and talk of a 'sin bin' nobody had expected. I studied the map, which was still on the screen. Behind the HQ building, to the right of what Waters called the Paddock but before you got to the Wood, was a small black circle quite close to the boundary fence. I raised my hand.

'What's that, between the bottom edge of the wood and the fields?' I asked.

The answer came from behind us, and I felt the hairs on the back of my neck go ping.

'That is an authentic World War II pillbox, built in 1940 under the supervision of a man called Fisher who actually used to own this farm. I would like to say that Pegasus Farm was of vital strategic value to the war effort, but I cannot. The truth is Mr Fisher was a prominent member of the local Home Guard and he managed to persuade whoever it was in charge of building anti-invasion pillboxes that Fisher's Farm was worth defending. It also meant he only had to walk across the Paddock when he went on night duty.'

There was some desultory laughter and a few heads turned to the back of the room. I didn't have to. The voice told me it was Cawthorne as much as if he'd said 'spade bitch.'

'Unfortunately, Farmer Fisher used the pillbox for other purposes after the war, notably as a toilet for his farmworkers. Consequently, it has been closed off and is out of bounds as far as the Exhilarator goes.'

Cawthorne walked to the front as he spoke. He wore the same khaki overalls as we all did, but he had a major's crown on each shoulder. He was more modest than I'd given him credit for.

Without meaning to, I found myself avoiding his eyes, slumping down in my chair and concentrating on the back of the one in front. Werewolf stayed upright, but then he'd never been as close to him as I had.

Cawthorne reached the overhead projector and turned to address us, one hand on the holster on his right hip.

'A word about your weapons, gentlemen,' he smarmed; then he went for the quick draw and levelled a long-barrelled pistol at all of us.

I was impressed. A guy on the front row broke wind. Werewolf whispered: 'He's faster when he moves.'

'This, gentlemen, is what we call the Equalizer,' Cawthorne said, turning the gun from side to side. 'It has been specially designed for the Exhilarator course.'

The handgun was a big one, or so I suppose, being no authority on these things.

Put it this way: it looked like something Clint Eastwood wouldn't have minded finding on his Christmas tree. It had a six-inch barrel, but a solid cylinder underneath it almost as long, so that from the business end it looked like an over-and-under shotgun with the lower barrel blocked off.

'It's a double-action revolver, which means you have to pull back the hammer to cock it before firing.' He broke the gun in half and showed us the cylinder filled with six red-plastic capsules. 'It fires paint capsules by compressed carbon dioxide in the tube under the barrel. Accuracy is about 30 yards and we have tried to make the guns as noisy as possible, though they still sound more like airguns than the real thing, I'm afraid. You will be issued with 24 paint balls and a spare CO_2 cylinder, although one is usually enough. You will be issued with a weapons belt and goggles or, for those wearing glasses, a visor for face protection.'

I sank even lower into my seat when he mentioned glasses, but he didn't seem to be looking at me.

'If you are hit on the torso, from head to knees but excluding the arms, that is a hit and you must return here for a penalty of five minutes. Other than that, as the Sergeant says, there are no rules. Out there, it's war!'

We trooped out and back into the changing-room, where 'Private' Boyd had opened a fire door on to what 'Sergeant' Waters had called the Paddock. It was supposed to be like going Over the Top, but it felt more like a gang of reluctant schoolboys setting out on a cross-country run with only the prospect of a quick smoke round the back of the bike sheds to sustain them.

I palmed the Olympus Trip into my overalls while pretending to tidy my sports bag and new suit. Then Ms Boyd called us to order and get in line for 'weapons issue.'

I shuffled along behind Werewolf and whispered to him, 'Head for the Wood to the right and wait for me somewhere near that big conifer.'

'Which one's the conifer?' he said out of the corner of his beard.

'The green one.'

'That narrows it down.'

The procedure was that Private Boyd handed us each a belt complete with pistol holster and ammo pouches, and then Sergeant Waters launched each of us through the door with a pat on the shoulder, telling us we had one minute's start. Werewolf and I were numbers three and four in the queue, and the Sergeant had to tap his watch a couple of times as Werewolf seemed to be requiring more help than the rest of us from Private Boyd in getting his belt on.

What he appeared to be doing was chatting her up. In reality, he was allowing the guy second in the queue to get a good head start *while* chatting her up.

Taking his time, he moved over to the door and paused. He was the only one of the game players not to have fooled around quick-drawing our paint guns as soon as we had got them. He just stood there with hands on hips until Waters raised a hand to tap him on the shoulder.

Werewolf looked him in the eyes and Waters thought the better of it, saying weakly: 'Go. 'And Werewolf went, running hard towards the wood.

One of the first two out had peeled off to the left towards the Orchard. The other had gone for the Wood but had entered well away from the large conifer Werewolf headed for. He'd just about made it by the time Private Boyd had strapped my gun belt on and issued me with a plastic face visor that fitted with adjustable straps at the back.

Then Waters hit me on the shoulder and I was off across the paddock, concentrating on the spot where Werewolf had suddenly vanished into the trees.

It was the sort of distance that Olympic sprinters can cover in less than a minute on their lap of honour. My time would be impressive only if clocked by sundial, but I was pleased with it, though I could have done with a couple of gym sessions to get in shape. I promised myself I'd never smoke again, and I didn't often do that twice in a morning.

I didn't so much take cover in the under-brush, I collided with it. I'd forgotten just how many sharp edges there were in the countryside. Then I felt my sleeve being tugged downwards and my feet swept from under me, and suddenly I was lying next to Werewolf.

'I thought you were going to walk all over me, yer clumsy shite.'

'Rubbish. I was coming straight for you,' I panted, misting up the inside of my face visor.

Werewolf had opted for clear plastic goggles, but he had already dispensed with them, tying them to his belt. He had remembered to bring a pair of gloves, unlike me. I'd also forgotten how many nasty sting-ing things there were in the country.

'It's a jungle out here,' I said to myself.

'Now what?' asked Werewolf.

He parted some ferns so we could look back across the Paddock to the changing-rooms, where the next toy soldier had just launched himself towards the Orchard.

'Can you keep them busy for an hour or so? Make them think there are two of us out here?'

'No problem. Give us yer gun and ammo.'

I unbuckled my belt. 'What colour ammo

did you draw?'

'Yellow.'

'I'm red, so that should give you a fair spread. If Patterson struts his stuff, he'll request a rider from Airborne just before eleven, so if anything is coming through, it should be before eleven-fifteen.'

I took off the stupid visor and placed it behind the conifer.

'Leave the belt here and head back around eleven-thirty. Okay?'

'Sure.' Werewolf checked over both pistols. Expertly. No comment.

'I'm going over there.' I pointed to the field Waters had told us was out of bounds. 'And circle round to the farm buildings to see what I can see.'

'If you're caught back there, what do you say?' Werewolf asked with what he thought was an air of innocence.

'Er ... that I'm a casualty?'

'Good thinking, man.' He levelled his pistol at me. 'So I'd better shoot you, hadn't I?'

'You're starting to enjoy this, you bastard, aren't you?'

Let's just say Werewolf shot me in the 'lower stomach' and leave it there. I know it didn't hurt, the paint pellet hitting and exploding with no more than a mild flick. It was the surprise and indignity of watching the yellow stain spread that made me wince.

I left Werewolf with a withering look and headed for the edge of the road, cutting back deeper into the trees so I couldn't be seen from the farmhouse when I reached the fenced-off field.

The fence was a four-strand barbed-wire job, and beyond it were rows of green plants about four feet high. Ideal cover running all the way to the farmhouse and the road.

Behind me, I heard two more shots. As Cawthorne had said, they were like airguns going off. Then there was a howl of protest, something like 'Hey, that's not fair!'

I dropped down and crawled to the front of the wood to have a look.

The guy with the hedgehog pullover, the one called Jenkins, was standing in the Paddock about 20 feet from the conifer where Werewolf had been hiding. He had both a yellow and a red stain across his chest and he was turning around with his arms out, appealing for a referee; then he turned and trudged back to the farmhouse for his time penalty.

It's a man's life.

I doubled back and picked a spot to vault the fence, using a post as a grip. I thought I did it quite well until I heard the khaki overalls rip. There was a horizontal tear four inches long just behind my right knee. People paid 60 quid for denims like that in the King's Road.

The field was laid out in strips about two feet apart, and only after pushing into the crop did I realise that the plants were trained up a trellis of almost invisible wires and that I was in a hop field – a 'beer field', as Duncan would have called it. Perfect cover. So perfect, I had to keep parting the hop bines and leaves to see how close I was to the farmhouse.

As I drew level with the back of the farm, I could see Jenkins remonstrating with Cawthorne and Waters. He was pointing at his chest, which had gone a bright shade of orange. Against the wall of the changing-room extension, Private Boyd leant against the door with her head bowed, trying to control the giggles.

I would never have a better diversion, I thought; then it did get better. Another player came out of the wood and began to jog across the Paddock. Even from this distance, it was clear he'd been hit several times in the chest and there was also red paint all over his visor. Werewolf seemed to be conducting some sort of slaughter out there. It was getting more like a grousemoor by the minute.

While the Exhilarator high command were busy dealing with another unhappy customer, I ruined some more perfectly good hops – I'm probably personally responsible for the rise in the price of a pint – and pushed through to the fence. I came over it below the farmhouse and hugged the side wall, like I've seen them do in the movies, until I could peer round into the farmyard.

Apart from the parked cars, it was deserted. There were two outbuildings across the yard; one looked like a converted barn and the other had at one time styed pigs. I was looking for a 4x4 vehicle, and either building could have housed this year's import quota.

I decided to go for the barn, and struck lucky twice in a row. For starters it wasn't locked, and for seconds it was obviously the farm garage.

Lined up, and obviously well serviced, were a small tractor, a ride-on lawn-mower, a small white Citroen AX with French number plates (presumably to impress the odd Frog estate agent) and, at the end of the line, a blue Shogun four-wheel with metallic paint job.

Duncan had guessed right about it being a Shogun, the smaller, two-door version. They were good little motors. I'd even driven one once – a mad, bass guitarist friend of mine, who'd hit the minor big league with a couple of records, had bought three of them to race around the M25 orbital motorway. (He'd also had each one stencilled 'TORA' across the back door, so that in formation on the three-lane motorway they read: 'Tora! Tora! Tora!')

I went straight to the hood of the Shogun, digging the Olympus out of the front of my overalls and trying to guess if there was enough light in the barn. I need not have worried. The front of the jeep was as clean as if it had just come off the boat from Japan. There was no sign that it had ever had a front cow-catcher roll bar fitted.

I took a couple of pictures anyway, not knowing what possible good they would do, then kicked the Shogun in the driver's door just for the hell of it.

Petty, but pleasurable.

Then I heard the slap-slap-slap of rubber-soled feet coming across the yard and did what any ice-cool undercover dude would do; I went into freeze-frame, rabbit-in-headlight shock. The one thing I didn't have to worry about was losing control of my bodily functions. Thanks to Werewolf, it looked as if I'd done that already.

Instantly, I just *knew* that the barn had closed-circuit TV and kicking a company vehicle was a firing squad offence. Come on, *think*. Barns were supposed to have hay in them – they did in the movies – where the hero could hide while the baddies, with a total disregard for blood poisoning or spread of HIV, jabbed a pitchfork in and out like a demented barman trying to get the last maraschino out of the bottle.

I glanced around. The last time this barn

had hay in it, Henry VIII took a tenth part in tax. Henry also had a go at stopping hops being used in good old English ale. Why do I know such stuff? Why did I have to think of it then? Sometimes I worry me. This wasn't a game.

But hang about, it was. What if I was 'discovered'? I was hiding, working my way round to the Orchard to try for the pennant in there. Okay, so I didn't have my gun. Would they notice? Risk it. Hadn't Cawthorne himself said there were no other rules? Where did it say I couldn't go unarmed if I wanted to? If you're daft enough to pay good money to have paint shot into your crotch, you're daft enough to do anything.

I scurried under the tractor as the doors began to creak open. The tractor had more ground clearance than the Citroen, which was settled low on its hydraulics, and being found under the Shogun might just be too suspicious. I wasn't desperate enough to get under the lawn-mower.

The floor of the barn was cold stone and slimy and smelled, of engine oil and damp cereals. I scuttered around until I was facing the doors and pulled my legs in just as they opened fully.

Sergeant Waters stood in the opening, his right hand reaching down to his side.

He produced a set of car keys and loped

past the tractor about ten inches from my nose. I could read 'Nike' quite clearly on his trainers until they disappeared one after the other into the Shogun.

The four-wheel started first go, and he reversed out into the farmyard. With the doors open, I could see Cawthorne walking over to him. He handed Waters a battery-powered megaphone and pointed towards the wood. Waters nodded a couple of times and set off.

Cawthorne walked back to the farmhouse and in through the front door.

I crawled out from under the back of the tractor just in case anybody thought to peer into the barn, and was about to use the lawn-mower for cover when my foot caught something hard and suddenly I was face down on the ground again

Only this was more painful than the barn floor and it had a different texture. I checked my camera to see if it was still in one piece and stuffed it back inside my overalls. Then I put my hands out to explore what I had tripped over.

After having looked out into the daylight, it took my eyes a few seconds to adjust. Then I realised I was kneeling on a tarpaulin that someone had carefully placed over what could have been a small metal gate – or the detached 'fun bumper' cow-catcher device from a small four-wheel-drive vehicle; say, a Shogun.

You don't have to give me clues on a plate. I fall over them.

CHAPTER TWELVE

I did the business with my camera, now there was plenty of light with the barn doors open, and was in the process of replacing the tarpaulin when the alarm bells went off and scared the hell out of me for the second time in five minutes. This was becoming Stress City, and I was too old for it.

It wasn't an alarm bell, of course, it was a telephone rigged to an extension bell fitted to the wall of the farmhouse, so that people working outside could hear it. There were four long rings and then it cut out, but before it stopped, Cawthorne was coming out of the farmhouse and walking quickly towards the Paddock.

I checked my watch: 10.40. That couldn't be Patterson calling for Airborne yet, but it might well be Airborne out on another document delivery somewhere else. The four rings and then cut-out sounded like a fax line connection. Why bother having an outside bell if the delicious Private Boyd was sitting on reception?

Cawthorne had disappeared around the northern end of the farmhouse, so I ran back the way I had come, around the south end, and climbed the fence back into the hop field. I ran between the bines, parallel to the farm, until I reckoned it was safe to crawl to the fence and risk a look.

I could see the Wood to my right, and way across the Paddock I could see Waters in the Shogun patrolling the edge of the Orchard. There was no sign of Cawthorne, and I thought I'd come too far. Maybe the fax machine was in one of the outbuildings; but they were the other side of the yard near the barn, and Cawthorne had been walking away from them.

Another 'combatant' suddenly appeared from the Orchard end of the course, hurrying towards the farm. Even at this distance, I could see he was liberally spattered with yellow paint. Werewolf was on the move.

Then I realised that I could hear an engine getting louder and the Shogun was bouncing across the Paddock straight towards me.

I was convinced that the grass near the fence was long enough to conceal me, so they couldn't possibly have spotted me. Not unless they had radar or heat-seeking missiles, which they didn't. Did they? I was less convinced about that.

I was about to dive back in among the hops, though I probably smelled like last night's barmaid already, when the Shogun veered off to my right, and then pulled up about 20 feet from me.

A very angry Sergeant Waters jumped out of the driver's door. I could tell he was angry, because he was red in the face and his fists were clenched and he was swearing like a trooper. Well, I suppose that was in character. I could see why he was angry: the windscreen of the Shogun was well-smeared with yellow paint, and he'd obviously reacted by turning on the windscreen-wipers, the worst thing he could have done.

What I couldn't work out was why he'd driven all the way over here. There was nothing here except the field and the old, disused pillbox Cawthorne had warned us about.

The door of the pillbox opened and Cawthorne stepped out, so close to me that if the wind had changed I could have sniffed his after-shave. Any closer and I would have fallen over him too.

'What's the panic? Don't you know to stay away from here?' Cawthorne was not pleased.

'Look at this!' Waters shook a fist at the windscreen. 'Just look. One of those buggers is deliberately spoiling the exercise.'

'Which one?'

'I don't know. I was over by the Orchard, and then this. He must have been up a tree.

We've had four reported in for penalty hits already. Two of them twice.'

Cawthorne nodded towards the farm. 'There's another one.'

Sure enough, another player was trudging out of the Orchard towards base.

'It must be those two in the BMW with the flash suits,' said Waters. I was glad we'd made an impression.

'I didn't rate the weedy one with the glasses,' said Cawthorne, 'but the one with the beard looked a hard case.'

'What do we do?'

'Has anybody asked for their money back?'

'Well, no.'

'Then let the game run and say nothing, but tell Sandy to make sure those two don't get another booking.' He turned to the pillbox. 'And don't come here again, I've told you this is private property. And go and clean my fucking vehicle, okay?'

Waters reversed the Shogun and did a backward handbrake turn, shooting off in a cloud of exhaust fumes and clods of grass and earth. Temper, temper.

I crawled closer to the pillbox. It was the same hexagonal design as any of the thousands you can still see along the south coast, or that you suddenly come across in the wilds of East Anglia for no apparent reason until you realise that the fields you're driving through were once airfields littered with empty Lucky Strike packets and B52 bombers. The whole concrete structure was sunk into the ground so it seemed only about four feet high. There were double firing slits on three sides and a metal door set in the side nearest to me. Cawthorne had had to duck his head to get in there, but he'd left the door wide open.

I had to get halfway under the bottom strand of barbed wire to see inside properly, and as I did so, my hand closed on something smooth and rubbery half-buried in the ground. I parted some grass and wondered why Cawthorne had bothered to run electric and telephone cables to a disused toilet for farmhands.

I could see why – and hear. There was a fax coming through. The machine had a plastic cover over it, like stereo systems used to have before they became furniture, I suppose to keep the dust out, but there was no mistaking the whirr-buzz sound. Cawthorne was leaning over the machine, blocking my view of anything else inside the bunker, and I slid around to check if I could see in through the slits.

No go. It would have to be the front door. But not while Cawthorne was in residence.

The door got me thinking. I crawled along the line of the fence to the nearest point I dared, so I could get a good view of it. There didn't seem to be any sort of lock on the door; wartime pillboxes wouldn't have needed one, would they? Sorry, lads, can't beat back the Nazi hordes today, Fred's left the key at home.

The door was metal, on hinges four inches deep. There was a metal grab bar and two bolts on the outside, one at the top, which could have had padlocks on at some time, to keep playful kids out. Then again, the pillbox was on private land, so maybe that hadn't been a problem. But I couldn't believe that Cawthorne would be so lax.

He wasn't. Above the door's right corner was a small black box burglar alarm, almost certainly wired back to the farmhouse, or more likely electronic, triggering a bleeper that Cawthorne could carry with him. It wasn't likely that it was connected to the local cop shop. He might have had to explain why he'd put a fax machine out here for the sheep to use on a quiet day. Perhaps the sheep were monitoring the futures market in wool.

I guessed that it was set back in the farmhouse, unless he had some sort of remote control toy. If it was, I reckoned I had a few minutes while he walked back there. If it wasn't, and he came back and caught me, then I'd have to fall back on my story as an over-enthusiastic games player. Trying that on Sergeant Waters was one thing. On Cawthorne, it could be a different ball game, and the balls on the line were probably mine.

The fax machine stopped whirring, and Cawthorne moved about, picking sheets from its output tray. Then I heard the snap of a lighter, and a cloud of blue smoke came out of the doorway, followed by a rattle sound. He was burning the fax message in a metal waste bin or my name was Roylance Maclean. Careful bugger, wasn't he?

He came out before the smoke had cleared and swung the door quietly on well-oiled hinges. He flipped just one of the bolts in a casual way and strode off towards the farmhouse across the Paddock.

He hadn't touched the black box alarm, so it was now or never. I guessed I had no more than four minutes before he got back to base, so I began to count on the old one-and-one, two-and-two, and so on principle in order to concentrate on the job in hand without looking at my watch. I told myself that I had up to two hundred and no more.

By ten, I'd crawled as far as the door. It took me to 20 to stand into a half crouch and reach up for the bolt. The door swung open and I scuttled in.

It wasn't as dark as I'd expected. The four-inch-wide gun slits let in plenty of light, although there were electric wall lights. Everything was covered in plastic casing to keep the elements out. Apart from the fax machine, there was an Amstrad PC with monitor and printer. No phones – Cawthorne would have mobiles – and apart from the two benches for the machinery and a single typist's swivel chair, nothing else. Except a long metal trunk on the floor, which removed a couple of inches of skin from my right shin as I scraped round it.

That got me to 30-and-five. Better do something.

I rattled the plastic cover over the Amstrad, but it was firmly locked in place. It was probably just as well. I am totally computer hostile, so I wouldn't have known what to do with the damn thing. I've nothing against them, they just hate me, so I became a founder member of the Campaign for Quill Pens and Ink. It's not a big organisation.

The trunk had a hasp and padlock, which looked new, though the trunk itself was war surplus. If I'd had my nail-file with me I'd have had a go at it.

Sixty. Don't hang about.

I wound up my Olympus and took shots of everything there was.

That took about ten more seconds. I couldn't think of anything else to do except get out.

That seemed sensible. I crouched down through the doorway and checked the coast was clear.

As I slid the door bolt home, I stopped counting at 92. A second later, there was a loud click and buzz, which could only be the black box alarm being activated.

Either I'd counted wrong or Cawthorne walked faster than I'd thought. Still (Rule of Life No 1), it's better to be lucky than good.

I worked my way back through the hop field until I could get over the fence and into the wood. It was just after 11.00 when I made the conifer where I'd split from Werewolf. My Exhilarator visor was still in the grass where I'd left it, and I sat down beside it to take stock of my stings, bruises and cuts. I didn't have time to get paranoid about blood poisoning, as my heart suddenly stopped beating.

The cause of this was somebody trying to spear me with a javelin, but a javelin with a yellow pennant tied to it. It landed six inches from my face, and before it had stopped quivering in the ground, a red one slapped down next to it. Before *I'd* stopped quivering, I realised that they hadn't been thrown, but dropped from above. And then a shadow passed over me and Werewolf came out of the tree to land perfectly balanced right in front of me.

'Jeeeesus Christ!' I said, holding my heart.

'Nice handle, but I'd stick to Roy if I were you,' Werewolf said matter-of-factly. 'Less aggro signing on at the Social Security.'

'Hey, if I ever did sign on, I'd need a pseudonym.' I looked at the pennants and so did he. He was proud of them.

'You had to get them both, didn't you?'

'I got bored,' he said. 'And you wanted a diversion. Find anything?'

'Some. Maybe not enough, though. But it should rattle him. I'll see what Sorrel's dad can turn up. Listen.'

In the distance, we could hear the outside telephone bell at the farmhouse.

I checked my watch and stood up so I could look across the Paddock.

'That should be Patterson's fax coming through if he did what I asked.'

'What happens?'

I explained rapidly about the pillbox, and sure enough we saw Cawthorne set out from the farmhouse, walking diagonally across the Paddock towards the fence. The pillbox roof was just visible, but you had to know it was there to spot it.

Just before he reached it, I used the last two shots on my film, though at that distance I didn't think I'd pick up much.

'We've done all we can, I reckon. Let's blow while he's busy in there.'

'Okay. You'd better have this.' Werewolf placed one of the paint pistols in my belt holster, then offered me one of the pennants. 'And one of these. It'd look suspicious if I took all the glory, now, wouldn't it?'

297

I stuffed the Olympus inside my overalls and we jogged back across the Paddock, studiously ignoring the pillbox off to our left. We were the first back into the changing-rooms, and we dumped our holsters and visors on the folding table near the door. I didn't know if we were supposed to check them in with Private Boyd or not. Maybe she was warming up the showers. Werewolf left the two pennants in the doorway, crossed like ceremonial assegais.

We peeled off our khaki overalls and hung them on hooks. Mine was ripped and stained around the knees and elbows and had a bright yellow crutchpiece. Werewolf's, with a quick press, could have come off the peg at any Army and Navy store.

I chivvied him into a quick shower. Ever since we'd been at university together, I'd known him as a bit of a shower freak, staying in there for ages. His idea of heaven would be for someone to design a device that would allow him to read a book in there. If you see Terence Conran, pass it on.

As we emerged wearing only our towels, the rest of the games players drifted in. Without exception, they were splattered in paint as if they'd gone in for action art. The guy with the hedgehog pullover – Jenkins – was probably the worst of the lot; even his visor was obscured.

Nobody said much. Werewolf softly

whistled Mark Knopfler's *Going Home* from *Local Hero* and didn't stop even when Jenkins walked up to him and said in a plummy voice:

'I know this is only a game, but there are rules, old boy.'

Werewolf stopped towelling his armpit and looked at him. I concentrated on zipping the flies of my trousers, head down, nothing to do with me. The other players carried on getting changed and opening lockers and stuff, but you could hear a pin drop.

'Who dares wins, old boy,' he said quietly.

Jenkins just stood there, unsure of his next six moves. He was saved by Private Boyd, who appeared in the doorway and began to scoop up the gun belts and equipment.

'Good game, gentlemen?'

'Fine, absolutely fine. We were just saying, weren't we?' said Werewolf loudly.

'Er ... yes. Exhilarating. Quite exhilarating,' said Jenkins, moving away.

Private Boyd walked through, unfazed by the half-clothed bodies scrabbling for cover. 'Good, good. Come again soon.'

Werewolf gave her a big smile as she approached. He was still stark naked, but had decided to get dressed. He started by putting his tie on. Private Boyd allowed herself a raised eyebrow as she went by.

Jenkins turned as if to say something, and Werewolf waved a hand at him.

'Hey,' he said quickly before Private Boyd was out of earshot. 'Do you know the sound of a truly satisfied woman after love-making?'

He said it like it was a joke to be shared, but I winced, knowing what was coming.

'No,' said Jenkins, going along with it.

'Didn't think you did,' said Werewolf.

With Werewolf driving the BMW, we covered the two miles to the village of Broughton Street at Warp Factor Five. I spotted a pub called the Hop Pole and asked Werewolf if he fancied a drink.

'Do fish swim?' he said, whipping the power steering over and bringing the car to rest in the pub car park in a shower of gravel.

Fortunately, the landlord hadn't seen our arrival, and he served us with a smile and an offer of menus. We ordered pints of bitter and ploughman's lunches and he brought them personally to us as we sat in the bay-window seat of the public bar. I wasn't used to such good treatment, then it clicked: we were wearing suits. Maybe there was something in this respectability lark after all.

Werewolf filled me in on his *blitzkrieg* across the Exhilarator course and had to admit that he'd enjoyed himself. He was getting more beer in when I saw a motorbike pull into the car park. The rider, in black leathers, stood the bike, a big Honda, near the BMW and began to remove a black crash helmet. Even from the back, I knew it was Private Boyd.

She left the helmet on the bike – how trusting people are out of London – and unzipped her jacket as she walked to the pub door.

She didn't look at me as she came in, just walked straight up to the bar. Without turning round, Werewolf said: 'What'll you have?'

I was impressed, then I noticed him clocking her in the mirror behind the bar.

'Pernod and blackcurrant,' she said.

'Glad you could make it,' he said. How had he managed that?

'Hello, Sandy,' said the landlord as he served her. So she was a regular.

'You two caused quite a stir back at High Command,' she said as she joined us. 'You're far too rough for most of our customers.'

'Now isn't that just too bad,' Werewolf said with a smile.

'I wouldn't try for a rebooking for a while,' she said, sipping her drink.

'Blackballed, are we?' asked Werewolf innocently.

She looked at him over the rim of her glass. 'I wouldn't say that.'

I bought her some lunch, and while Werewolf flirted, I tried to pump her about

Pegasus Farm and the operation there. When Cawthorne was mentioned by name she put her forefinger and thumb together in a circle and made the universal sign for self-abuse. Not the sort of thing you see in the sign-language translations for the deal.

'He gets off playing soldiers like you wouldn't believe,' she said between mouthfuls of cheese. 'Even has a secret little den where he takes the other members of his gang. The big kid.'

'Is that the pillbox?' I chanced.

'Yeah,' she said, without a flicker of suspicion as to why we were interested. Maybe I'm too cynical. 'No *girls* allowed, not in the boys' secret camp!'

'What do they get up to, then. Songs round the campfire?'

'They play with guns, don't they?'

'Is one of them a guy called Sorley?' I asked.

'Yeah, that's right, and there are a couple of others. Any chance of the other half?' She held out her empty glass to me.

'So they have private games of the Exhilarator, do they?' I asked as I stood up to go to the bar. 'What do they do? Use luminous paint after dark?'

'Nah,' said Private Boyd. 'Real guns.'

She held her hands out as if she held a sub-machine-gun and went 'Rat-tat-tat-ta.' I was grateful the bar was empty.

'Cawthorne collects them. Thinks I don't know. Keeps them in a tin trunk in his pill-box. He's got grenades and smoke bombs and other stuff like my kid brother had a box of toy soldiers.' She smiled up at me, 'Not so much blackcurrant this time, eh? Ta.'

Sandra, but she preferred Sandy, told us that she'd worked at the Exhilarator for five months but was just biding her time before she could move away from her mother and get her own place in London. Werewolf admired her motorbike; I asked her about weekend games at the farm. She'd been into hiking since she went out with a Hell's Angel called Rafe when she was 16. She didn't work weekends, she said; Cawthorne and Sorley handled things then.

And then it was thanks for the drinks and time to get back as another gang of wallies was booked in for one o'clock.

Before we left, she wrote her phone number on a beer mat, and in the car park she slipped it to Werewolf before she put her crash hat on and fired up the engine.

As she roared down the village street, Werewolf unlocked the BMW. I looked at him over the roof.

'Watch it, Sundance,' I said. 'Sorrel wouldn't like it.'

'Ah, don't fret yourself.' He shrugged. 'We have the same philosophy. Get your appetite where you can, just remember to eat at home.'

Werewolf pulled up near the Barbican and said he would walk to Sorrel's flat. I said I would get the BMW back to Patterson before the police helicopters were called out.

'Do the suits have to go back?' he asked, fingering a lapel.

'No way.'

'Shit. I would've picked a good one.'

'Thanks for this morning,' I said. 'I owe you one.'

'I know you do. Just add it to the list.'

'I'm on a promise to meet Sorrel's dad tonight,' I said casually.

'We'll be out all night. And tomorrow.'

'Going anywhere nice?'

'Nope. Staying in her flat with a crate of wine and the lights off. She doesn't know it yet, though.'

'Message received and understood.' Sorrel was to be kept out of things. 'See yer when you get back from Ireland.'

He paused at that, and I'll swear he almost looked behind him to see if anyone was earwigging.

'Actually,' he said, 'I'll need to borrow your gaff on Sunday, if that's okay.'

'Sure. You know me. Open house.'

'Thanks. I'll be on the first flight on Sunday. I've no intention of staying over there longer than I have to, and Sorrel's away for the weekend herself.'

I wondered if she was hunting up an appetite, but I didn't ask, just like I didn't ask about Werewolf's trip to Dublin. My teeth are one of my best assets, and I'd like to keep them that way.

'Okey-dokey. I'll get something in for breakfast – you bring the duty frees.'

'Yer on. Take care, Angel.'

Don't I always?

As I drove into the underground car park of Pretty, Keen, Bastards, the garageman looked (a) amazed that I had returned at all, and (b) staggered that there were four wheels and no obvious dents on the car.

I took the lift up to Reception, and Purvis delighted in telling me that Patterson was still at lunch.

'I'll wait,' I said, and headed off towards the postroom.

Michelle was the only one on duty there, but she put down the latest James Herbert long enough to tell me that yes, they had sent for an Airborne messenger just after 11.00, and that Anna kept asking if I'd called.

I slunk through the dealing room to Patterson's office and got there just as he did. His tie was askew and his breath smelled of brandy. If I was a less trusting soul, I'd have said he'd had a good lunch.

'You,' he said, and I nodded agreement. 'What did you find out?'

'Just what we thought. It's Cawthorne all right. The other end of the leak is down at his farm.'

Patterson sank down into his chair. 'Get any evidence?'

'Nothing that would stand up in court.'

'Court? Who said anything about a court?'

'Calm down, man. Keep the blood pressure down to a dull roar. It was a figure of speech.'

'Is my car all right?'

I wondered when we'd get round to that.

'Yeah, yeah, don't get your knickers in a twist, it's in one piece.' I flipped the keys on to the desk to reassure him. 'We've got enough to let Cawthorne know we're on to him, or we have by tomorrow night. All you have to do is send a couple more things by messenger.'

'What sort of things?' He looked suspicious.

'I'll tell you tomorrow.'

He shrugged, losing interest.

I perched on the edge of his desk.

'Whatsamatter, Tel? Come on, cough it.'

'It's just—' he reached for a paperclip to fiddle with – 'I – we've been thinking. Now we know how stuff is leaking, we can plug the leak – get another delivery service. Cawthorne cuts his losses and goes somewhere else. Leaves us alone.'

I gave him my killer look; the one I reserve for Springsteen. It didn't work on Patterson either.

'Makes sense,' I said. 'No fuss, no inquiry in the City, no cops.' He was nodding. 'No need to worry the senior partners, 'specially not Mr Keen and his son Snow White, the Homepride Flour Grader. But what about Alec Reynolds, Tel? Well, he's out of it, isn't he? Got him buried yet, or cremated and his ashes scattered down Threadneedle Street or round the corner in your wine bar on the floor with the sawdust? But there's Salome to think of, Tel; don't forget her, because I won't.'

'Now look.' He pointed a finger at me. Werewolf would have snapped it off. 'She's getting the best attention money can buy. Strictly speaking, I should have informed the Kent police when she was fit for visitors, or rather the hospital should have. But I told them not to, protecting her...'

'She's conscious?'

He'd pulled his finger back or I would have bitten it. Springsteen is always showing me how.

'Yes, this morning. I've been meaning to phone her husband, but...'

I was halfway out of the door.

'You shitehouse!' was what I yelled over my shoulder.

Or so the girls from the postroom told me later.

They'd heard it quite clearly.

I bus-hopped back to Hackney, feeling a bit of a prune sitting there in my suit in between a gaggle of wrinklies who'd been blowing their pensions down the supermarket. They probably thought, at that time of the afternoon, that I'd just been made redundant. It was too early for me to be a Yuckie – the tabloid newspapers' shorthand for the young city slickers who celebrated the end of a day's trading with too much lager and then reverted to type as the football hooligans they really were under the skin. They were supposed to terrorise London Transport after dark. Maybe they did. Certainly, it was almost impossible to get a taxi in the City after about 8.00 pm these days. If I'm ever strapped for cash, I'll cruise around. You never know who might mistake Armstrong for a real taxi and offer me a few quid as a friendly gesture for giving them a lift.

My third bus dropped me two streets away from home, which gave me a chance to call in at the local florist's and buy a 20-quid bouquet on PKB's Amex card. Normally, I get my flowers on Oxford Street just after 7.00 pm when the barrowboys have knocked off and gone to the pub, leaving loads of blooms for the Westminster Council rubbish collectors later on.

Nobody could have recognised me walking up Stuart Street. I don't think anybody could see me behind the bouquet, and I had trouble finding the keyhole.

I don't know who frightened who more. I almost dropped the flowers when I saw Lisabeth on the phone in the hallway as I kicked the door shut. She jumped back a pace and would have gone further, but the phone cable prevented it. I couldn't blame her; I must have looked like a platoon of Japanese snipers behind all that foliage. She clutched a hand to her ample bosom – actually not so much a bosom, more a shelf (a cheap shot) – and motioned that the phone was for me.

'Just one moment, Mr Angel is free now,' she said into the mouthpiece in a voice I hadn't heard since Fenella's parents had paid us a visit once.

We pantomimed an exchange of flowers for phone, which resulted in her crushing about half a dozen carnations and me getting the phone cord wrapped around my neck. It was Innes McInnes.

'Angel?'

'Yo.'

'How did it go today?'

'We survived the Exhilarator, and I think we got some candid camera shots that may come in handy. You had any ideas?'

'A few. What do you think Pegasus Farm is worth on the open market?'

That threw me for a minute. So now I was an estate agent. Well, I had the suit for it, but then, you see, I'm basically honest.

'I dunno. Million and a half?'

'Mmm. That's what I thought. Come and see me later, at the office, about six-thirty. Know where it is?'

'Houndsditch, isn't it? Near the Clanger.'

'The what?'

'The pub, the Clanger. Best pint of draught Bass for – ooh, two hundred yards.'

'Er ... yes, if you say so. Parking is impossible around here, I'm afraid.'

'Not for me it isn't. See you.'

Lisabeth handed over the bouquet, her nose twitching a warning of hay fever sneezing on the Richter Scale.

'So you've remembered Salome at last, have you?' There's appreciation for you. 'Well, Frank was there all night, and then he went straight to the office, but they sent him home at lunchtime. He looks very ragged, so I made him go to bed and get some sleep.'

'He'll get up for me,' I said, moving towards the stairs.

'Don't you go disturbing him. He's had...'

'Salome recovered consciousness this morning.'

Lisabeth squealed and advanced on me, beaming.

I backed rapidly up the stairs, holding the bouquet between us like Peter Cushing used to hold a crucifix up to Dracula.

Frank sat in the back of Armstrong, occasionally kneeling up on the rumble seat so he could yell in my ear, but all the time talking. Before we reached the BUPA hospital in Paddington, I felt I knew every temperature change Salome had gone through in the past five days, what her grandmother – phoning twice daily from Jamaica – thought about life, the universe and young people driving around in fast cars, and how difficult Frank had found going to the launderette.

The one thing he didn't ask, for which I was grateful, was what Salome had been doing with Alec Reynolds at midnight on a Saturday down in darkest Kent. Then again, he'd no reason to think I knew.

A nurse in a pale blue designer trouser suit (how unlike the dear old National Health!) gave Frank a dirty look, as he had rushed out in T-shirt, jeans and trainers. I still had the suit on – and Fly's glasses if I needed any props – so I got a 'That'll do nicely' sort of smile and the up-from-under look that tells you that there are advantages to private medicine. I made a mental note to ask for an application form on the way out.

She asked us to wait and indicated a nest of Bauhaus leather armchairs. I'd hardly got

311

comfortable when another lady – older, but still born after the Beatles had their first Number One – wearing a pink trouser suit with waistcoat, announced herself as the hospital administrator and told us to follow her.

Frank saw me watching the sway of her buttocks as we trooped down a corridor.

'That reminds me,' I said out of the corner of my mouth, 'I must get my watch fixed.'

It was an old one – one of Groucho's actually – but he smiled and relaxed a bit, so it did the job.

The administrator took us one floor up in a lift big enough to ferry a helicopter to the roof. Maybe some of their patients arrived that way.

'Mrs Asmoyah is in Primrose,' she said to Frank. I thought she was being sarky about my bouquet, but then I realised all the rooms were named after flowers. Primrose was second on the left after Violet if you hung a right after Tulip. I wondered if they had one called Hemlock for the really ill.

'We moved her there just before lunch when she came to.'

'Has a doctor seen her?' asked Frank anxiously.

'Of course,' said the Obergruppenfuhrer administrator in her 'What-do-you-think-we-are?' voice. 'Two in fact; the duty doctor and a consultant – a very distinguished one,

I might add.'

'You see, Frank,' I said, slapping him on the back. 'Nothing's too good for our Salome. I told them to spare no expense.'

The administrator smiled. I'd said the right thing, and she'd buttoned me as the one who signed the cheques. I was in there.

We discussed the administration of the hospital, especially the shift times of the nurses, to allow Frank a few minutes alone with Salome. I tell you, I'm always thinking of others. Then I asked the administrator, who was called Lucy (I was right about the Beatles), what the real form was on Sal's case.

'Nothing unusual really, although of course it's not usual to get yourself smashed up in a car accident in the first place. But for people who do suffer head injuries like Mrs Asmoyah, it's not uncommon for them to suddenly come round a week or even ten days later and be perfectly okay. There may be problems: damage to the eyesight, loss of sense of smell, perhaps amnesia. That's why we'll keep her in for a week or so, for tests, but our consultant is very pleased with her - and very optimistic. She's very lucky, having a caring employer like you.'

I had to agree. I was the soul of philanthropy as I entered the Primrose room. Strike that. Make it Primrose Suite.

There was a flat-screen TV and video

recorder on a two-tier trolley, both remote controlled, headphones for a radio and tape system, remote-controlled blinds and curtains and a small fridge with the words 'Personal Bar' printed on the door. So this was how the other half got sick. I could handle it.

'Angel!' croaked Salome from the bed, which seemed to have Frank draped across it like a spare duvet.

There was a lot of hand-clasping, cuddling and a few tears, some of them from Salome. Then she asked what had happened to Alec, because nobody had told her, and I just looked at a spot about a foot above her head and let Frank do the dirty work.

When Sal stopped sobbing, I asked her how much she remembered about the accident. It wasn't much.

'We'd done the Exhilarator course in the evening, but we hadn't found anything – except that Cawthorne doesn't like women much, and blacks not at all.'

Frank tensed, but I lifted a finger slightly to shut him up.

'We were staying in a hotel in Maidstone and we went back for a meal, then later, about tennish, we sneaked back to see if there was anything going down. Cawthorne seemed to be having a private party. There were a lot of cars at the farm but nobody around. They were all off in the woods somewhere.

'We got as close as we dared, and we could see torches and they were using... Alec called them thunderflashes...' I nodded to show I understood. 'And then we heard guns. Real guns. Alec said we'd better get out of there, so we did. I'm sure we weren't seen, but I was pretty scared.' Her brow creased in puzzlement. 'I remember getting in the car and driving through the village back to the main road but ... nothing else.'

She reached for Frank's arm and grabbed it with both her hands.

'Frank! I just can't remember anything else! I just don't recall the accident.'

'Good,' I said, patting her arm. 'Let's keep it that way.'

CHAPTER THIRTEEN

McInnes's office was a suite on the second floor of a four-storey block sandwiched between other late-'60s developments, all now owned by Japanese or Canadian banks for some reason. Most of them had bistros or wine bars on the ground floor or in the basement, but they came and went. Above them, business went on.

A big, black security guard practised his mean look on me through a plate glass door, but eventually released the electronic lock after I'd asked for McInnes through a squawk box. He pointed to a door at the end of a short corridor. I smiled at him, but he didn't look a better person for it.

There were three or four offices, all with doors open but lights off. I got the impression that McInnes had let the staff go early. His door simply had 'Chairman' embossed on it. I knocked and there was another electric buzz before the door clicked open. Another careful man.

His jacket hung on an old oak hat-stand, probably the only thing in the room not electronic or plastic, apart from the chunky gold cufflinks on his blue-striped shirt and a digital watch that looked as if it not only gave you the exchange rate for yen but ran the traffic lights in Tokyo as well. His desk was modern pine and no bigger than a baseball diamond. Most of it was occupied by a word processor and printer, leaving just enough room for two small televisions and a multi-purpose phone console. There were no personal knick-knacks or executive toys, but with that little lot, he didn't need them.

'Angel! Hello. Good man.' He wasn't looking at me, but at the VDU screen on the WP. 'Come and look at this.'

I sauntered round the desk to get a view of the screen. The only chair in the room was his swivel one, though there were two sofas near the window. Good psychology. Your visitors were either friends you could relax with or minions you made stand. I stood, but put my hands in my bomber jacket pockets just to show I was chill.

The screen showed a balance sheet for a company headed LTN, but it might as well have been in Chinese for the sense it made to me.

'Linton's,' said McInnes. 'You must have heard of them. Surely?'

I looked as if I was thinking. He wasn't fooled.

'Holiday camps, man. Linton's-by-the-Sea. Oh I Do Like to Linton by the Sea-side...'

'Does that thing play the organ as well?'

'Oh, come on...'

'Yes, okay. Linton's holiday camps. I've heard of them.' Then I added quickly: 'But I've never been to one.'

'Och, I have,' he said, laying on the Highland Mist accent. 'When I was a wee boy.'

'I know, you could have a week's holiday, ice-cream and fish 'n' chips every day and still have change from 25 pence.'

'It was called five shillings in those days, but I don't suppose you remember the old money.'

'I wouldn't own up to it if I did.'

He smiled.

'Sir Frederick Linton started his holiday

camps just after the war...'

'Well, there were plenty of guards looking for work.'

'There isn't one we haven't heard, Angel.'

'Sorry.'

'He was never as big as Butlin or Pontin, with far fewer sites, but they generated a good cashflow and he was able to move upmarket. Farmhouse holidays in Dorset, salmon fishing in Scotland, even grouse-shooting.'

'But?'

He looked at me.

'There has to be a but...' I said.

'You're right. The problem was Sir Frederick himself. He got his knighthood for services to the Countryside Commission, not for being a good businessman. He disliked credit, so any expansion was paid for by generated cash and consequently he got left behind by the operators who didn't mind borrowing. Sir Frederick also has a profound distrust of marketing and advertising, so – surprise, surprise – very few people ever heard of his expansion into holidays abroad.'

'He doesn't sound to be the Club 18-30 type.'

'He isn't. He still thinks there is a sedate lower middle class out there wanting communal family holidays. Over the past six years, he's bought eight derelict farmhouses in northern France and attempted to turn them into blocks of self-catering flats with pretty basic amenities. He's been taken for a ride by every French builder south of Dieppe. The units are not up to standard, late, and in the wrong place. Britanny Ferries showed what you could do if you marketed them right. Sir Frederick just bumbled along.'

'And now he's in trouble?'

'Going downhill, shall we say. Profits have been lousy for the last couple of years and he can no longer generate cash to reinvest in his property.'

'Can't he borrow?'

'He could, but he doesn't want to. He's 68 now and looking to retire. The French venture was meant to add value to the company so he could sell up and settle the proceeds on his three daughters.'

'What about the Linton holiday camps in this country? Surely they're worth a bomb nowadays?'

McInnes pushed his chair back from the screen. 'You'd think so, but Freddy's a funny old cove. I told you about the Countryside Commission. Virtually every site, every piece of land he owns, is tied up to the National Trust or is in a green belt or nature conservancy area. His major asset – his only asset – was his land, and he virtually gave it away. I wouldn't mind having a piece of it myself, but there's nothing you could do with it. There's no way it could be developed.'

'But that doesn't apply to the property in France, does it?'

He winked at me. 'You're catching on.'

McInnes gave me a quick lecture in company share structure, followed by a seminar on desk-top publishing. The last bit I found interesting; the bit about the company went in one ear and almost straight out of the other without a pit stop.

Roughly, though, it went something like this.

Linton Plc – the LTN abbreviation on his screen – had a thin spread of shares, about 42%, publicly owned, Sir Frederick and his family owning the rest. McInnes had identified five dealers who were market-makers in LTN and three major institutionals with an interest who were also clients of Prior, Keen, Baldwin.

'If we use PKB to leak the suggestion that I am considering going into a partnership with Sir Frederick to develop the French end of things – I'm known to have interests in France as it is – then an unscrupulous person would have a good go at buying up any stock on the market, maybe even approaching the family for some of their allocation.'

'And before the news got out, so the price wouldn't rise.'

'Naturally, and by taking out the market-makers all at once, you could guarantee that.'

'How much would the price rise – normally?'

McInnes swivelled to the WP keyboard and tapped away.

'Shares today closed at 113p each, but there hasn't been any trading for weeks. I'd guess that if a merger was announced they could go to 350p. If the land didn't have so many restrictions, a lot more than that.'

'But you'd double your money?' I said, wishing I had a cigarette.

'Yes, you'd expect to.'

'And you think because of the French connection, Cawthorne won't be able to resist it? Given his speculations over there near the Tunnel, could this be another branch of the same thing? What do you call it?'

'A fit. Yes, it could seem as if Linton's French properties would fit with Cawthorne's Yuppie commuter homes.'

'So – let me get this straight – we're leaking to Cawthorne the opportunity to at least double his money, possibly even get control of more land in France?'

'Mm-mm.' McInnes smiled and nodded.

I shook my head. 'Well, he'll certainly go for that,' I said.

'So would I,' said McInnes, 'if I could raise nearly five million on a credit line quickly enough.'

'You probably could.' He made the modesty gesture, palms up. 'Can Cawthorne?'

'I think so, but it'll stretch him badly. He'll have to put the Exhilarator and his French land up to do it.'

'But he could walk away with ten million.'

'If he's willing to take the risk.'

'Just how much of a risk is it?'

McInnes looked at his fingernails.

'A stupid one. If you know that the French government is about to announce plans for a nuclear reactor near the prime Linton site in east Normandy *and* you know that Sir Frederick Linton is going to declare himself bankrupt next week.'

If I'd had a hat on, I'd have taken it off.

'You devious bastard,' I said.

'Why, thank you, Roy.'

McInnes drafted himself a letter. Well, not actually a letter, more a press release. He headed it for his attention only, marked it 'Draft Announcement: For Approval' and dated it for the next day. The text outlined a merger between Linton Plc and Glen and Island Securities, which I presumed was one of McInnes's companies, to take effect within a week. The date of the announcement was for Monday at 11.00 am, and there was also a lot of stuff about share options and cash alternatives.

He put all this up on the WP himself and

then took a wedge of PKB circular paper out of a drawer and fed it into the printer. He tried one out, adjusted the margins and pressed a few buttons until a perfect copy came out. He put it in an A4 envelope without folding it and stuck a pre-printed address label on it.

'Get PKB to send this to me by messenger first thing tomorrow, and I'll guarantee Cawthorne will be buying Linton stock before the pubs open.' As he spoke, he ripped up the first version he'd printed off and dropped it in a waste bin. Then he fiddled with the WP keyboard again.

'Wiping clean?' I asked, tucking the envelope inside my jacket.

'Yes. I told you, I'm staying squeaky clean on this one. When that comes tomorrow, I'll burn it. PKB won't have any knowledge of it and Cawthorne could never admit where he got his copy from. I don't have any shares in Linton. No comebacks.'

I remembered what he'd said at Sorrel's place.

'Didn't you say it might cost you?'

'It has. A day of my time – how do you cost that? Plus it will cost me for the information on Linton and for keeping that info out of the City until Monday at least.'

'I won't ask how you got it.'

He levelled a finger at me, like a gun. 'Good.'

'But I'd like to know why.'

He sat down in the swivel chair again and did a couple of complete turns.

'Cawthorne had a thing going with Sorrel once – a few years back when he was starting out in the City. They met on some skiing trip and went at it like knives for about six months, then he dumped her for some Sloane Ranger with a quarter claim on some title nobody's ever heard of.'

There was bitterness there.

'And Sorrel got hurt,' I said knowingly.

'Oh no.' He shook his head. 'Sorrel couldn't give a monkey's. She shacked up with a heavy metal bass player two days later and forgot all about him.'

I bet she forgot where she lived, her name and other stuff too.

'So...?'

'So nobody – but nobody – treats my daughter as second class.'

'I see,' I said truthfully. I could relate. 'But I thought all decisions in the City were taken on a cold, rational, logical, profit-motivation basis.'

'They are,' said McInnes. 'Until you're rich enough to indulge yourself a bit.'

McInnes wouldn't join me for a pint in the Clanger, even though you could see it from his office. I went anyway, partly because it really does serve a decent pint of draught

Bass and partly because it has a relatively private pay-phone. I got a pound's worth of change from the barman and tried Lloyd Allen's number in Brixton. Amazingly, he was in.

'Lloyd, it's Angel.'

'My man. Did your scam go down?'

'Partly, but I need more help from our motorbike friend.'

'Lewis Luther is yours to command. For a fee, that is,' he added.

'Agreed. You might also tell him to scout around for a new job. He shouldn't have a problem. And I'm going to need some muscular help for about an hour on Friday.'

'What d'you mean, man? Anything heavy and you should talk to the Yardies, not me.'

I had no intention of talking to the Yardies full stop. Never would be too soon. Their homespun Jamaican blend of violence, thuggery, extortion and more violence for good measure made the Triads who now ran Chinatown look like graduate social workers.

'I want a few lads to cause a diversion, that's all. A bit of steaming, but innocent like. Definitely not World War III, okay?'

'In dat case, honey–' Lloyd laid it on – 'I can offer you the Dennison boys. Three for the price of four.'

'Sounds reasonable. Where can I reach them tomorrow afternoon?'

'Here, if that's where you want 'em, my man.'

'Good enough. Oh, and Lloyd...'

'Yes...'

'There's something else.'

'With you, my man, there usually is.'

I did one more thing before I soaked under the shower and slept the sleep of the truly shattered. I checked my personal war chest for cash and liquid assets and made sure my passport (well, one of them) was in order. You never know.

The first thing I did on the Thursday morning was get up. As stiff and bruised as I was after the Exhilarator, that was no mean feat. I vowed that I would get myself back into shape, and even thought about rejoining the Gym 'n' Tonic club again. They should have got over the incident in the ladies' jacuzzi by now.

I was nosing Armstrong through the City by 8.00, and even with stopping off to leave the film from my Olympus at a quick-photo booth, I was outside PKB by half past.

Patterson was emerging from his early morning conference by the time I'd blagged my way past Purvis. He didn't exactly welcome me with open arms. I couldn't think why.

'What do you want?'

'Cup of coffee and a minute of your time.'

He thought about this, but not for long.

'In here.' He nodded towards his office and led the way. I closed the door after me.

'I know you're bursting to ask, so I'll tell you now; Salome's vastly improved. There, I knew you'd feel better.'

'Is that it?'

I do hate it when people get overemotional.

'No. I want you to get me an Airborne bike to deliver something this morning.'

'What?'

'An envelope.'

He snorted at that.

'To whom?'

'You don't wanna know.'

'Then no bike.'

I took McInnes's envelope from my jacket and showed him the address label. His eyebrows shot up and he reached for it but I leaned back. I can do that quite well since Springsteen taught me.

'What's in there?' Tel licked his lips.

'A leak.'

'About what?'

'You don't want to know,' I said slowly. 'Watch my lips: you do not want to know.'

He narrowed his eyes.

'Did you bodge something together? You know bugger-all about how things happen.'

'Oh, I wouldn't say that, Tel. I know you

327

shouldn't wear Argyll socks with a dinner jacket, you should never tell an Irishman that Guinness is exactly the same over here, and you shouldn't listen to Leonard Cohen if you're anywhere near a razor.'

'I meant about the City,' he said nastily. 'You're clueless.'

'Oh yeah, I admit that, but he isn't.'

I pointed to Innes McInnes's name on the envelope.

'What's that got to do with it?'

'He wrote what's inside.'

'To himself?'

I nodded.

'Then I don't want to know.'

'Knew you'd see it my way, Tel,' I beamed.

Anna was on duty in the postroom, and she phoned for Airborne to collect the envelope. I had been a bit worried, because McInnes's office wasn't more than a brisk stroll from Gresham Street, but nobody in the City worried about biking stuff next door.

'It sounded as if Tel was giving you a rough time,' said Anna as she handed me coffee.

'Aw no. He's a pussycat,' I said. Then I thought about Springsteen and realised that was a stupid thing to say.

'He's about as threatening as a Chris de Burgh LP.'

That was better.

The rider wasn't Lewis Luther. I couldn't see him because of the riding gear and the helmet, but he was much shorter than Lewis. Perhaps it was the Lenny Emerson that Lewis had mentioned and that Lloyd had said had just come out of chokey. What the hell, I didn't want to meet him, I just wanted to be sure that he did the usual dishonest thing. It would be a real pain if this one turned out to be a legitimate messenger.

He wasn't. He pulled in near Liverpool Street station behind the red Transit and Sorley's hand came out of the back to do the business. The envelope, resealed, was delivered to McInnes's office no more than a minute or so later than you could have reasonably expected.

The scam was rolling. It was also more or less out of my hands now.

I collected my photographs on the way back from following the despatch rider. I'd asked for enlargements, and they'd obviously had two or three goes trying to get the quality better, but for me they did just fine.

A pleasant young lady with her hair ponytailed with a rubber band to keep it out of the machinery, apologised like mad and charged me half-price.

Back at Pretty Keen Bastards, I played around with a couple of prints on the Xerox machine until I had A4-size paper copies.

By that time, the grainy prints were even grainier, but one of the shots I'd taken inside the pillbox was still detailed enough, if you knew what it was.

I kept the photocopy and the negatives, but put the prints in an envelope for Patterson, then took Anna out to lunch and bent the Amex card some more.

It's all go in the City.

I called in to see Salome again in the afternoon and, I have to admit, was relieved to find she was asleep. Still, Lucy the administrator and I got on famously. I think she was flattered that I took such an interest in medical working conditions, such as how long the shifts were and when did they finish, whereas most men would just have tried to chat her up.

Before I drove down to Brixton to see Lloyd that evening, I rang McInnes at his office and told him things were moving.

'If you can get to a Topic screen tomorrow morning, you'll see if he's taken the bait,' he said.

'That quickly?'

'He won't be able to resist it. He just can't. And if he thinks he's stuffing me, so much the better. He'll go for a dawn raid before the market opens tomorrow.'

I thought he was winding me up.

'A what?'

'A dawn raid – that's what it's called. A Monday would be better, but he won't dare leave it that late, and from what I've heard about Linton's business, the sooner the better. There's one thing we should take into consideration.'

'Somebody else catching on and getting drawn into the con?'

'So you had thought about that?'

Yes. Just then.

'Is it likely?'

'Well, I think Sir Frederick Linton will jump in and stop things if he sees innocent money going after bad. You see, he's basically a very honest man.'

'I guessed that.'

He must be. He was the one going bust.

When it happened, it was with a whimper.

Nobody opened champagne or jumped off a skyscraper. No one dipped their Vick inhaler in neat coke, no one rushed out to order a Porsche. By City standards it was probably chicken feed. It made a few paragraphs in the papers but nobody yelled, 'Hold the financial page!'

I arrived at PKB before 8.00 on the Friday and, as I was wearing the suit, I walked straight in. I put on Fly's clear-glass specs and straightened my tie and became totally invisible.

Patterson said he hadn't time to mess

around with me, and I told him all I wanted to do was watch the market. Despite the suit, he didn't trust me with PKB equipment, so he called Howard Golding – the fax expert – to sit with me and press buttons.

'What are we looking for?' asked Howard, as we sat on swivel chairs near a terminal.

'Linton Plc. I want to see if there are any movements.'

He made a 'What the hell for?' sort of face but began to whistle up the details on the screen.

The dealing room was the busiest I'd seen it, and by quarter past 8.00 most of the guys were in shirtsleeves and the empty coffee cups were piling up.

'There's nothing much going on,' Howard told me. Then he yelled across the room. 'Hey, Sean, anything doing on Linton?'

I flapped at him to keep his voice down.

'Not a lot,' yelled back Sean. 'Somebody bought small yesterday. Price rose on spec to 119 but fell back to 116 at day-end. First movement for ages. I'd class it as moribund stock if you're asking.'

Sean yelled all this back without looking up from what he was doing.

Howard shrugged. Then he picked up a phone. 'Let's see if we can get one of the dealers. What are you after?'

'Just interested,' I said dismissively as he dialled.

'That's funny,' he said, puzzled. 'I can't get through.'

That was the start of it.

As soon as the Exchange opened proper, there was a public announcement that Pegasus Investments had acquired over five percent of the stock of Linton Plc and was still buying, though by then the price had gone up to 280p. By mid-morning, Howard estimated that nearly 15 percent of Linton shares had changed hands.

He had a furtive meeting with Tel-boy and I distinctly heard 'Somebody took out the market-makers in a dawn raid...'

Patterson looked worried for a second, then shut himself in his office.

What did cause a stir in the dealing room was the announcement at 11.00 by Sir Frederick Linton, or rather a financial PR company acting for him.

Basically, through the jargon, it said that because of untoward speculation in Linton shares, Sir Frederick had advanced the news (scheduled for Monday morning anyway) that he was seeking a suspension of his company listing on the Exchange prior to calling in the receivers.

'There is, as we say around here,' confided Howard, 'a distinct smell of burnt fingers in the air.'

I was whistling to myself – maybe 'Satin

Doll', but something jolly – as I sneaked out of the dealing room and took the lift down to meet the Dennison boys.

I had primed Anna to send for an Airborne messenger when I tipped her the wink (okay, so I hadn't mentioned that Patterson knew nothing about this one), and Lloyd had primed Lewis Luther to make sure he was the Airborne rider in the area.

That was the chancy bit, of course, as I hadn't been able to specify a time exactly.

The Dennison boys were in place, in the sandwich bar round the corner, pigging out on Danish pastries. I paid their bill for them, although Sel – but it could have been Mel – insisted on a tea to go. I told him not to spill it over Armstrong as they piled into the back.

I moved Armstrong to the front of the PKB building, and we had only a minute or so to wait before Lewis Luther pulled up, parked the Kawasaki and dismounted.

I called him over before he got to the entrance.

'There's nothing for you to collect, Lewis.'

He stopped in his tracks, then sauntered over to the passenger window I'd pulled down. I wouldn't need the Dennisons for Lewis, but it didn't hurt to let him see them.

'But I got the call...' he mumbled through his helmet.

'I know, Lewis, relax. Get on the radio and

fix a rendezvous. Here you are.'

I handed him an empty envelope on which I'd written McInnes's name and office address.

'Then what?' asked Lewis, though it came out as 'En ot?'

'Then tell us where it is and go home, put your feet up.'

Lewis sighed. He was probably wondering if there was time to get down the Jobcentre that afternoon, but he removed his helmet and activated his collar radio.

'Liverpool Street,' he said after getting the reply, 'just round the corner from Blomfield Street.'

I nodded. The same place as the other messenger checked in yesterday.

Lewis put a gauntlet on the window.

'Hang about,' he said, as he unclipped his radio. 'You'd better give this back to Sorley. Don't want anybody saying I tea-leafed the office equipment.'

I took it from him.

'Lloyd'll see you right, Lewis. Thanks.'

Mrs Luther would have been proud of him.

I briefed the Dennison boys as I drove. All I wanted was a bit of steaming in the back of Sorley's van: lots of bodies, noise and confusion. I did *not* want Sorley putting in hospital.

'But I thought somebody needed a good seeing-to,' moaned Del, or maybe Sel.

'Not today, lads. We just get in there, out of sight of Joe Public and Mr Plod, and you lot sit on the guy until I've done my bit of business.'

By the time they'd finished grumbling and rapping among themselves, we were turning into Liverpool Street.

The red Transit was parked near a bus stop opposite the Railway Tavern, on the Broadgate side of the street. They were still building the Broadgate development, so there were cranes and trucks around and it wasn't the sort of place you'd get a ticket or get clamped for dodgy parking.

I nosed Armstrong to within a yard of the back of the van, and the Dennison boys were out on the street before I'd killed the engine.

Poor Sorley never knew what hit him. One of the boys knocked on the van door and as it opened, the other two piled in. By the time I got there, Del and Sel (I think) had him pinned against the shelves where he stacked spare envelopes. I climbed in and Mel (possibly) closed the door, staying outside to keep guard.

'Just what...' Sorley began to bluster.

He was wearing khaki slacks and desert boots and an army-style pullover with patches everywhere. The Dennisons had an arm each, freezing him in the crucifix position.

'Is your fax on?' I asked, reasonably enough.

'What? Now look here...'

I ignored him and examined the fax. A red light glowed in one corner, so I assumed it was ready to go. There was a digital dial pad and then buttons marked 'SEND' and 'RECALL' and 'AUTO.' I guessed that it was automatically programmed to go through to Pegasus Farm. But, better be sure.

'Do I just press "SEND" to get through to Cawthorne?' I asked him, though I didn't look at him. We all had to bend our heads because of the van roof, and you can't be threatening from a crouched position. Well, I couldn't. The Dennisons could.

'Answer the man!' shouted one of them, and then the other one butted him on the upper arm, on the muscles below the shoulder.

He yelped at that. So would I.

'What are you doing? Who...'

Young Sel made ready for another head-butt, and Sorley saw the better part of valour, though his arm was probably quite numb by now and the second wouldn't have hurt so much.

'It's "AUTO" – the "AUTO" button. That's all you need do.'

'Thank you.'

I opened the A4 envelope I'd brought with me and slid out the Xerox of the photo I'd taken of Cawthorne's pillbox headquarters. I slid it into the fax's feed tray and pressed 'AUTO.' It hummed, then whirred, then beeped and clicked, and then the sheet began to move through.

It took only a few seconds, and I left the Xerox in the out tray of the machine, placing Lewis's radio on it.

'Just serving notice, Mr Sorley.' I looked at him over the top of my fake specs. 'You're going out of business. Now just sit down on the floor and be quiet and we'll be on our way. Get his keys.'

I'm almost positive it was Sel who dug his keys out of his trouser pocket, none too gently, then twisted the arm he was holding up Sorley's back to force him to the floor of the van.

I knocked on the back window, and Mel let us out; me first, then his brothers. Sel gave me the keys, and I locked Sorley in there without saying anything else. He had the look of a man trying to remember where he'd seen someone before. And that always makes me nervous.

I threw the keys inside the front of the van, through the driver's window. Let him work that one out.

He could look on it as an initiative test.

CHAPTER FOURTEEN

Friday night. Party night.

Frank was hospital visiting, Werewolf was across the sea in Ireland, Sorrel wasn't answering the phone (well, you never know till you try) and I couldn't think of anyone I particularly wanted to get drunk with, so I went out on the town with Lloyd and the lads.

The Dennison boys came with us and so did Beeby. One of the brothers – I forget which – said he wanted to be a Moslem when he grew up, so he'd given up booze, which made him the driver for the night. Lloyd may walk more on the narrow than the straight but he wasn't daft enough to go pub crawling in a pink '64 Zephyr without a sober pilot.

We started off in a pub in Barking. It had an upstairs room where a black trio were jamming on two alto saxes and a portable electric organ. Well, I thought they were jamming, until one of them stopped playing and said their next composition was called 'Seabass' and would be played in 13/11 time. At that point I lost interest and Lloyd gave up any thought of signing the band for a record contract.

After Beeby had whispered in Lloyd's ear for a good five minutes, we moved on. She was wearing a T-shirt with a yellow Smiley face over each nipple, so it didn't need a genius to work out our next port of call.

It was an old warehouse near the Ripple Road railway sidings in Dagenham. It had been swept out, but that was about all you could say for it. A posh-voiced young lady wearing a tweed jacket (the real Harris is back in) was about to charge us a fiver each for entry until she recognised Lloyd and waved us through. Inside, half a dozen dry ice machines were working overtime and the disco was belting out house music at around 150 beats per minute.

We didn't stay long; just long enough for Beeby to score some ecstasy and flap her arms around for a while – there's no way your whole body can keep up with that rhythm. Lloyd and I declined to buy anything from the resident pusher, agreeing that we both thought drugs very retro these days. Maybe we were getting old. I'd certainly never seen as much stuff openly flogged since I was a student.

There was nothing to drink – there never is at acid house parties – so around midnight-thirty we split, although everybody assured us things hadn't warmed up yet.

They were well-hard at the party we gatecrashed in West Ham. A bouncer asked Lloyd if he'd brought a bottle. Lloyd nodded to one of the Dennison boys and they produced two cases of Red Stripe lager from the boot of the Zephyr. As long as you liked Mackeson or dark Jamaican rum, there was plenty of other refreshment, and the music was revival reggae, some early Marley and a lot of Desmond Dekker. And, of course, there was the holy ganja weed, which we indulged in just to show we weren't religiously bigoted.

It felt good to relax, with no more cares, no more executive stress. No more job at Prior, Keen, Baldwin. Still, why worry?

We piled into the Zephyr around 4.00 am. Beeby was just about coming down from her ecstasy round trip to Jupiter, one of the Dennison boys was missing and one was asleep, and Lloyd and I were deciding which eight records we'd take to a desert island. I was on number 73, but Lloyd was having real trouble making up his mind. They dropped me off at Stuart Street just as dawn was getting a parking ticket somewhere over the Thames Barrier, and there was a lot of hooting of horns and shouted merry quips and I think it was Chaka Khan on the in-car system, which rattled the windows and completed the job of annoying the neighbours.

To avoid their wrath, I got inside quickly

and tiptoed up the stairs to the flat. Springsteen was lying in the bed, having burrowed under the duvet, and didn't move when I entered, but sighed deeply in a sarcastic manner.

The dirty pawprints he'd left across the pillow weren't even dry, though, so he hadn't been in long himself. But like I said, Friday night is party night.

Saturday was mostly devoted to sleep, but I surfaced in the afternoon long enough to do some shopping and laundry.

Frank zipped in and out running errands between visits to Salome, twice appearing with huge bunches of flowers. He called in once to ask how to use the microwave, so I went upstairs and showed him and remarked what a tip he'd left the flat in. He shrugged his broad shoulders and looked confused, so I said I'd clean it up for him. As soon as he'd gone out again, I went downstairs and told Lisabeth he needed help. She said she wasn't a skivvy, and I said I knew that, but Frank was only a man after all, and she nodded wisely and sent Fenella upstairs with an armful of dusters.

Ruth rang about 5.00 and said she was on late shift again, but did I fancy supper at the Nurses' Home before she went on duty? Are frogs waterproof? I said I'd be there at 8.00. Shortly after, Fly rang to remind me to return the glasses frames I'd borrowed, and would she see me at the Ward Bond Retrospective? I promised I'd try and make it, but I'd be late.

As I opened a tin of Whiskas for Springsteen before I went out, I reflected that being unemployed again wasn't so bad now life was getting back into its old routine.

'This working for a living is very over-rated,' I said to Springsteen, and he seemed to agree.

I remembered that I'd promised to visit Salome on Sunday, so I set the alarm for 10.00. Then I remembered that Werewolf was coming to stay early, so I reset it for 8.30. I'd been woken up by Werewolf before, and it's not a pretty sight.

That was why I was bringing in the milk from the front doorstep – something I usually do only when coming home – and why it was me that Cawthorne picked on.

God knows where he'd been hiding. Probably he'd crouched down behind one of the parked cars, maybe even Armstrong. Fine watchdog he turned out to be. I mean, he could have honked, couldn't he?

I was bending over to pick up the milk bottles – Gold Top for me, semi-skimmed for Frank and also Lisabeth and Fenella, none for Mr Goodson in the ground-floor flat as he never appeared at weekends – when I heard his footfall on the pavement.

'Is this...?' he said, and I made the mistake of looking up.

In the time it took for me to straighten up, I realised who it was. Unfortunately he recognised me too, and came up the steps at me like the Miami Dolphins defence.

I wasted a few vital seconds just taking him in visually. Maybe I could have got the door shut in time if I hadn't paused to wonder why he was wearing a dinner jacket, black trousers with a satin stripe and a white, frilly shirt with the bow tie undone and hanging loose. He also had a raincoat wrapped over his right arm, like policemen do when they demonstrate how their dogs bring down runaways.

By the time it clicked with the few brain cells I have left that he was intent on doing somebody serious damage and I was in his flight path, it was too late to do anything sensible except hang on to the milk bottles.

He cannoned into the door with his shoulder and slammed the rolled-up raincoat into my stomach. I remember thinking he must have had some lead piping in there from the way the breath suddenly left my body, then I was rolling backwards across the hallway, banging the back of my head on the skirting-board underneath the wall-mounted phone, which gave a ting in sympathy.

Cawthorne swayed on his feet, giving a passable impression of a drunken bull in an arena, then he kicked the front door shut and leaned over me, pointing his overcoat at my head.

'Where is she?' he hissed.

'Hey...'

I was looking at the milk bottles, all three still intact, and wanting him to notice how clever I'd been doing a backward roll and bouncing off the wall without breaking them. He didn't seem too interested, just insistent about waving his coat at me.

Then my head cleared and I could see the gun barrel protruding from the coat.

'Where is the black bitch?'

He shook off the coat and leaned closer. I could see the gun clearly now. It had a barrel at least nine inches long with a square fixed sight at the end. It didn't look like a big calibre gun, but I wasn't going to ask how big. I was on the business end, and that was what mattered.

Cawthorne pushed the gun at my face, scraping my right cheek with the sight. On the cold metal breech I could read the engraved words: .22 Rim Fire Long. It didn't make me feel any better.

'Last time, whatever your name is. Where's that spade cow?'

He stopped stroking me with the gun then, and a puzzled look came over his face.

'I know where I've seen you before. The party ... Watling Street last week. You were with her then ... before...'

'Before you tried to kill her with the Shogun,' I said, perfectly reasonably.

'You're the bastard who sent those pictures...'

He pushed his face closer to mine, and I noticed there were smears of white powder in the indentation in his mouth just below the nose. I knew that it was odds on he hadn't spilt talcum powder, and I realised I ought to be more frightened than I was.

Somehow, I just couldn't handle the possibility that I might get shot and end up seriously dead here on the floor of my home on a Sunday morning holding three pints of milk. I decided to treat it as a distinct possibility.

'Salome's not here,' I said, finding it suddenly difficult to swallow.

'I know *that*. Where is she?'

He pressed the long gun barrel to my forehead. He was serious. It was time to come clean.

'Jamaica,' I said, looking through his legs and up the stairs, hoping that Frank didn't decide to come out for his morning jog.

'Jamaica?' He said it distantly, disappointed.

'Gone to convalesce with her mum.'

I hoped Frank stayed indoors, but why

didn't Lisabeth come looking for her milk? She could handle him. A quick drug-crazed gunman before breakfast was right up her street.

'How did she fix the Linton scam, then?' The gun jammed harder, hurting.

'She didn't.'

Through his legs I could see Springsteen at the top of the stairs. Go on, my son, leap on his back, sink the claws in, get his veins in your teeth...

Springsteen sat down, gave his private parts (private – there was a laugh; ask any female cat in the neighbourhood) a lick and then trotted off back into the flat. Thanks, pal.

I tried to play it cool. Ignoring the gun, I began to stand the milk bottles on the floor in a line. One of them I could use to belt him with if he got a bit closer, but I couldn't do anything holding three.

He didn't seem to know what to do next, so I kept talking.

'I thought that one up. I knew you couldn't resist it.'

'You? You're nobody. You don't have that sort of pull.'

The gun withdrew a millimetre.

'I had help, sure. A friend of mine has good information, and that's what it's all about, isn't it? You did me a favour, you know. My friend and I made a few grand on

Friday. We'd just bought some Linton shares ourselves.'

He let this sink in, then he straightened up and his left hand dived into the pocket of his dinner jacket. He brought it out with the thumb and forefinger clenched together and put it to his nostrils, snorting loudly. White dust fell on his lapels. If he sneezed, I was going to have a go. He didn't. He just sniffed and shook his head slightly.

He took a couple of deep breaths, keeping the gun rock-steady on me. I'd never seen one like it before; it seemed to be all barrel and nothing else.

'A few grand, eh?' he said, nodding as if agreeing. 'You punk. You're so small-time it's not true. You have no concept of what I've lost.'

He was shaking his head the other way now, in disbelief.

'And it started with that black bitch, that...'

There was no way I'd distract him from that train of thought, but Springsteen could.

I'd left the flat door open when I'd gone to get the milk, so when Springsteen did his usual trick of climbing over the sink to get out the kitchen window, we could hear him as he sent a pile of dirty crockery crashing over. (Well, who do you know who does the washing-up on Saturday night?)

Cawthorne looked around but was back

on to me before I could move. He didn't know where the sound had come from; he just assumed it was someone with two legs. If he'd shot me then, I could have died knowing it was Springsteen's fault.

'Get up,' he said.

I did so willingly. It was better than being shot.

He grabbed me by the shoulder. I was wearing a Tunnel of Love Tour T-shirt and jeans and some old trainers I slopped around the flat in. He bunched up some of the T-shirt in his left hand and stuck the gun in my ribs.

'You're coming with me. Open the door.'

I did as I was told.

We walked down the steps together and then crossed Stuart Street to where he'd parked his red Porsche. He gave me the keys and told me to get in the driver's side, then he hopped round the front, pointing the gun at me all the time.

An oik in T-shirt and faded 501s and a man in a dinner suit with a gun, getting into a Porsche and driving off at nine o'clock on a Sunday morning. Nobody gave us a second look, nobody phoned the cops, nobody even twitched a net curtain.

I suppose that's why the rates are so high in Hackney.

He told me to drive and jammed the long-barrelled gun into my left side so that I'd have matching bruises on both kidneys. He snapped out directions and emphasised them by jabbing a forefinger into the windscreen. When he wasn't doing that, his left hand was dipping into his jacket pocket and coming out with pinches of white powder, which he sniffed avidly, though messily, a fair few quid's worth going down his lapels.

As if the drive wasn't nightmare enough, Cawthorne turned on the radio. Loud. It was the *Morning Service* on Radio 4, broadcast live from some extremist wing of the Scots Presbyterians demanding to know if I'd made my peace with Ghawd. In between hymns, it sounded as if the congregation was passing around a rattlesnake in a bag, but that was probably my imagination running riot. Still, if you've gotta get religion, I prefer the hellfire no-doubt-about-it variety to the guitar-strumming all-touch-hands sugariness.

Once south of the river, it was clear we were heading for Kent. I'd more or less guessed that from the off, when I'd managed to string a coherent thought together.

Cawthorne had not fastened his seat-belt and I hadn't tried to do up mine, partly because I'm out of the habit driving a taxi where you don't have to, and partly because I would have had to ask Cawthorne to withdraw the gun barrel. On any other day, knowing my luck, the Law would have had me pulled within half a mile for not buckling up. And weren't they supposed to have a down on red Porsches anyway? Where were they when you needed them?

I even kept the speed up in the hope of getting a ticket.

No such luck. Kids doing 31 miles per hour on a skateboard were probably being loaded into Black Marias somewhere in the city, but not down Sidcup way. I was doing 90 as we hit the motorway and I put my faith in the Kent County Constabulary. Maybe they were on church parade. They sure as hell weren't on the M20.

'Turn off. Up here.'

'I know,' I said.

Cawthorne hadn't said much during the trip. Well, not much that made sense. Now something clicked inside the bit of his brain still working on demist.

'You were snooping for the black bitch the other day. Did she put you up to it?'

'Nobody put me up to anything, Cawthorne. I found out how you worked your little scam and I set you up. Look on it as private enterprise.'

I felt oddly calm. The guy's hatred seemed to be reserved for Salome – he said 'spade bitch' to himself a million times – and I was a poor substitute. But then I was the one with the gun in my side.

'Why? What's in it for you? You're nothing in the city.'

I took umbrage at that, then I realised he meant the City as in financial. In the real city, I reckoned I had more street cred than wheel clamps.

'I told you, I made a few bob buying Linton shares that you then bought off me.'

'Chicken feed. Peanuts. Small fucking change.'

'Maybe,' I said cautiously.

'So why take the risk? Eh?' Jab, jab.

I thought about saying 'What risk?' but that might have destabilised him. Keep it conversational. After all, he wasn't going to shoot me while I was driving his car, was he? Did he know how much an upholstery valet on a Porsche cost?

'You took all the risks, Cawthorne. Especially trying to get rid of Salome and Alec Reynolds. Why did you do that?'

My ribs told me that was a mistake. He jabbed so hard this time, the Porsche weaved across two lanes. Fortunately there was no traffic to speak of.

'So that's it,' he said more to himself. 'You're sniffing after that black whore. You like a bit of chocolate, do you? Do you?'

He went on in that vein, getting cruder and more excitable, until the sign for the Wrotham turn-off. I suppose I could have spun the Porsche or driven into a field and risked it, but I didn't. I just followed his instructions until we were going up Blackberry Hill and then turning left on the unmade track and coming out at Pegasus Farm and the Exhilarator.

And I knew – I think I had all the time – what he had in mind for me. It was no consolation that I was there because I'd gone for the milk that morning. He'd been after Salome in his coke-zapped imagination.

Still, if I was here, Salome was safe. It was going to be a far, far better thing, and all that.

Heroes – aren't you sick of 'em?

He made me park the Porsche in the courtyard and give him the keys. The main gates were shut and chained and the farmhouse and changing-rooms deserted and locked. It looked like the creditors were in already.

Cawthorne withdrew the gun an inch and looked at his watch, then showed it to me.

'I'm leaving here in exactly 55 minutes. I'll be in France by lunchtime.' Via Dover, most like. 'And I'm not coming back.'

He dipped his hand into his pocket and fed himself another snort. 'So I'm treating myself to one last game here before I go.'

He waved the gun around, indicating towards the Paddock and the Exhilarator course.

'What–? A paint gun against that thing?'

He shook his head. 'You don't even get a paint gun. All you get is two minutes' start.'

There were a hundred things I wanted to say – pleading, threatening, joking to defuse the situation – but a look in his eyes told me there was no point.

I got out of the Porsche and started running.

I was banking partly on the fact that he would be operating below par. It was obvious from his clothes and the stubble on his face that he'd been up all night, and a fair chunk of the Colombian economy had gone up his nose since then.

I worked out that if I could get to the wood, I could cut across to the hop field and hide in there. With my luck, they would have harvested it yesterday. No, they don't pick hops until the first week in September. How do I know this stuff? Why did I think of it then?

I'd reached the edge of the courtyard when a bullet smacked off the cobblestones about six inches from me.

I wasn't going to get my two minutes.

I stopped dead and slowly turned around.

Cawthorne was sitting on the bonnet of the Porsche, pointing the gun at me. I'd managed about 40 yards.

'You said two minutes,' I shouted.

'Just getting my eye in!' he yelled back,

quite friendly all of a sudden.

I took a pace towards him without really knowing what I was doing, and his reaction surprised me. He stood up and began to back away, fumbling in his jacket pocket. But this time, the right one. Then he stopped and worked the action of the gun. I saw a cartridge case eject and even heard it ting on the cobbles, then he was feeding another in and working the breech. Confident again, he levelled it at me.

'Clock's ticking.'

I ran to my left, towards the corner of the farm building, and dropped from his line of sight. That meant the wood was that bit further away for me, but it might delay him for a minute just checking to see if I'd tried to hide in the farmhouse. If he was rational, that is, and *not* in the process of rapidly leaving his skull.

I didn't stop running, just veered left again and into the Paddock.

If I'd realised early that the long-barrelled gun was a single shot target pistol, I'd have had a go at him in the car or on the street back in Hackney, I told myself. Made him fire one and then got away or even disarmed him. Of course I would. I almost convinced myself. In a fair fight, he wouldn't stand a chance. Well, not if he took about an ounce more coke and I could have first go from behind with half a brick.

If he didn't have a gun – or if *I* had one

I damn near twisted my ankle veering right and heading away from the wood towards the pillbox.

I should have known as soon as I saw the iron door hanging open.

Cawthorne had probably spent the night there. He'd been covering his tracks but at some point had realised that he couldn't fit the personal computer and the fax machine and stuff in an overnight bag, so he'd gone bananas and lashed out.

Everything that could have been smashed or just satisfyingly dented, had been. The Amstrad's VDU had an empty bottle of vodka through it. The fax machine was upside down in a corner, its plastic cover shattered into slivers like broken glass. There were a couple of other bottles rolling around under an upturned chair, an empty Tequila bottle and a half-full Scotch. From the smell, most of the contents had gone on the floor rather than into Cawthorne. There was also a strong smell of the copying fluid the fax used.

The metal trunk I'd come for lay open. Whatever Cawthorne had had in his private armoury had gone now, probably to the bottom of the farm pond if he had any sense. Since the last police armistice for unregistered guns, the penalties for being nicked were seriously heavy.

It wasn't quite empty. Rattling around on the bottom were some cardboard tubes that looked like sticks of dynamite but were probably thunderflashes and a couple of boxes of loose ammunition. Maybe he'd just forgotten them. I suspected that he'd come here in the night – the internal light was still on – and started to remove any traces of his Airborne operation. Then he'd thrown a wobbler, decided it was all Salome's fault and gone looking for her. And found me.

I stuffed one of the thunderflash tubes into the back of my jeans. If all else failed, I could wave it at him, but there was nothing else there for me.

I crouched as I went through the door, and pushed it so that it almost closed behind me, then went down on all fours to sneak around the back.

'I know where you're hiding...'

Then a bullet spanged off the concrete and convinced me that I'd better start being scared stiff.

I felt safer behind the pillbox, because it offered great armfuls of lovely, thick concrete to hug.

I levered myself up cautiously and peeped into one of the gun slits. Through the box itself and the slits in the opposite wall, I could see Cawthorne reloading his pistol and walking towards me. He was no more than 20 yards away.

'Not much of a game, Maclean,' he was saying loudly. He must have got that name from the Exhilarator booking. I wasn't going to correct him. I wasn't going to say anything.

'I bet myself you'd last at least a quarter of an hour in the woods. I didn't think you'd trap yourself like this.'

It dawned on me that he thought I was inside. It was the only thing I had going for me.

I risked another look and almost died on my feet. Cawthorne was standing, feet apart, aiming right at me, like between the eyes. I ducked as he fired and cringed as the sound of a dozen trapped hornets buzzed what seemed like an inch from my head.

'You'd better come out. It'll be quicker in the long run,' shouted Cawthorne, walking closer, reloading again.

There was another shot, and more hornets.

He was firing into the slits of the pillbox, and the ricochets were bouncing off the walls inside. I wondered what the odds were of a bullet going in one slit and coming out the slit on the other side where yours truly was.

I looked behind me. The fence and the hop field looked too far away. He would see me if I broke that way. The wood was even further, and a run there would put me on a diagonal line of fire for him. I'd have more chance in a shooting gallery. The only thing to do was keep the pillbox between us. He was moving to his right, coming round to the door. He couldn't fire directly in there, because I'd almost closed it. He knew there weren't any weapons inside, so eventually he must get bored with pumping bullets in and have a look. As he got closer, though, my view of him would get less and less.

I risked another look and saw him moving out of my view through one of the slits. He was quite close now. So close, I could hear the snap of the breech as he worked the action of the gun.

I edged my way anticlockwise, away from the door end, hugging the rough concrete until spots of blood appeared on the palms of my hands, checking the slits as I went.

There was no sign of him, which I took to mean he was in line with the door. I hoped it did. I was running out of concrete to hug. If I went much further, I'd be heading back round towards him. But there was nowhere else to go.

Except up.

I stood up between two slits and put my hands on the roof of the box. At that edge, it wasn't much taller than I was, and I estimated I was opposite the entrance. I held my breath.

Cawthorne wasn't saying anything. Maybe he was too busy talking to the voices in his head. Then I heard him sniff quite distinctly. Then silence. In the distance, I could hear church bells and the drone of a car engine.

And then what I'd been waiting for; the metallic creak of the door being opened.

I risked a look through the slit to my right and, sure enough, the box began to fill with light. That convinced me. I scrabbled and heaved myself up onto the roof and rolled and scrabbled across the concrete.

I didn't know if he could hear me through the eight-inch thick roof. I never gave it a thought. Suddenly I was at the far edge and looking over.

The left shoulder of Cawthorne's dinner jacket was just below me. The gun, his head and one foot at least were inside the box. That would have to do.

I put both hands on the top of the door frame, which he'd opened to an angle of 45 degrees, and pulled as hard as I could.

The door hit him and propelled him inside. From the noise of crashing and breaking, right into what was left of the fax machine. There was a magnified boom as the gun went off, and a spang as the ricochet hit the door. I felt it vibrate as I scrabbled and snapped fingernails to get the bolt shut.

As it clicked home, I rolled on my back

and looked at the sky and exhaled. Then I looked at my hands, scratched and pitted with bits of concrete, and wondered if I'd be able to play the violin now. It would be a miracle, as I couldn't before.

There was no sound from below me in the box, but I could hear something else: an engine. A diesel engine.

I turned my head, and round the corner of the farmyard I saw Armstrong bouncing across the Paddock to the rescue.

Late as usual.

I was on my feet and waving both arms in the air when Cawthorne opened fire.

I didn't see which slit the shot had come from, nor whether it hit Armstrong or not. I couldn't tell even if Werewolf had noticed he was being shot at.

It had to be Werewolf. No-one else would have such a blind disregard for Armstrong's suspension.

I scuttled to the edge of the box and saw the gun barrel emerge. I think I yelled in frustration and swung a kick, almost over-balancing and falling right under his gun.

It put him off, though. I was sure that shot went wild. Then I was going wild, leaping and yelling a warning to Werewolf that I knew he wouldn't hear over the engine noise.

He slewed Armstrong to a halt about 30 yards away, killed the engine and got out.

'Get down!' I yelled.

'What the fuck is...?' he shouted back. Then Cawthorne shot him.

I saw Werewolf clutch his right leg and go down, but after that I think all I saw was red mist.

'I'm up here, you bastard!' I yelled down.

'Don't worry, you'll get yours, shitface. You're dead. Dead!'

The gun barrel reappeared, pointing upwards this time, and he fired, but the angle was far too steep and the bullet zipped away harmlessly. I wondered how much ammo he had left, or how much coke.

Then I remembered the thunderflash stuffed in the back of my jeans, except it wasn't a thunderflash, it was a smoke stick. Well, that's what it said it was, and just above where it said 'Made in Korea' was printed 'Twist top and pull.'

I did just that, and pungent orange smoke began to pour out. I knelt down and, holding my breath, leaned over the edge of the box and stuffed the thing through the nearest slit.

Cawthorne shouted 'You fucker' and burst out coughing. He fired once more, wildly, anywhere. Then I was off the roof and running towards Armstrong.

Werewolf had rolled right underneath and had propped himself up against the front wheel arch so he had the engine between himself and the pillbox. I scrambled round the bonnet and threw myself down beside him.

'This is definitely not in the fucking rules, man,' he said.

'How bad is it?' I asked, not really wanting to look.

He held his leg with both hands, just above the knee.

'Flesh wound,' he said.

'You're supposed to say "It's nothing, just a flesh wound," like they do in the movies.'

'It hurts like buggery, but they don't say that either. It went straight through. I heard it go into the door.'

He saw my expression change.

'Oh, that's nice. Best mate turns up and gets shot and you don't turn a hair. The pigging cab gets scratched and...'

'Oh, shut up, you great nance. Let's get out of here.'

'What was it you threw in there?'

'A smoke flare.'

'I've got something better in my bag, if you can get it.'

He rolled over so he could look under the chassis.

'We're gonna need it,' he said.

I got down and looked too. Cawthorne had thrown the smoke stick out of the box, but not more than a few feet. It was still spewing out orange clouds, which drifted to and fro around the pillbox.

The gun appeared at the end of Cawthorne's arm and he fired. I ducked instinctively, but the shot was aimed higher than ground level, and the result was a tinkling crack.

'He just shot your wing mirror,' said Werewolf, 'He's going to take it out on Armstrong if he can't get us.'

'Maclean!' shouted Cawthorne, then he coughed again. 'It's time we did a deal.'

I looked at Werewolf and he looked at me. We must have taken too long about it, as Cawthorne fired again, and the tinkle this time said he'd hit a headlight.

'Okay, okay. What did you have in mind?'

I peeked under Armstrong. The orange smoke was wafting away from the pillbox if anything. I could see the gun quite clearly. Which meant he could see us.

'If you try and drive that thing,' he bawled, 'I'll shoot your eyes out. You know I can.'

Werewolf shuffled closer and whispered, 'Keep talking, but get my bag out.' He motioned to the passenger door and I squirmed over him and grabbed the handle.

'So we wait here until somebody comes, Cawthorne. You got time, haven't you?'

I had the door open. There was a large Aer Lingus flight bag on the floor where a passenger seat would go in a normal car.

'Has your friend?' Cawthorne replied. 'This place is closed up. Nobody will come here and nobody will say anything about the noise or the smoke. They're used to it round here. Can your friend wait it out? Just how bad is he hurt? I know I hit him.'

I had the bag out and the door closed now. 'What did you have in mind?'

I slid the bag towards Werewolf and he unzipped it. Some socks, a paperback and a couple of packets of Sweet Afton spilled out.

'I need to get out of here,' shouted Cawthorne.

'He does,' I told Werewolf. 'He has a ferry to catch.'

'So what?' I shouted.

Werewolf reached into the bag until he found what he was after. It was a clear glass bottle with a plastic stopper and a hand-printed label proclaiming 'Kerry Mist.' He handed it to me and went back to holding his leg. His green cords were well soaked by now and his face pale.

'So you let me out of here and you go your way, I go mine. Simple as that,' came Cawthorne's offer.

'Poteen,' whispered Werewolf. 'Hundred and twenty proof if it's a day.'

'It's a bit early, even for me,' I whispered.

Werewolf sort of snarled. 'Tell him to throw the gun out and give us that pack of Kleenex.'

'Lose the gun,' I yelled, handing Werewolf a pack of paper tissues from his bag. 'Then we'll work something out.'

He fired again and something metallic bounced on to Armstrong's bonnet. The radio aerial.

Werewolf took a handful of tissues and scrunched them into a wad. He pulled the plastic stopper from the bottle with his teeth and splashed the clear liquid over the tissues, then crammed them into the neck of the bottle.

'A de Valera cocktail,' he said. 'Light the blue touch paper and run like stink.'

He reached into his jacket and fumbled out a disposable plastic lighter.

'Get up close and bung it through a slit, then hit the ground.' He winced again at the pain in his leg. 'Don't forget to light it.'

'All right, Cawthorne,' I screamed. 'That's enough. I'm coming out.'

'Just what are you doing here anyway?' I asked Werewolf, taking the bottle from him and pushing it down my T-shirt, cold against my chest.

'I was coming down Stuart Street as you drove off. I told you I was getting the early flight. I was out of Thiefrow by half past eight and I got a lift almost to the door.' He tried to smile. 'A young lady I met on the plane. You damn near ran me down in that cherry red Porsche. I knew whose it was straight away, and I guessed this was where you'd end up. Thought you might need help. He's not going to let it go, you know. It's him or us.'

Or Salome. If not now, then later.

'I know. How did you get Armstrong going?'

'The spare key you keep on that magnetic pad behind the nearside back wheel.'

'How long have you known about that?'

'Since the week you soldered it on. Why?' He looked genuinely puzzled.

'Oh, nothing.'

I stood up and moved to the rear of Armstrong.

'Don't shoot, Cawthorne!' I bawled. 'I'm coming to open the door.'

Werewolf tugged at my trouser leg. He was offering me the lighter.

As I took it he said: 'Massive retaliation. That's the plan. 'Okay?'

'Yeah,' I said.

Rule of Life No 59: Get your retaliation in first.

CHAPTER FIFTEEN

I set off at a cracking pace. Once out from behind Armstrong, there was no way I was hanging around. I couldn't run, because I had the bottle of poteen balanced against my stomach like a bizarre pregnancy, but hopefully invisible from the front under the T-shirt. I was also convinced I was going to drop the lighter, which was slippery with sweat in my hand.

I headed straight for the pillbox door, knowing the closer I got, the worse became Cawthorne's angle of fire. Over the last few feet, I could see his dinner-jacketed arm and the gun hanging out of the concrete slit like a broken wing. It was a surrealist painter's dream, but my nightmare.

The gun weaved figure eights in the air.

'Just unbolt the door... That's all... We can do a deal...'

Cawthorne's voice was almost unrecognisable. He was flying now, but I wasn't trusting to it affecting his aim. And I wasn't trusting him at all.

I virtually jumped the last yard to the door and put my back to it. There were gun slits to my left and right at eye level, but because of the angles in the walls of the box, I was pretty sure I was in a blind spot. I took the bottle out of my shirt and put it on the concrete square at my feet, but I held on to the lighter.

There was a metallic clang behind my left ear. Cawthorne was beating on the inside of the door with something.

'Open the fucking door... Let me out!' He was shrieking now.

The orange flare had more or less petered out by now, or maybe the wind had changed. There was nothing to stop Cawthorne getting a clear shot at Armstrong at all. I could wait him out, I thought, until a few more snorts of electric snuff made sure he couldn't hit a barn door. But you never know with snow, as they say.

I didn't trust Cawthorne – let's be frank, I wouldn't spit in his ear if his brain was on fire. But I couldn't just blow him up, could I?

'I'm going to pull the bolt, Cawthorne,' I shouted at the slit, 'but I want to see the artillery out here first.'

'Get stuffed!'

'Nobody's going anywhere until you throw the gun out. That's the deal. Non-negotiable.'

I thought he might have liked that. Non-negotiable. It had a reasoned, businesslike ring to it.

He tried to shoot me instead.

His arm came right out of the slit to my left – he'd switched sides – and was holding the gun upside down, his wrist twisted, to get the angle. I saw the barrel and the foresight out of the corner of my eye and slammed myself back into the door, pretending to be no thicker than a coat of paint.

I'll swear I saw the bullet leave that barrel and fly across my face. I was so relieved it hadn't hit me, I would have signed affidavits admitting anything, from being Kurt Waldheim's PR man to having read and enjoyed the Booker Prize winner.

So why did I scream? Then my ears stopped ringing from the sound of the shot and I realised it wasn't me screaming, it had been Werewolf.

I couldn't see him behind Armstrong, but Armstrong had been in the direct line of fire. That did it. No more Mister Nice Guy.

There was no point in calling him names, no point in trying to talk him down.

Cawthorne had drawn back his gun arm and I could hear him working the action for reloading while he stumbled about inside the box.

I bent down and put the lighter to the tissue fuse and flipped the wheel. It caught immediately, and I swept up the bottle with my left hand and pirouetted through 180 degrees. Keeping the damn thing well away from my face.

It went through the gun slit sideways on and I was diving for the ground before it hit the concrete floor and exploded.

'Are you all right?'

'I might not make the Irish skateboard team.'

'Where did he get you?'

'In the leg, Dumbo.'

'No, just now, when you screamed.'

'Oh, he missed me by a mile,' said Werewolf through clenched teeth. 'I only screamed so you'd have an incentive to torch the bugger.'

I stared at him for a minute without saying anything. I didn't want to look back at the pillbox.

'You'd better unlock the door,' he said. 'It'll look suspicious if it's bolted when he's found.'

'Yeah. Okay. You're right.'

I put my hands under his arms and helped him up. 'You need a doctor,' I said.

'Think we'll get a cab this time of the morning?' he asked with a sickly grin, resting his head on Armstrong's wheel arch.

'This far south of the river? No chance.'

I tied my handkerchief around my face for the run back to the box. There was black acrid smoke coming out of the slits now, and more orange smoke from flares that were cracking and going off inside. Great whoofs of flame would billow out and bubble off into the smoky pall as things like the inking fluid for the fax went up. There were loud cracks, which I thought at first might be ammunition but were probably the plastic casings of the wrecked machinery flexing and snapping in the heat. The whole thing looked like an overheating Aga in a satanic kitchen.

My eyes were streaming by the time I reached the door and my hand closed over the bolt.

I had a bizarre thought. If this was *Elm Street* or any one of a dozen other horror flicks, Cawthorne would come staggering out of the flames, his blackened, clawlike hands...

I almost didn't do it.

The bolt came down easily enough. It wasn't even warm, as I'd half expected, and the door wafted open an inch or so, more smoke and fumes curling out and sweeping up to join the pall that now rose 30 or more feet up in the air.

But by that time, I was halfway back to Armstrong.

I could still see the smoke in Armstrong's rear-view mirror from the motorway, but Werewolf said I was imagining things.

I'd piled Werewolf into the back seat, and he'd taken a shirt from his bag and tied it around his leg. He kept saying he was okay, but he had lost a lot of blood and he was furious that I'd used the poteen before he'd thought to take a drink. I leaned over to the glove compartment and almost ran us off the road fumbling for the quarter bottle of vodka I always keep there for emergencies. I handed it over my shoulder to Werewolf, and he did it severe damage. I wasn't sure that it was good medical practice, but Werewolf bleeding over my back seat was Emergency with a capital E in my book.

Medical treatment had been the subject of another brief debate as we'd careered down Blackberry Hill.

I'd opted for the hospital in Maidstone because it was closest and I knew where it was. I was beginning to call there on Sundays more regularly than the chaplain. But Werewolf vetoed that straight off.

'Hammersmith, and put the pedal down,' he said.

'Hammersmith? Is there a hospital in Hammersmith?'

'I don't know, but there's a pub.'

'Hey, come on, man...'

'I'm serious.'

Ever known an Irishman joke about booze?

'The Robin Hood and Little John.'

'What?'

'It's a boozer near the Hammersmith flyover. The Boys use it. They'll know what to do.'

'Christ, if we're going that far, you can go to Charing Cross Hospital.'

'I could go to Hammersmith Cemetery, but I ain't gonna.' I heard a painful intake of breath. 'Look, neither of us wants to have to explain this hole in my leg. This way, it's no questions asked.'

'It's run by the Boys, isn't it?' I knew how little Werewolf enjoyed the prospect of being in debt to the Boys from across the Irish Sea.

'Relax, man. They owe me one, but the bastards don't own me.'

'How deep are you in with them?'

It was something I would not have dared ask if he'd been on two legs.

'Nowhere near as deep as they'd like, old buddy. And believe me, it's going to stay that way. They think they can use anybody they want to, and sometimes you have to go along with them or there's trouble back home. Damn it, man, let's use them for a change.'

'There must be another way,' I said, as Armstrong juddered up to 75.

Who said the FX4S cab was as aero-dynamic as a brick?

'Relax,' said Werewolf. 'It'll be okay. Just get this crate out of second gear, will yer?'

I cut across south London, through Dulwich, and we hit Wandsworth just as the

374

doors were opening in the pub next to Young's Ram brewery. The company mascot, a prize ram, was tied up outside the front door. Pedestrians wisely chose to pop in the pub for one rather than try and sneak by it. That's what I call marketing.

We crossed the river by Hammersmith Bridge, and Werewolf directed me from there. Our speed had hardly ever dropped below 50, and I'd run at least two red lights, but we'd been lucky.

The Robin Hood and Little John was a dark brick building now standing alone at the end of a street, but at one time would have been the end of a terraced row of houses. It had a faded plastic sign in one of its dirty windows saying that you could play pool there. That seemed to take care of the nightlife in the area. The whole impression was of the sort of pub you might have called in to get change for a pay phone so you could ring the tourist board for directions to the nearest museum.

'Round the side,' said Werewolf faintly.

I parked Armstrong but left the motor running. The pub had a side door, with a bell and a hand-written sign saying 'Function Room.'

I propped Werewolf up against the wall and got his bag for him.

'You'd better blow,' he said. 'It would take too long to explain you to the management.'

I looked up and down the street. It stayed empty. Then I looked at Werewolf.

'You look like your passport photograph,' I told him.

'I feel like it.' He grinned faintly. 'Now blow.'

How could I leave him there, clutching his leg, blood dripping on to the pavement? My oldest mate, my auld mukker. The guy I'd been through thick and thin, mostly thick, with. The guy who'd just saved my life. I couldn't just walk away, could I?

'See yer,' I said.

I got Duncan the Drunken to fix Armstrong's headlight and aerial and to patch up the other damage, which included three bullet-holes in the bodywork. Duncan actually found a spent .22 bullet on the floor and offered me it for a souvenir. I took it and dumped it in a Keep Westminster Tidy litter bin.

While Armstrong was off the road, hidden in Duncan's lock-up garage in Barking, I borrowed a set of wheels from him – a five-year-old Fiat Uno. If my luck held, nobody I knew would see me in it. And when I say 'borrowed,' it did cost me and over the odds, but then I could rely on Duncan to be discreet.

Werewolf reappeared on the scene after two days and five phone calls from Sorrel asking where he was. Whatever he told her about his limp and the bandage on his leg, she never said anything. I took them out to dinner a couple of times, and we talked about everything except Cawthorne. Then he got word of a roadie job with a band on a short tour of northern Europe, ending in a jazz seminar weekend in Zurich, where Gene Krupa used to hold drum schools.

Sorrel said she had the use of a flat in Zurich and she'd go on ahead. Maybe there was still some skiing to be found. Werewolf said he thought that sounded dangerous.

I saw Innes McInnes once, at his invitation, to try the Bass in the Clanger near his office one evening.

'It'll take months to sort out Cawthorne's affairs,' he said between sips of beer, though he looked ill at ease handling a pint.

'What happened to Linton Holdings?' I asked.

'Oh, the company went down, taking Cawthorne with it. But that was inevitable. I'm putting Sir Frederick on one of my boards next week. I think I'll send him to France to look over Cawthorne's properties there. They'll have to be sold to someone.'

'Of course,' I agreed sympathetically.

'You did all right for yourself,' he said, narrowing his eyes.

'A modest punt, is the expression I think.' Then I tried to change the subject. 'Did you ever hear what happened to Cawthorne exactly?'

He shrugged. 'Took it worse than I thought he would. On the Saturday – the day after – he rang just about everybody he knew to try and offload the Linton debt. When he didn't get anywhere, he went on a lone bender down at that farm of his. The word is he was playing with his guns and there was some sort of fire. Nobody else was involved, from what I hear.'

I looked at him, but he wouldn't meet my eyes.

'It's being put down as a nasty accident. There's no hint of suicide.'

Well, that was true enough.

'And the Kent police found a ... cache ... a ... what-do-you-call-it? A load of cocaine...'

'A stash,' I said. Then added: 'So I've heard.'

'That's right, a stash worth nearly 100K on the street.'

Then he did look at me. 'Just how much did you make on those Linton shares?'

'That's for me to know and you to wonder, bonny lad,' I said in a hammy Scottish accent as I finished my beer. 'Another?' I held up my glass.

'You were right about one thing,' he said, then polished his off.

'What?'

'This is the best pint of Bass around here.'

I held my arms out.

'Would I lie to you?'

Lloyd came round one evening to hand over, as he put it so delicately, my 'winnings.'

I'd taken nearly four thousand pounds from my war chest (actually a copy of Hugh Brogan's *History of the United States* turned into a fireproof combination safe) to help Lloyd buy a few Linton shares. He gave me nearly six grand back, which he said was less commission, whatever that meant. I didn't ask how much he'd made.

He agreed to stay for a drink, having left one of the Dennison boys outside watching his car because he didn't trust the neighbourhood.

I popped a couple of cans of lager and gave him one. Springsteen had curled up on his knee and was having his ears scratched. If he clawed Lloyd's trousers, that was probably my share of the profits blown.

'I've had another idea, Mr A,' said Lloyd. 'A money machine, got to be.'

'Do tell, do tell,' I said, flipping on a tape of the Andrews Sisters singing 'Rum and Coca Cola', one of the best anti-imperialist songs since Trotsky gave up writing lyrics.

'I'm gonna start a messenger company. Motorbike riders, all with mobile phones – leased, of course – and all delectable young females aged between 18 and 22 with fine, firm bodies. Gonna call it City Angels. Hope you don't mind.'

'Not at all. Listen, there's a friend of mine called Sandy, lives in Kent. Recently been made redundant...'

I called in to Prior, Keen, Baldwin on the Monday but got no further than Sergeant Purvis at the reception desk.

'Mr Patterson is tied up,' he said before I could open my mouth, 'for the foreseeable future. He asked me to give you this.'

He was grinning inanely, which I should have taken for the bad sign it was, as he handed over a plain white envelope.

There was a cheque inside, for £1500 with the payee line left blank; just the way I like them. There was also a PKB 'With Compliments' in there as well, with just the words 'In lieu' written on it.

No goodbye, good job well done, thanks for everything.

Still, he hadn't asked for the American Express card back, had he?

It really annoyed Purvis, who couldn't work out why I was grinning as I got in the lift. He didn't wave back.

Salome's recovery took about five weeks in all. It was considerably speeded by the news that the Kent police were not going to press charges about the accident that had killed Alec Reynolds.

On my advice, she saw the assessors from her insurance company in the hospital, and naturally she won them over from her sick-bed (I also advised on which shorty nightie she should wear) and her claim was settled in full. Soon, she and Frank would thrill to the patter of tiny VW Golf wheels in their parking space outside.

Before that, on the Saturday after I'd been made unemployed again, Frank knocked on the flat door and charged in as he usually did.

I was sitting in the middle of the floor, wiring up some new hi-fi gear. Springsteen was asleep across my Habitat sofa-bed. (How do cats make themselves longer at will?)

'Hi, Angel.'

'Hi, Frank. How's the invalid?'

'Fine. Hi, Springsteen.'

He was in a good mood – he didn't normally talk to animals – and Springsteen noted it too. I distinctly saw his eyelid move.

'That's a nice CD player. Is it new?'

'Er ... yes,' I said, scrunching up the American Express receipt and stuffing it into my back pocket. 'What can I do you for?'

Frank stuck his hands in his pockets and rocked back on his heels.

'This BUPA hospital that Sal's in has visiting privileges.'

He grinned a lot and his eyebrows shot up

and down.

'Let me guess,' I said, taking a screwdriver out of my mouth. 'Tonight is *the* night!'

'Right on!' Frank punched the air like a footballer.

'And you want a few tips. That it?'

He gave me a sour look. 'No thanks, white meat, I'm well equipped!'

'So I've heard.'

He wiggled his hips. He *was* in a good mood.

'No, it's just that Sal asked me to bring the birthday present you gave her tonight. I didn't know you'd given her anything.'

'It was a surprise,' I said.

'Where is it? I can't find a thing. She said she'd put it back in the wrapping paper.'

Thoughtful old Sal.

'It's in the bottom left-hand drawer of your wardrobe,' I said. 'I noticed it when Fenella was tidying up during the week.'

'Oh, fine. Thanks.' He made to go. 'What is it anyway?'

'Keep it wrapped. Let Salome surprise you.'

'Okay. See you around.'

I let him get to the door before I said: 'Hey, Frank. Does the hospital have any spare beds?'

'Why?' he said over his shoulder. 'Not feeling well?'

'I'm fine, Frank. I was thinking of you.'

This Large Print Book, for people
who cannot read normal print,
is published under the auspices of

THE ULVERSCROFT FOUNDATION

... we hope you have enjoyed this book.
Please think for a moment about those
who have worse eyesight than you ...
and are unable to even read or enjoy
Large Print without great difficulty.

You can help them by sending a
donation, large or small, to:

**The Ulverscroft Foundation,
1, The Green, Bradgate Road,
Anstey, Leicestershire, LE7 7FU,
England.**
or request a copy of our brochure for
more details.

The Foundation will use all donations
to assist those people who are visually
impaired and need special attention
with medical research, diagnosis
and treatment.

Thank you very much for your help.